51 Pegasi – Sister Tiffany
A Life of Service

A story in the 51 Pegasi Series

by

Roger Haller

51 Pegasi – Sister Tiffany
A Life of Service

9780981685366

This is a work of speculative fiction. As such, real and fictional people, places, and events are applied as background, but this tale is fiction; every character is fictional and does not or should not reflect on the real lives of anyone.

This book is not designed to apply judgment but to look at these events through the lens of an assortment of diverse characters. If I did it right, you will hear several voices, not just the narrator.

Distributed by Ingram, Amazon.com, and Cowboy Logic Press at www.cowboylogic.net/books

Edited by Annie Viall and Smedley Smith

I dedicated this book to my wife, Joni, and the fantastic readers, editors, reviewers, friends and family who have adopted these stories into their lives and are helping me drive the bus.

I hope this book inspires them to make a positive difference in their world.

Cover Illustrated by Roger Haller

Special Thanks to Smedley Smith and Annie Viall for beta reader feedback and to the great reviewers who shared their thoughts on the book with their friends.

Sister Tiffany's Map

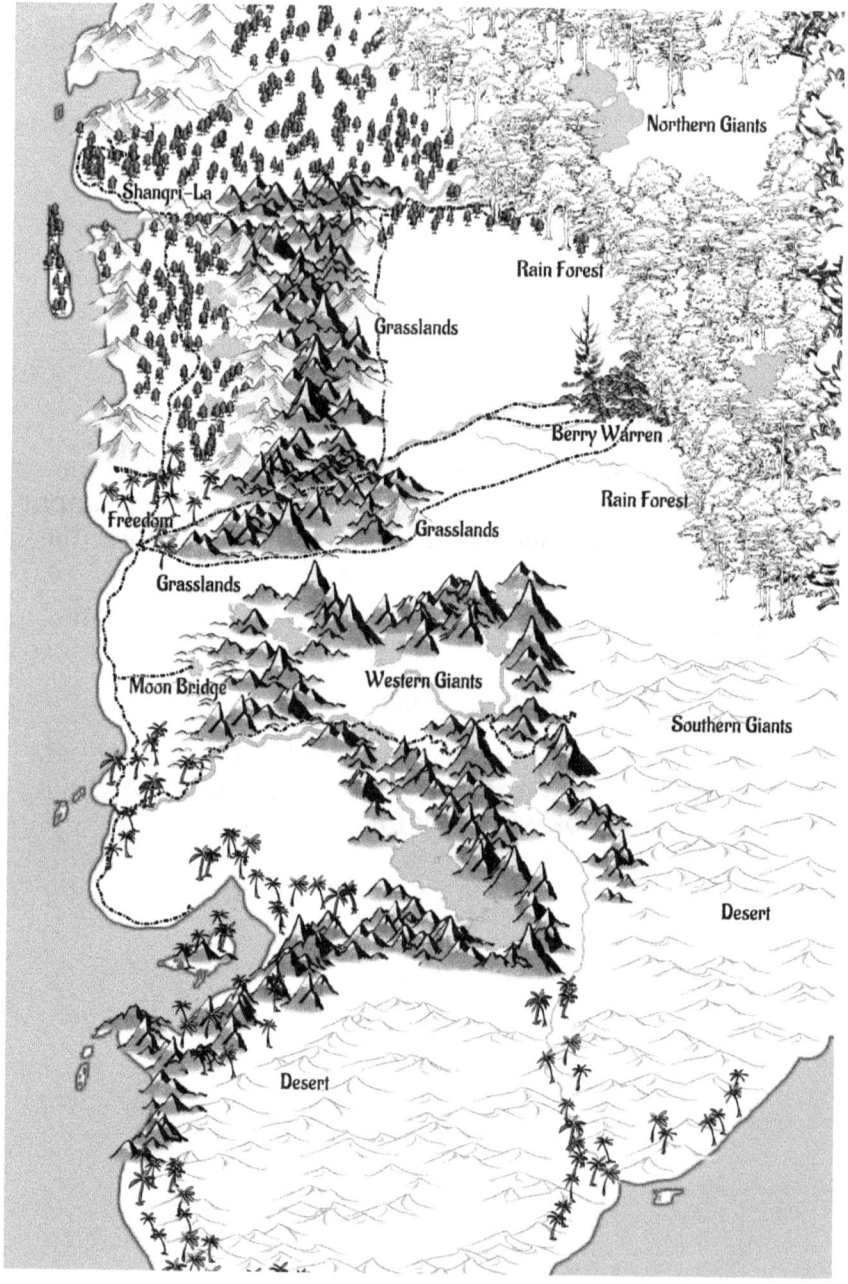

Chapter 1

A Life of Service

Tiffany could still speak fluent Swedish; the language she used to tell her parents she would be a missionary in Africa. They were unsurprised when she announced she was entering the sisterhood as their focused daughter graduated from Catholic University. However, they were shocked when she announced she would leave Wisconsin.

Marquette University had inspired her to "Be the Difference," and the school charged her with thinking big. Officially she was a Sister rather than a Nun. Rather than cloistering in a convent or monastery, she was dedicating herself to a vocational journey.

Tiffany decided the poor in a third-world country needed her most, and Africa was her first choice. Northern Uganda needed help in the wake of the Kanungu massacre.

Tiffany made sure her parents knew how passionate she was about the calling; and to do that, she needed to use their native tongue.

Roger Haller

Her mother cried. She knew the history of Uganda and was terrified of what could happen to her only child. Her father was stoic. He knew her determination, inspiration, passion for the Church, and massive heart. He and her mother had helped make her who she was.

He pulled his family into his arms. "Var försiktig, skriv och kom tillbaka till oss en dag. – Be careful, write, and come back to us one day."

"Självklart, Pappa – Of course."

Tiffany's mother just wept and nodded.

Within two weeks, Tiffany was in Northern Uganda. She joined two other Sisters already in the mission. Sister Beatrix and Sister Anne became instant mentors, trainers, friends, and, in a more profound way, sisters of the cloth. Beatrix was from Lyon, France, but spoke English well, and Anne was from Leeds, in central England.

They became known in the mission as a collaborative unit dedicated to repairing the lives of the genocide survivors.

It was an uphill battle as the Church's reputation had taken a beating from the locals since the leaders of the Kanungu cult had wrapped themselves in the Church's beliefs, notably the Ten Commandments. The cult centered their indoctrination on the Commandments, which they modified to their use.

The tragic church fire in the Southwest of the country had deadened the lives of the survivors. They fought for the memories of what their family members had taken to heart.

Ultimately, the doomsday cult indoctrinated the victims to the strictest interpretation of the church teachings, but with the caveat that the world would end in the year of the millennium.

A Life of Service

The end of present times became a reality for seven hundred innocents who had been locked into a church. The doors were nailed shut and set ablaze. This tragedy was on the heels of thousands killed by Idi Amin's armies in the seventies. Missionaries took much of the heat during these times, and the rhetoric escalated with the latest atrocities.

Tiffany, Beatrix, and Anne fought diligently with love, tenderness, understanding, and empathy for the drained lives of those around them. This ministry was hard work. The missionaries had enemies. Many in the country and from other countries did not want these people to get the help they needed.

The sisters were reminded many times in a day that they were not welcome. The ones who reached back, desperate for support, kept them helping.

The missionary's lives were threatened. They were verbally and physically abused, spit on, slandered, and ridiculed while they did their work. Tiffany remembered evenings when the sisters would pray together and cry together from the weight of so much hate, mistrust, and stress. They relied on each other and the rest of the missionaries for the strength to stand firm and respond with love and resolve.

The mission evolved into a refuge where the struggling could come to hide from oppression and hate.

A large percentage of these refugees were widowed women and children. Tiffany and the sisters became known for the sanctuary. They began hearing more about the "Lord's Resistance Army," or LRA. They also began to hear the name Joseph Kony.

They became aware of a few Americans who wanted them out of the way. They hadn't heard names yet, but some of their charges began to warn them of traitors from their own family.

Roger Haller

51 Pegasi - Sister Tiffany

Tiffany and her sisters weren't sure what that meant. Sometimes, the language barrier can lose the essence of a statement when the subject is close or extended family, or even nationality or race.

The result was a feeling of vulnerability as they could not be sure of the needed support when it became crucial to have it.

Joseph Kony was becoming a more significant factor in their stress, as the aggressions were daily now, and the locals often warned the sisters that Joseph would make them pay for their interference in Uganda. The missionaries never met Mr. Kony, but the threats were coming from a cohesive militia as the harassment began to come from well-funded soldiers in Land Rovers, uniforms, and military long guns.

Tiffany's letters home slowed down as she didn't want to share the stress with her parents. Her letters from them stopped altogether, so she suspected someone else was reading her mail. The last letter she received before the strife told her that her father was very ill, and her parents were moving to an assisted living home.

The mission received one more letter from that home, explaining that her father had died of Cancer and her mother was in the late stages of dementia. They didn't expect her to last through the month.

Tiffany was angry. She was angry with herself for leaving them behind and with Uganda for allowing these type of people to take command. She was also angry with her religion because the all-powerful Catholic Church was not funding its mission to the degree, she knew was needed to make a difference.

While she felt she was losing faith, she was also ramping up her drive to make a difference for the people in her care.

A Life of Service

Her quest was more personal than ever. She felt it was time for God to notice the effort needed and help her.

I felt her numbness as everything she lived for crumbled. She needed a miracle.

***

Roger Haller

51 Pegasi - Sister Tiffany

The refuge was surrounded by roaring Land Rovers and yelling soldiers shooting into the air. Everyone in the compound ran into the sanctuary for shelter. The doors were quickly blocked by men with automatic weapons. Rifle butts smashed the windows in, and men roared orders through the openings with their barrels aimed at the milling women and children.

The militants ordered the captives into three groups. Twenty-three children, all under sixteen, were forced into the back of a military truck.

The leader of this ambush singled Tiffany out and, nose to nose, informed her the children would learn to serve their new masters very well. In broken English, she was told she wouldn't need to worry. They would be well-fed… If they obeyed orders.

Twelve weeping Ugandan women were loaded into another truck, and it quickly sped away. The leader told Tiffany they would have new husbands taking over their care. As the truck disappeared, the wailing women held their arms outreached toward the sisters. That would be the last she would see any of her charges. The militants directed the sisters back to the leader.

He pointed at a small table and chairs and said, "Sit."

He then went outside while the men stood station in each window and doorway.

Beatrix reached across the table, and the sisters joined hands and prayed. A half-hour elapsed before the leader returned with a portly man in civilian clothes. The man was dressed very well and presented an attitude of superiority. Somehow, he looked familiar. It seemed he was used to commanding others. He spoke to the military leader in Ugandan and sat at another table.

A Life of Service

The leader ordered the sisters to stand. Militants moved the table and chairs to the side of the room. The leader began giving them orders.

"Disrobe."

As one, the sisters replied. "No."

The leader pulled out a pistol and shot the floor between Anne's feet. Other than the startled jump at the gunshot, the sisters stood their ground. Feeling that Beatrix was the elder of the sisters, the militant walked up to her and pistol-whipped her across the face, causing her to splay out on the floor.

"If you do not comply, she dies first."

He stood over her with his pistol aimed at her head and looked back at the standing women. When they were slow to respond, he cocked his gun and focused again on the dazed sister on the floor.

"No…" Tiffany began. She began removing her head covering. "I'll comply."

The men watched in amazement as the striking blond Swede emerged from the habit like a butterfly from a cocoon. Anne followed suit, and Beatrix stood with them in solidarity and disrobed. The civilian silently stood, approached the militant leader, and paid him a large roll of American bills.

The sisters were handcuffed together and led to a Mercedes van without side windows. They were placed naked on bench seats, and their cuffs were attached to tie-down rings on the van wall.

The militants drove quickly out of the compound. The civilian climbed into the van's passenger seat, and the driver left the empty compound.

Roger Haller

51 Pegasi - Sister Tiffany

Tiffany watched the dust plume filter the image of the refuge through the small back windows as that chapter of her life and the Church faded from her life.

Anne started praying. Beatrix joined her, but Tiffany could only sit and watch the landscape fall away behind the car in a veil of dust. She didn't feel scared, angry, bitter, sad… she didn't feel. It would take some time before she would feel again.

The sisters were taken to a compound on a hillside.

Once locked inside, the men marched them through a dusty compound into a palatial villa with all the amenities, luxurious furniture, and art. Their captors led them to a windowless lounge with an attached bathroom, bedroom, walk-in closet with harem costumes, and a large mirror. Tiffany assumed it was a one-way mirror. She also noted security cameras in every room.

Their daily life became a blur of on-call sex slaves for a rotating group of lowly slugs who would call day or night for sex acts that had nothing to do with intimacy and everything to do with control. This routine continued for a few weeks as the women sought ways to end their lives, even though it meant damnation. Hell would be a better fate.

As life became mundane, Tiffany found she was a favorite of their purchaser, and she finally figured out where she knew him from. He was a priest from a convent a few kilometers from the sanctuary. She said nothing for a few weeks, but he opened the subject. "You look so much better out of the habit, Sister Tiffany." He tried to be witty, but she had never spoken her name.

"How did you know my name?"

A Life of Service

He was stumped momentarily, but he said, "The militants told me."

Tiffany looked up at his eyes. "Aren't you Father Lukwiya? I think we met at the mission office last year."

"Enough. I am not Lukwiya."

He got up, dressed, and left. None of the sisters saw him again. When he left, Tiffany discussed the conversation and her revelation about his identity with her sisters.

"I know," Anne said. "He was far too friendly with me before you came here. I would always stay in company when he visited, so it never escalated."

Beatrix nodded.

"Why didn't you tell me?"

"Would it have made any difference?"

"Yes. While I still had faith, it would have. It doesn't matter now, though."

One of the regulars, however, commented.

"I don't know, ladies. The boss isn't interested in you anymore. I think he will sell you. You might want to try harder to please. Not many places so nice as this."

As the human snail walked out of the room and latched the door, they heard a hiss.

The sisters woke in a cage hanging from a tree. The heat was intense, and the humidity made it hard to breathe.

The sisters were naked and wet from the hot mist.

Roger Haller

51 Pegasi - Sister Tiffany

The scene took me back to my introduction to this new world. Even though the Sisters had lived through hell to this point, I felt their shock through my soul.

***

Chapter 2

Caged

Tiffany had to fake her courage as she calmed her sisters' escalating panic. The women noticed they were not alone as they managed to lower their voices to whispers. A cage across from them appeared to hold a group of mature men and women.

They were trying to communicate in a Slavic language. None of the sisters could understand the words, but the people in that cage were in the same condition.

All were naked, scared, and on the verge of panic.

To their right was another cage.

That one seemed to hold a family with an older couple and three younger adults. They were speaking English with a British accent. Sister Ann gravitated to them immediately, but they quickly connected with all the sisters. Before Tiffany could object, Sister Ann introduced them as Catholic Sisters.

Ben, the patriarch of the English family, had some history in Ukraine, so he could translate roughly.

Roger Haller

51 Pegasi - Sister Tiffany

The other cage held five unrelated people from Crimea. Some were Russian, and some were Ukrainian, and they were not pleased to be in the same hanging pen.

Beth, the wife and mother of the small English group, warned the sisters that their captors were due shortly, and she made a point to let them know their keepers were monsters. They were as big as a town-home and covered in fur. She also facilitated introductions. The sisters met Richard, Benjamin II, and Sally.

The younger generation was quiet, still very embarrassed to be naked along with their parents and now a trio of Catholic Sisters.

Ben, the elder, explained, "The enormous Yetis will be feeding us shortly, but once they leave, I will introduce you to the Slavic cage. The evening will be a good time to fill you, new folks, in with what we know or suspect of our situation."

Sister Beatrix mumbled, "Thank you." She wasn't sure she was ready.

The conversation was interrupted by a rumbling they could feel as their cages shook. Grunts and guttural noises that were alien to their ears accompanied the arrival.

Suddenly, fur filled the space between the cages. Giant primate faces with a variety of expressions, from glee to quizzical frowns, injected fear into the scene. The sister's shock rattled as the Yeti pressed raw, white meat into their cell.

It looked like a massive turkey breast with stems of gigantic celery, rhubarb, or something similar. Also rolled into the cage were red globes the size of small melons or pumpkins that turned out to be berries from the thorn thickets below.

Caged

The fur-covered towers moved to the other cages to repeat the feeding ceremony. Once done, they returned to observe the sisters and made encouraging motions with hairy digits akin to fingers. Anne started for food but stuck to the vegetation. No one was excited about the raw meat.

Tiffany expected they would need to get used to it, as they would need protein to survive. Looking around, the sisters could see the other captives begin to eat.

Tiffany assumed her leadership role again and tore off a handful of the meat. She tentatively tasted the offering and reported that it tasted like fowl.

The giants seemed pleased. They did another short tour around the cages and rumbled off through the trees.

The sisters noted that dusk was quickly falling and started to look for the most comfortable way to rest through the muggy, steaming evening. The cages quieted down as each cell found its routine.

The evening quickly darkened to night as the sisters discussed a bathroom routine at the back of the cage. They agreed to screen for each other as best they could to preserve any small amount of dignity they could scrape from this strange new life.

To their surprise, the sisters found relief through sleep that night.

As the temperature eased. In fact, they found they needed to hold each other to preserve body heat in the damp, bare cage. However, sunrise brought quickly climbing temperatures, and they were almost grateful to be naked. The light breeze through the canopy was necessary.

The other cages began to stir, so introductions continued.

Roger Haller

Ben introduced the Slavic cell. The intensity of the discord in the Slavic cage became evident to the sisters. They now observed two factions, one to the left and one to the right of their cell. One side identified as Russian, the other Ukrainian, both from Crimea. Ben, the elder, voiced the issue to the sisters.

Sister Beatrix asked Ben if he would help with a translation. When he agreed, she started. "We are Catholic sisters kidnapped from a mission in Africa. Please tell us who you are and where you are from."

When everyone knew the dynamics, she said, in a friendly but direct way, "I think we get it now. You are all Crimean, but you now live in this strange new place where we all must be brothers and sisters to survive.

You also bring two languages to the rest of your new family, which will help each of us expand to become bigger and better and survive in our new environment."

Ben successfully translated to the Slavic cage, and it became clear that the message resounded with them. It took a few minutes to settle in, and they quietly discussed her logic in their cage.

There was still a lack of trust and many wounds needed to heal.

Both sides of the cage studied each other, but the look was not hatred. It would take time, but sister Beatrix successfully sewn the seeds of brotherhood with amazing skill.

The next few days proved to be stranger and more frightening. They set the stage challenging new lives in this strange place. It seems the Giants had plans for them.

My mind went back to my introduction to the cages.

Roger Haller

Caged

In particular, I remembered three strangers looking for reasons to live. Suddenly, we were on a path we had not chosen. It was a path, however, none of us would regret. The time we spent on it turned out to be the most important time of our lives.

***

Roger Haller

51 Pegasi - Sister Tiffany

They lived as a novelty in their cage for more than a month. The sisters were separated and placed in mating cages and supplied with mates.

The Giants coupled Tiffany with one of the Slavics and paired Beatrix with another. Ben, the younger, was put into a cage above Tiffany with Sister Anne. His sister, Sally, was housed with another of the Slavic group, but their brother, Richard, disappeared in a cage by himself.

Sister Ann conceived, but Sister Beatrix and Tiffany didn't. Sally and her mate were carried off, so it seemed she may have conceived as well.

With Tiffany, the mate respected her calling and would not force her. They both knew what would happen next. The Giants would not settle for nonproductive couples.

Finally, the giants removed the men from the unsuccessful sisters, and the two were together again. They never saw Sister Ann again, but Beatrix and Tiffany found solace in each other for a few fleeting days.

They were worried. By now, they had seen a pattern where unproductive couples were disappearing. A few new couples arrived and took their place. Their wait would not be long.

After watching a new couple set up where the British family used to live, the Giants grabbed the sister's cage and moved it to a tree high over the edge of the berry thicket. The cell slipped and jolted as the Giant grabbed it like a packing box and hooked it back into the tree. This heart-pounding event left the sisters on their bellies, scrambling for the cage bars to hold on.

There was another cage with the parents of the British family and a couple of the men from the Crimean pen. Sister Beatrix said a silent prayer and made the sign of the cross.

Roger Haller

Caged

She looked at Tiffany and whispered. "Sister, I don't have a good feeling about this. I know what happens to livestock when they are no longer producing."

She looked startled as she leaned back and looked into Tiffany's eyes. "I'm so sorry, Sister. I should have kept that in my head."

Tiffany cupped her friend's face in her hands, pulled her close, and kissed her forehead. "Don't fret, sister. It was already heavy in my head."

They looked across at the British couple, hugging much like they were. It was easy to see they understood the move as well. Beatrix excused herself and went to the back wall. By habit, Tiffany moved to a point on the front cage wall between her friend and the nearest neighbors and grabbed the bars in thought...It wasn't necessary to block because the abbreviated dusk in this new world was so short. In the time it took to discuss their prediction, darkness had fallen.

Before Beatrix finished her task, the cage dropped from its hook in the tree. In the aftermath, Tiffany assumed it had not been hung properly. The roof lid came off, and the cover on the cage wall crushed Beatrix. She never uttered a sound and never moved during or after the fall. The roof effectively pinned her to a corner.

Tiffany landed roughly in a corner against the ground. It took her a moment to regain her senses, stand, check for injuries, and call for Beatrix.

The prisoners couldn't see what happened, but they heard it and understood. They called out to see if the sisters had survived as Tiffany climbed over to her last connection to her old life, crying her name. There was no response from Beatrix, and the prisoners were panicking.

Roger Haller

51 Pegasi - Sister Tiffany

The cage's lone survivor informed those still in the trees that Beatrix was dead. She urged them all to be quiet and find a way to escape and scrambled over the bent wreckage of the cage. Tiffany escaped into the berry briars, guided through an animal entrance by a dim blue light along the warren floor.

In the dim light, she could see three and four-foot thorns sticking out in all directions, so she had to focus on her path and slow down. The noise from the camp died out, and she was alone. Tiffany decided not to go further than she had to. She needed light and time to think.

The liberated Sister knew her task was to free people from these giants. For the first time in this new world, she had a mission. First, she would need to survive.

The tall, fit, Nordic Amazon felt she was no longer on the Earth she knew. She had more strength, stamina, wind, and a new cause.

Tiffany swore to herself that she would find out where and why they were here and disrupt the kidnappers that had brought them here.

She suspected the LRA. Whoever they are, they had just created a warrior.

She found a smooth hollow in the ground and curled up to cry.

She wasn't crying for herself but for the children back in Africa, her sisters in the cloth, and her lost religion. No, Tiffany didn't need pity.

She needed tools, weapons, shelter, self-sustainment, and troops. Tiffany was already planning to recruit. Deep in thought, as she curled up in the soft blue light, she was startled by scuffling behind her and a bump against her backside.

Roger Haller

Caged

She almost impaled herself on a massive thorn as she jumped up and spun around. A small animal, the size of a lap dog, tried to scurry past her along a well-worn trail. She reached up to grab a horizontal thorn on a dead tendril to pull herself up and out of the way. The small animal scampered down the trail, and she fell to the ground for the second time tonight.

She sat dazed in the dirt, holding a light, effective, and dangerous javelin. Things were beginning to go her way. She studied the brambles above her and recognized the structure of a rabbit warren, only magnified several times. She found a busy crossroads of massive vines that provided a platform above the trail to sleep on. With her newly acquired spear wedged into the platform, she stretched out and reached above for one of the smaller berries she had been eating since arriving.

Tomorrow would be a big day one way or another. Either the giants would find her and rip her out of this sanctuary, or like a rabbit in its den, they would look for easier quests. Tonight, she needed rest. Her past life came tumbling through her mind when she slowed down, and she cried some more in her solitude. It would take some time to sleep, but it finally found her.

I knew she was safe, and I felt I was watching the birth of a warrior. Even though she was moving from piety to war, Tiffany was the same woman. She had always been a warrior for those who needed her. Her challenges had always been daunting, but it had all contributed to the heart and soul driving her tonight. By now, I knew Tiffany had no use for revenge, hate, or anger. Higher callings drove her to the logic of the heart. Her love for the people who needed her would be a force many would underestimate to their peril.

***

Roger Haller

Chapter 3

Breakout

Tiffany woke in the thicket. She was surprised she'd slept long enough for the sun to rise, but she noted the much cooler temperature in the briars. The multiple layers of shade acted like blackout curtains. Even though the sun shone through in spikes of radiant light and heat, the overall feeling in the thicket was safe, cool, and calm.

Between sleep and awake, her brain had been working. Several ideas had surfaced. Some had filtered away as they came in, but a few stuck and gave her material to work with.

Tiffany did a short inventory of her immediate needs. She had berries, shelter, and a weapon. She wouldn't starve.

Her cover may or may not be sufficient, but she should soon get some sign, one way or another. She would be testing it. The Nordic Amazon needed more weapons and tools.

A knife would be helpful, and Tiffany would need some variety in her diet to perform at her peak.

Breakout

Looking around the berry warren, she found a form of ivy twisting through the berry vines. Closer to the ground, the ivy had died and provided a tough but pliable strand that could substitute for rope. She pulled a length of the fibrous vine into the path at her feet, but it held fast. She noted that it was secured to a green branch of the vine at a junction that acted as an anchor in the thorny thicket.

To inspect it closer, Tiffany attempted to climb the jumble to the stuck junction. She grabbed at a thorn bud that looked like a handle and promptly let go as her hand was bleeding at the base of her pinky finger. It wasn't deep, but after closer inspection, she found the thorn bud had a razor-sharp edge hidden in the base.

A knife!

Her mind jumped into gear as she looked for a way to break the bud from the thick stem of the berry vine.

She ran her thorn spear through the hook of the bud and pried, but it simply crushed the sharp edge and did nothing to pop the bud off the vine. Tiffany then plucked a potato-sized rock from the path at her feet and struck the side of a bud from both sides with no effect. Finally, she hit the bud from the base end, which popped it cleanly off the vine and fell at her feet.

Smiling, she repeated the magic strike on another couple of buds, and the smooth harvest of biological knives was perfected. Tiffany gathered a half dozen. The tool builder set her attention back on the fibrous vine.

Trimming the makeshift rope with one of her new knives became easy, and she soon had six 30-foot vines laid out in the trail. She found the best sections were the dead but still pliable sections. Tiffany found the hardened ends could not be easily manipulated, and the living ends were not as strong.

Roger Haller

Tiffany cut a short section of green vine and tied it around her waist. She now had a belt from which she could hang her bud knives. They attached well, and if she didn't add pressure, they didn't cut through the vine.

Now, she needed to go back and better understand the cages from the outside. Tiffany returned to the entrance she had escaped into and peeked tentatively through the cover.

She towed three vines with her and left them a few yards from the opening to the giant's camp. She could hear activity, so she made sure to be silent, stay out of view, and be ready to run back down the warren path.

The cage that had fallen was still on the ground, bent. The beasts had removed the broken cover and dropped it upside down beside the damaged pen. Sister Beatrix's body was gone. Tiffany was relieved. It was not a good time to get emotional again.

The giants were busy feeding the captives. One of them turned toward her, sniffing the air. She held her breath and froze to ensure no movement would catch their attention. The beast was looking directly at her, but after an eternity, it turned and lifted the cage it was tending and left with it perched on its shoulder.

The giant was removing a mating pair. Another beast carried away another.

Tiffany recognized Sally peering back over the camp from the first cage, and in the second, she recognized a young man and woman from the Slavic's cell.

Neither cage contained Sister Anne, the Brits, or any of the Slavics.

Breakout

The cage camp grew quiet, with only murmurs while the captives ate. Tiffany stepped carefully out of the warren to inspect the broken cage.

She was particularly interested in the latches. The pens were four-sided, and in the middle of each side was a simple latch secured on the roof that pulled up over a fulcrum, looping tight on a hook.

Pulling down on each lever would open the latch and release the respective wall. In the center of the roof was a hook hanging on limbs. Attaching the hook to the top was a metal bolt secured by a metal loop inside. Tiffany assumed the loop served as a thumb screw for the giants to unscrew or separate from the hook on the outside. Threaded bolts were a very human.

Tiffany's plan was coming together. After another quick look around the camp, she softly called out. "Hello in the cage!" Her call was met with silence. Even the murmurs stopped.

She called again. "Hello!"

Finally, several sets of eyes peered over the edge of the closest cage floor. "Hello?"

This reply won her some more audience. There was one more cage with people watching.

From where she stood below, Tiffany soon learned that these were not the Slavic people or the Brits.

Her escape had started a stream of pairs being hauled off to another location by the giants. These people did not know her.

"People, I have escaped those cages and plan to free you too. Are you with me?"

51 Pegasi - Sister Tiffany

A man from the first cage replied. "Yes. What can we do?"

A woman from the second cage agreed. "Yes… Please. Help us."

"Okay, this is what I need you to do. I will throw up a vine, and I need you to lift someone to tie it securely to the ring on your ceiling. It must bear your weight, so double and triple the knot." Tiffany pointed at the ring on the overturned cover. "I'm going to get the vines."

As she disappeared into the entrance to the berry warren, I noted that she had found secrets to this world I wish we had seen when we went through this hell.

***

Breakout

In moments, the Amazon was back under the edge of the first cage, hanging about a story above her. She couldn't quite reach the floor, even though she could jump her height. Tiffany began swinging the vine and launching it up toward the cage bars. On the second try, a wiry young man snatched up the end, and hauled it into the hanging pen. His efforts had the enclosure swinging gently from the tree.

"Got it."

"Okay, now you need to get someone to climb up to the metal loop in the ceiling."

A young black woman scampered from his knee to his shoulders, and fastened the vine to the small but sturdy hoop.

"It's tight." She jumped down, climbed up a few feet of the vine, and bounced. They were beginning to see the plan as the rest of the vine lay coiled on the floor.

"The vine is easy to hang on to. It's shiny but dry. I've got a good grip."

This show was not wasted on the other swinging jail. Tiffany repeated the procedure with the second cage, where a bigger man captured the flung end and lifted a small Asian woman to tie it off.

Tiffany stepped onto the damaged lid of her former cage, and pointed at the wall latches. She ensured her audience understood as she worked the latch up and down.

She demonstrated the loop they had to free on each door.

"Tie knots in the vine every 6 feet or so. This will help you hold on and climb down once your cage falls away from its roof." She pointed to each vine-rope.

Roger Haller

They got it, and as they worked at the vines, Tiffany climbed a tree that ran up against the side of the far cage, with another vine looped over her shoulder. Her time in Africa and her new-found passion for making this work became evident as she scrambled out a limb, caught a bigger branch, and climbed to a sturdy limb above and between the two cages. She secured her rope-like vine.

Tiffany went back to the cage's roof with the man and two women inside, down the slope of the far side to her secure point, and stopped to check progress. Everyone in both cages stood stationed near their ropes. She attached the vine in a loop under her shoulders and swung over the lid to the first latch. Without ceremony, she flipped the latch up, and the cage dropped a few inches. Her charges gasped, grabbed harder to their purchase on the vine, and nodded.

Tiffany scrambled to the next latch, and the cage dropped to a precarious angle. This step showed the captives what would happen.

"Get on the vine. The last one may break when I let the next one go."

As she slipped around to the third clasp, the cage contents pulled themselves up onto their vine. The bottom belonged to the older woman in the cage, who was a bit heavier. She nodded, and Tiffany flipped the third latch. The pen wall fell open, but the last latch held.

This was a good thing because the lady on the bottom knot dropped off the vine and fell to the cage's wall, which was mostly horizontal.

Her legs dangled through the bars, but she was able to grab the vine, pull herself to the edge, and let herself down the rest of the way. The two left on the vine followed suit.

Breakout

The three freed captives ran to the entrance of the berry warren as they watched Tiffany swing off the cage and grasp a bar near the top of the second hanging pen. With a nod from the captives, she flipped the first latch off. She got the same results, but the escapees knew what to expect this time and were ready.

Tiffany moved around to the second latch. There was little drop this time, so she quickly continued to the third. Again, the hanging cage stayed latched to the fourth clasp, so there was no crash to alert the Giants.

This pleased Tiffany. To the concern of the captives waiting below she cut the vines loose with her new bud knife, wedged onto her belt, and climbed down the way she had climbed up.

"They won't know how we did it without the vines, which may be useful in the future," she explained as the men helped her drag them back into the thorn thicket.

Tiffany led the escapees back to her little nest in the warren and learned who she had saved. She left off her former vocation as she opened introductions. "I'm Tiffany Henderson. From Milwaukee and Uganda. I'm heading somewhere they don't have people in cages, so if anyone wants to join me, you're more than welcome."

The shorter, wiry man said, "I'm Randy Weinstein, from New York City. I don't want to be anywhere near here. I'm in."

The bigger black woman agreed. "I'm Ann, from Detroit, and I can use a diet, but not that one.

I'm a little beyond prime and don't want to be having babies. Lead the way."

The smaller Asian woman just nodded. She wasn't much for words and seemed to be in shock.

Roger Haller

"You have a name?"

"Kia…, Dallas."

"You okay?"

"No, but I am better now."

The younger black woman said, "I'm Penny. I am an office manager and accountant. I need to get back home. Since I don't know where we are, I'll hang with you guys till I can find a way back. Is there anywhere we can get some clothes?"

Tiffany shook her head. "You know as much as I do, but one thing I am sure of is I do not want to be at the mercy of those hairy giants."

The next introduction was from a middle-sized, mid-American named Stacey. "Stacey - I'm a farmer. I'm not sure who's feeding my chickens right now, but I guess I've got bigger issues to deal with. First, I want to leave this place."

Dan was the last to speak. He seemed like he was as quiet as Kia. "I am a Cellular Engineer. The name is Dan, and I'm from Atlanta. I want to get back to work. I miss my computer, my wireless network, and my idea of the perfect discussion is on a Zoom meeting."

Tiffany noticed Kia perked up. "I am RAN engineer. I work cellular, too."

Dan smiled and shook her hand. "As soon as we get settled, let's chat."

Tiffany felt it might be some time before they got settled but was happy there were some connections started. "Folks, those hair mountains are going to be angry. We need to get some distance on them while we can.

Breakout

It's getting dark, but these berry bushes come with night-lights. The fungus is luminescent. We might be safe here for a short time if we stay away from the edges of the thicket, but they will find a way to flush us out if we don't get away."

Everyone agreed, so they headed deeper into the warren, eating berries to build strength while discussing their options.

I was happy to see that Tiffany's natural leadership caught on. No one was arguing. Tiffany found a way to inspire me every day I knew her in this world.

***

Roger Haller

Chapter 4

Swimming Through the Grass

When night fell on the steamy berry warren, the escaped humans met the small reptiles that called the thicket home. At first, they were startled and afraid of the strange creatures, but Tiffany eased their fears. She told them about her experience the previous night and assured them the animals seemed harmless.

The creature appeared to be a cross between a Halloween cat and a frog. When startled, they moved like cats but with a comical arch to their backs that belied their speed. They had padded feet like a cat or dog, with short claws for quick getaways and stubby teeth more suited for vegetation, insects, or softer food.

They did, however, have a barbed tail like a Stingray, but from what they observed, it was used only for defense. It avoided contact instead of posturing for protection, particularly when confronting the much bigger humans.

At this point, no one had considered eating the animal because they hadn't been hungry enough to eat raw meat.

Swimming Through the Grass

However, that night in the warren, they did taste the blue, glowing mushrooms to see if they were edible. They opted to be satisfied with a taste until they knew if there would be effects from the fungus. They filled up on berries and used the neon night lights to explore for exits away from the rain forest camp.

They found three spots where small streams came and went from the thicket and agreed that leaving in a stream of sun-warmed water might hide their tracks. They settled on an exit near where they could watch the sun go down. The stream left the berry warren on what felt like the North side, and they could see it arched around to the West as soon as it left the cover. They also noted that tall grain stalks surrounded the creek. The rain forest opened to a vast grassland to the West.

The runaways were concerned with visibility at night. They may not have the luxury of the blue mushrooms, and they did not know how much they could see. The dense canopy of the rain forest had kept them from seeing the night sky. It even kept the full power of the Sun from reaching them. They did agree that they had the best chance to avoid discovery from the Giants at night.

They settled on a plan. They would assess the stream path from within the safety of the thorn thicket, and as soon as the fast-moving dusk hit, if all were clear, they would head west and get as far as they could in the night. They hoped they could find shelter, food, and safety away from the rain forest.

The small band of fugitives spent a restless night getting to know the little creatures they named Humpbacks. They also witnessed a few other small animals who inhabited the berry briars.

Through the sleepless night, they observed a migration outward into the grasslands, and back into the warren as soon as light began sweeping over the prairie.

35

Roger Haller

They also observed a pair of moons from the security of the briar. There would be enough light. A pair of moons prompted the epiphany to all of the little tribe. They were no longer in the world they had known. The evidence had been mounting. Two moons made a strong statement.

"It looks like the grass is safe from predators at night but not during the day." Tiffany mused the observation with Dan. "At least, the predators we know."

He nodded. "Yes, we don't want to be out during the day."

The assessment was interrupted by a roar from the East. The Giants had discovered the open cages. More voices magnified the outcry as the escape news echoed through their tribe. The cacophony spread as the Giants raced around the berry warren and through the forests behind the camp.

The rage continued for over an hour, and the openings to the thorn thicket were smashed and thrashed with long poles and clubs. The escapees could tell the captors did not know where they were but suspected the briar they were trembling in.

The noise subsided, but for most of the day, massive shadows swung past the openings as the humans stayed well back from the outlets.

There was no sign of the Humpbacks or small rodents they had seen during the migration through the night.

Tiffany suggested they try to get sleep because the night would entail moving as fast as they could from their tormentors. She felt it would not be long before the Giants would find a way to flush them from the thorns. She remembered how the Giant had seemed to smell her as she watched the camp earlier.

Swimming Through the Grass

She suspected they knew approximately where they were, and they needed to be outside the circle of the Sasquatch senses. Since no one knew what their range was, they must gain distance.

The day was hotter than usual, so rest was fitful. The cooler evening finally arrived, and they staged by the small stream that would be their vehicle away. As the light waned, Humpbacks began filing out. Watching them for a few minutes, convinced the tired fugitives the animals knew what they needed to know. They were more wary than before but moved out in the stream, through the tall grass.

It was finally safe to begin their journey. Tiffany eased into the refreshing water, still within the briar, and found she was waist-deep in the middle of the stream.

The rest of the tired escapees found the water welcoming, refreshing, and comfortable.

Tiffany suggested that they do not talk; if they had to, they would sign or whisper lightly.

Making gestures, she automatically started using American Sign Language, a skill she had learned to communicate with the deaf citizens of the Ugandan villages she had served.

Randy, Dan, and Ann knew some of the language, so at first, they began teaching each other the letters of the alphabet. Tiffany instructed everyone to stay lower than the surrounding grasses, stay quiet, and dip down to swim with the current as much as they could.

The little gang made good time, quietly breast-stroking away from the berry warren. The dusk had become dark quickly, and the stars were powerful support as they drew farther west. They could see enough to make their way.

Roger Haller

51 Pegasi - Sister Tiffany

Shortly into the journey, the sky lightened behind them with the rise of the first moon, filtered by thin clouds. Their view opened enough to see a tall tower off to the North. Beneath it was the black shape of a cabin.

Randy tapped Tiffany's shoulder and pointed. They all stopped to see what he was directing them to. He softly whispered. "People made that."

The moon showed itself now, and the cabin came into clear view. Reflections suggested a window. Penny jumped up and down, splashing more than she should. Stacy quieted her down by grabbing her shoulders. "Shh."

Tiffany turned to the swimmers. "Team, we can't stop here." She whispered. "You can bet the Giants will be all over that cabin. We will come back and investigate when the excitement dies down. For now, please stay quiet, stay down, and swim hard."

Penny looked dejected but agreed and settled back into the water. The runaways made excellent time for another hour. Suddenly, they stopped in awe. The sky grew lighter. In moments, the prairies lit up. As they turned to look back, the second moon greeted the trekkers.

Tiffany and her band of escapees had met Alpha and Beta, the twin moons of their new world, in their full glory. They had trouble understanding the paradox. They had just swum past a cabin and tower built by humans but now were stunned by the power of the twin moons.

Seeing the shock on the faces of her charges, Tiffany knew she had to break the trance and get them moving again. She whispered softly. "Folks, I don't understand why we have two moons, but there are many strange things about this place. Just remember, we need to get away from here. We need to live long enough to understand what's happening."

Roger Haller

Swimming Through the Grass

As she swung around and launched her breast stroke downstream again, she muttered, "Maybe it's the mushrooms."

I watched the resolve in her shoulders and back muscles as she powered downstream with the tenacity a natural leader unconsciously carries. Everyone followed quietly.

***

Roger Haller

For what felt like hours, they swam. The work paid off. By the time the moons had gone to bed and the light of the pending sun was creeping up behind them, they could see tall mountains looming ahead.

Tiffany thought they should be worn out by now. Maybe the adrenalin of flight kept them striving, but she felt there was more to their strength and stamina. She made a note to talk it over when they could. She remembered thinking of her increased strength earlier.

Dan must have been reading her thoughts. "Tiffany, I think we've made enough distance to talk a little. Have you noticed how far we have come without tiring?"

"You're right, Dan," she said over her shoulder, "We need to keep pushing until we can find shelter in those foothills, but I think we can start discussing our observations and goals when we see opportunities."

Dan agreed. "Yes, we need shelter before we stop. I have noticed a few tributaries join our stream. The water's force helps us make good time and takes a lot of the load off our arms."

Ann surged up beside him. "Still, I have never felt this strong."

There were a few grunts of agreement around them.

Tiffany looked back at the swimmers. "Tribe, let's hug the left bank. It looks like this stream turns into a river as it flows into that canyon ahead. We may be in danger if we are out in the middle of that stream when we get there. I see some lowland shrubs on the left side. They may give us the cover we need. The other side looks like a cliff. I don't think we would stand a chance there."

Swimming Through the Grass

Penny was the first to reach the left bank, but Tiffany advised her to stay in the shallows. "We don't want to leave tracks. I'm certain those Giants will be here looking for us eventually."

No one answered, but everyone took her advice.

Things went smoothly until they reached the canyon entrance, then Kia lost her footing, slipped, and fell into the rushing current. Within moments, she was struggling to stay above water.

Dan launched after her, quickly caught her, and helped her drive for the shore. In moments, they disappeared around the first bend in the canyon torrent. Penny started to panic, so Stacey herded her and Ann to the shallows. They scrambled in ankle-deep water, stumbling toward their lost comrades. Tiffany found a rocky beach around the bend, where they lost sight of Dan and Kia. The river-worn rocks of the shore divided the roiling river from a scrubby brush of hardy shrubs, small trees, and debris that the river and the elements had tortured.

"Let's try not to leave evidence of our path. Step one rock to another, and let's get up into that cover." Tiffany got no objections.

Once the partial tribe was secure, she asked them to stay put. She would scout the river's edge to find Dan and Kia. She promised to try to be back while the daylight held.

Tiffany retraced her stepping stones back into the water and swam downstream near the bank. Stacey and Randy tried to keep everyone calm as Penny and Ann spent the afternoon fearing the worst. Downstream, a bend or two, Tiffany found Dan and Kia perched precariously in the wide open. They had found a landing on a lump of clay at the bottom of the clay cliffs of the South shore. This was the end of the line.

Roger Haller

51 Pegasi - Sister Tiffany

The only way forward was the torrent of the unknown river, and the current was too strong to swim back to the rest of the crew.

Tiffany pulled herself up to join Dan and Kia on their small perch. She looked up as Dan helped her settle against the sheer wall. "There is no purchase above, is there?" She knew the answer before Dan and Kia shook their heads.

While contemplating the finality of their position, a massive splashing broke their dilemma from downstream. A giant, wading upstream toward them, broke out in a lopsided grin. Another two giants broke the current directly behind it. The first giant reached them, perched his huge fists on his hips like a reprimanding mother, and chortled.

The desperate humans had never heard that reaction before. The giant held out his hand, palm upward, to within inches of the stranded escapees. When they made no move, he raised his other hand and signed "Hi." in American Sign Language.

Startled, Tiffany signed "Hi." Back. The giant chuckled again and wiggled his outstretched fingers. Tiffany climbed onto his hand and clutched the fur on his wrist to avoid falling off. Dan and Kia followed suit. The giant tucked them carefully into a pocket in the strap he wore over his shoulder like a Miss America pageant winner.

"We save you." He signed and started downstream.

"Wait!" Tiffany objected. The giant stopped and looked at her as she signed. "We have four more." She pointed upstream.

The giant raised his eyebrows, turned, and headed upstream. Tiffany pointed at the rock beach, and the giants waded to the shore. Tiffany called, but her crew wouldn't come out of hiding.

Swimming Through the Grass

She signed that she needed to go and convince them to come. The giant set her on the shore and signed, "Hurry."

Moments later, Tiffany returned to the giant with the rest of the tentative escapees. Ann, Penny, Stacey, and Randy were squeezed in with the rest, and the Giants headed downstream.

My heart grew two sizes watching the natural love and dedication she showed the tribe, which depended on her strength of body and character.

***

Chapter 5

Friendly Giants - Chuckles

Tiffany and crew were deposited gently on the South shore of the powerful river, just beyond the twin clay cliffs. No one believed they were safe yet, but the fear was beginning to subside. The new tribe of escapees was starting to hope they would see life continue and even a chance to flourish.

Now, with all on the ground, the giants sat cross-legged above the rocky shore. The lead giant began a deep conversation with Tiffany, and Dan helped to translate to the others as the conversation commenced. During the dialogue, the other giants remained silent but for an occasional grunt or deep rumble from their chests. The lead punctuated its signing with its trademark chortle.

With a detailed exchange, Tiffany explained she would call the leader Chuckles. Not sure how that would translate, the whole team sighed in relief as it resulted in an extended chuckle. This warm exchange was magnified when Chuckles turned to explain to the other giants.

It was evident they found it funny.

Friendly Giants - Chuckles

The escaped crew learned that Chuckles and crew were a separate tribe from the Tower Giants that they had encountered in the cages and that he and his tribe meant them no harm. In fact, when they had learned of the escape from the Tower Giants, they decided to move the humans to safety if they found them.

Chuckles made it clear, however, that they would not interfere in the affairs of the Tower Giants in their territory. It was important in their culture to live and let live to prevent challenges, conflict, or even war. Their culture had survived thousands of years without war. He also explained they were all part of the bigger society of Forest Giants. To the South East, there were also Desert Giants

Once Tiffany and Dan explained the Giant's social structure, they all agreed to respect the Giant's relationship and expressed thanks that they were saved from a horrible end. The human tribe began to feel more secure in their relative safety. They began to look around at their new surroundings.

The intuitive nature of the gigantic beasts noted that the humans were beginning to accept their freedom and planning for their next steps. Chuckles began explaining their new environment, options, challenges they may run into, and opportunities. The Giant recommended the local landscape at hand would be suitable for nesting.

It provided shelter from the Screamers, from the air, and the Forest Giants, who seldom visited this canyon, as they had no use for the coast land to the West. Chuckles explained that this is where he came to build his tribe because it was a good place to whelp.

The humans gained two important epiphanies from Chuckle's details. First, Chuckles was male. The heavy fur around the primate genitals concealed their sex, and males and females had much the same build.

45

Roger Haller

His priority was to have a safe place for children. The Giant behind him, his mate agreed with a nod and a pat on Chuckle's shoulder. She understood his message. Secondly, they learned about the monstrous birds, the Giant's called Screamers. Chuckles explained that humans would be perfect prey for Screamers.

Their giant benefactor suggested they build shelter in the abundant trees on the mountainside and stay out of open spaces. He pointed to the rocky outcrops in the trees and signed that there were holes in the mountain's wall. Caves. This was particularly important when they heard screaming in the distance. The Giant leader advised them to keep watching the skies.

Chuckles knew little about the coast to the West but said Giants hated the smell of the bitter waters. A strong odor that interfered with their acute sense of smell.

Dan locked on to the idea that the Giant's primary sense was smell. He explained this to the crew, challenging them to imagine trying to negotiate the landscape in blinding light. It wasn't hard for the human tribe to understand the Giant's aversion to strong smell.

Tiffany asked about the trail to the West. Chuckles explained that they had been there a couple of times, looking for whelping grounds, so he knew the river would fall over two waterfalls on the way, but it wasn't too far to the coast.

He also noted that the Screamers seemed to have the same aversion to the coast. His tribe didn't have any reason to go back.

The lead Giant turned to his tribe, grunted, rumbled, and gestured, and they stood and left. He explained that his tribe was off to get the humans some food and tools to get them started. Chuckles signed that they would not be long.

Roger Haller

Friendly Giants - Chuckles

Tiffany asked where the Giant's camp was, what they suggested for food to forage in the canyon, what predators, other
than the Screamers, they should look for, and any defenses
they would recommend.

Chuckles chortled again and answered slowly, one at a
time. He signed that their camp was up a steep canyon to the
south. His tribe had settled in a high valley overlooking the
clay pass. He suggested it would be difficult for the humans to
climb to their valley. Their home had a vast view of Screamer
territory, and the massive purple raptors were their primary
food source.

He suggested that the berries, the mushrooms, and the
celery stalks their captors fed them in the cages could all be
found locally. The little reptiles were plentiful in the canyon,
but the berries would be smaller, and the celery stalks would
be in open spaces. They would need to be careful when har-
vesting. The meat they had been fed was from the little reptiles
they had met, and the longer, stringier meat was from the
giant purple Screamers.

However, the captives had been fed mostly Screamer
meat, as the little humped-back animals were far too small to
be feasible for the Giants to supply.

He was relieved to see Tiffany and company could harvest
and process them on their own but was surprised to see they
preferred to burn their food. He pointed up the hill to their
cooking fire and wrinkled his nose.

Tiffany explained they had managed to find rocks that
would spark when struck together and with much effort and
dry tinder, had kindled their first fire, She signed they needed to cook their food. Chuckles shook his head in confusion.
Tiffany finally understood. Giants eat raw. For the humans, the
raptor would take much more effort and danger to hunt.

Roger Haller

The purple predators and the Forest Giants would be their biggest danger, but there were rumors of larger reptiles west of the first waterfall they came to. However, because they rarely went that way, no one in his generation had seen one.

The other Giants came wading back into camp again with a large chamois sack. In it, they found fresh and dried versions of the food they had just discussed. Surprisingly, they also produced a few knives, a hand saw, dishes, and pots and pans.

Chuckles chuckled again. These unusual tools had been 'borrowed' from the human hut near the tower. They had been saved as a curiosity, but the Giants had no use for them, as they wouldn't fit their massive digits.

The little band of humans was overjoyed at the food and tools delivery. This bounty would give them time to set up camp and prepare fresh food.

Chuckles and his tribe stood, waved a friendly salute, and stepped into the river. Momentarily, they were out of sight downstream, and there was no trace of them having ever been on the little landing. Tiffany urged the little tribe into the trees.

Randy was ecstatic over he kitchen tools. Three of his favorites were flint lighters. His past life as a chef made him the obvious lead cook, although Stacey was a happy right hand. They had their first meal in their new home. By the time the sunlight was ebbing, they had a rudimentary roof over a sleeping area in the hillside moss under cover of massive evergreens.

I wondered how much of this dedication Tiffany was born with and how much of it was cast in her soul by the trials she lived through in Africa.

***

Friendly Giants - Chuckles

The little band of freedom fighters began the chore of building their camp. The next few days were full of activity as they carved out a new home on the lush mountainside. Chuckles and his mate showed up in a few days with more supplies and some dried Purple Screamer meat, feathers, and tanned hide.

The two Giants seemed invested in the success of the little human tribe, and they spent many hours educating them on the life and society of the Giant species. Tiffany, in particular, was fascinated with their massive neighbors.

They also brought news.

Some Rain forest Giants had searched the grasslands and forest around the berry thicket and were convinced the humans were still hiding in the brambles. They had seen no sign of the escapees. Others were beginning to wonder, though, because they didn't smell them as strongly in the thickets anymore, so they were searching farther South and North, looking for tracks.

The Pass Giants shrugged shoulders but said nothing about the little band of refugees. Chuckles hadn't expanded the conversation but promised to watch out for the humans. He didn't suggest what he would do if they were seen. The Giant did sign to Tiffany, however, that he felt the little tribe would be safe in the canyon pass for now. The Canyon Pass Giants felt the humans had more to worry about with the Screamers.

Several days later, with rudimentary huts built and purple feather kilts on Dan and Randy and soft chamois robes on the ladies in the evenings, the human tribe felt much more comfortable.

They were now finding their own food: berries, celery, mushrooms, and the strange little humped-back animals.

Roger Haller

49

The little village was enjoying evening meals cooked over a fire. Kia had developed a strong cord from the intestines of the little reptile, and Dan and Randy had created long bows from green hardwood saplings. Arrows were too rudimentary to be of much use yet, but they continued to work on them. The crew's imagination expanded as they found rigid willow suckers hardened on the ends in the embers of the fire, made primitive arrows. They began practicing the hunt by adding split purple feathers wrapped to the bow end with the same gut.

Tiffany and Randy became particularly successful. With the help of Penny, Ann proved her artistry with their clothing. Kia and Dan were avid builders, so more huts, furniture, and tools became their contribution. Kia and Dan had also explored the animal path heading West along the river.

Life was settling in the little camp when Randy raised the alarm.

"People!" His shout echoed off the canyon walls and startled two men struggling to come to shore at their camp. Adding to the surprise, the skies opened up with far-off screams. The men looked back at the screams and panicked toward the little band of humans running to meet them.

At first, the newcomers were happy to see the humans but struggled to understand, the urgency in the din, as their new friends became saviors and rushed them off into the trees and a small cave at the base of the mountain.

They understood soon enough as the massive raptors tore at the shrubs and trees protecting the mouth of the cave.

The tribe and their visitors huddled all day in the cool, dark cave as the mind-numbing screams raged in the camp. It wasn't till dusk that they could hear each other talk when the Purple Screamers finally gave up and left.

Friendly Giants - Chuckles

This was the moment they found out they could not understand each other.

The two men were Asian, but no one knew what language they were speaking. They resorted to drawings in the sand around the cooking fire as the camp shared food and feather kilts with the naked men. The tribe welcomed the men to the camp, but the two insisted they would continue West in the morning. They made it clear they were still too close to the Tower Giants and now gigantic Raptors. The two would be moving on. Randy tried to convey there was a coast to the West, but the tribe wasn't sure the men understood.

The two moved on in the morning with a pack of dried meat, dried berries, and a handful of celery stalks. Dan had shown them the path heading West. As they waved and disappeared into the trees, Dan turned to Tiffany and the rest of the village, "You know, we will need to explore that path too. The coast may offer a lot of opportunities. Particularly if the Giants and Raptors avoid it."

Tiffany agreed. "Yes, once settled here, we must explore the coast. I like that these great bodyguards are watching out for us, but oceanfront property has appeal."

The Screamers didn't return, so the little village settled into a routine.

Evenings were spent expanding and innovating the tribe's tools, food collection, security, and living conditions. Roofs on their huts were improved. The arrows became more effective at short range, and clothing expanded with donations of hide and feathers from Chuckles and her tribe. The village began to feel optimistic about its future.

The little tribe was confident now that they were on another planet. Dan and Kia were technologists and scientists, so they dealt with facts.

Roger Haller

51 Pegasi - Sister Tiffany

Tiffany had lived a life of service before this world, and her nature kept her on that path. She was still a natural leader who listened carefully to her followers. Since living in the canyon, in particular, she had focused on listening. These people were all leaders in their own right.

Dan and Kia wanted to get back to that cabin to find out what technology had been involved in this transition. They felt a human-built building would supply ample clues. Randy was all about their diet. He was satisfied with life in this world and wanted to make the best of it.

The Chef was constantly experimenting with their food and types of cooking, and he wanted to explore more options. He wanted to see the coast, and he wanted to understand the seafood opportunities.

Ann had been irreplaceable in the invention and manufacture of their clothing.

The environment didn't demand much so far, but evenings cooled down, so covering at night was helpful. Tiffany noted that no one was in a hurry to cover up completely. They had arrived naked; the shock had worn off, so now, when the village covered up, it was for a reason. The ladies had their needs, so the Chamois and Moss were helpful.

The cooler evenings welcomed the robes, but the breeze across their skin was essential in the bright, sunbaked canyon. The little tribe had become accustomed to living barefoot, but they all agreed sandals would be most helpful. Ann was determined to solve that problem soon.

Penny was a little lost in this environment. She struggled the most to adapt but had no choice. She talked more about what she missed than what she was gaining. Tiffany often thought about the slight, talkative young black woman.

Friendly Giants - Chuckles

The natural leader in the reinvented Sister hoped to find the spark to inspire Penny to challenge herself and grow. Tiffany felt, somehow, there was no going back. This would be the rest of their lives.

I believe Tiffany was the first human in this new world to voice that personal decision. I know my resolve to live out my life in this world was partly inspired by her adoption of the new life.

I saw her dedication to building something better than she had lived through. I felt her desire, and it became mine. This world was where I was meant to be.

***

Chapter 6

West to the Coast

A few days passed as the little camp formed. Relief turned to actual happiness as the village began to enjoy their surroundings for the first time. This canyon pass was beautiful when the residents weren't trying to eat you. The short days were hot and muggy, but the cool mountain breeze flowing down the forested hill behind them swept comfortable breezes across the busy river and up the baking canyon wall across the valley.

Tiffany went off to the solace of her hut early after the eventful day. She thought how thankful she had been that the two additional men had decided to move on. Today, the striking woman recognized some bias in her thoughts, words, and actions. Her Scandinavian blood demanded she be faithful to her sense of right and wrong. She wanted to spend a little time talking to herself.

Perhaps this was the first moment she didn't feel the need to run. Maybe this was what it was like to get rest. At last, she had time to think… Possibly to overthink.

Still, she had to sort out feelings she did not fully understand.

Roger Haller

West to the Coast

She laid on her soft bed of evergreen bows, folded her fingers behind her head, and studied the thatch in her roof as though they were tea leaves. Tiffany worked out an epiphany. She decided she wasn't too fond of Dan or Randy, even though they were nothing but polite, helpful, and non-threatening.

Tiffany had no issue with Ann, Stacy, and Penny. She worked through their strengths and weaknesses, and found them to be very human. In a way, she felt responsible for their wellbeing.

The soul-searching Amazon bombshell couldn't see why she felt the way she did at first, but she could tell she did feel off about men in general. When she couldn't think of anything bad about Dan or Randy, she turned the finger toward herself. She pondered the religion she left smoking in her rear-view mirror and the perpetrators of that terror. They had primarily been men.

Tiffany recognized now that she had built a bias against men because of the ones she had to deal with. She remembered the numbness that had enveloped her when she was owned by men who violated her body and her soul. The troubled leader made a pact with herself to remove the "Original Sin" label from Dan and Randy. She hoped that would help keep the tribe cohesive, allow her time to work out her bias, and mellow out for her second lease on life.

Still… There was something else. Now that Tiffany was no longer married to the church, she was not attracted to the men as she felt her human nature would have suggested.

She wasn't attracted to Ann and Penny, but she admired Stacy's self-owned nature. She could tell Stacy would not rely on anyone to manage her life. She was self-directed. Although that didn't lead to romantic thoughts, Tiffany was beginning to find insight.

Roger Haller

The revelations may have made sense in these circumstances, but she felt more maternal to Ann and Penny, even though Ann seemed older. Penny seemed to be about her age. Ann seemed more like a supportive personality. Strong-minded but not built for leadership. Penny didn't seem to know what she wanted yet, but it was apparent she didn't have a strong sense of self-worth. Tiffany felt she could support them best by leading them to tasks and challenges that suited their natural drive.

She had to think harder about the men, though. She had naturally fallen into a leadership role, which meant she was a leader of men as well. Dan was much like Ann. He was more comfortable in a supportive role, except for his love of technology. The engineer may have even had some feminine traits. He was probably the cleanest, most organized of the tribe.

Randy was amiable, but she noted his testosterone drive. He was more assertive and tended to show off a little with the bow, the building, and the physical chores. She felt his interest but was sure she hadn't encouraged it. He may have been a bit intimidated.

Tiffany finally faded to sleep to dreams of a smooth but powerful partnership with a featureless person who loved and nurtured her. Her fantasy was not about sex as much as love.

During the night, she woke gently from time to time in wandering combinations that featured a smorgasbord of scenarios. All being warm, romantic, exciting, relaxing, and meaningful, but no image of this person revealed itself through the night.

The accidental warrior needed somebody. Not anybody she knew, but somebody. The epiphany she woke with was that she was lucky to belong to the tribe she was with, but it was clear she had not yet met the person who would manifest her dreams.

West to the Coast

"Let's get that trip to the coast under our belt, team." She voiced the thought as she joined Dan and Ann at the morning tea fire.

Dan jumped up, smiling. "Yes, I'm in."

Ann smiled, too, but kept her seat. "I think I've had enough adventure for a while. You go ahead, but I'll stay here, keep the fire going, and stitch up some more robes and kilts from our stock."

Tiffany nodded as she poured her tea. "Yes, maybe just a couple of us should scout it out while the rest stay as safe as they can as we figure this place out."

The conversation inspired Randy, Stacy, and Penny to emerge. Randy asked, "Did I hear something about scouting?"

"Yes, Randy, Dan mentioned yesterday that he wanted to check out the coast. It seems he was inspired by the guys going through. I agree. Chuckles said it is not far to the coast, and we need to know as much as possible about where we live."

"Well, I had my eyes on a berry thicket up the hill, and I do love the dried berries. I had planned a little day trip with this cool new paperboy sack Ann made me."

Tiffany grinned. "That's okay, Randy. We just agreed that only two or three should go. We want to keep the camp safe and productive."

Penny looked back and forth through the conversation. "Randy, can I help? I love Fruit roll-ups, too."

Stacy had plans for some rich dirt she found under the mountain bluffs. She wanted to see if her berry seeds would take off, and she wanted to try a couple of new tea combinations. She had ideas about the local orange moss.

Roger Haller

51 Pegasi - Sister Tiffany

Randy was only too happy to have company, so they settled the plan. Tiffany and Dan would scout the coast, and Randy and the ladies would hold down the fort. With the stage set, Randy asked, "Who's up for a little Humpback sowbelly and mushroom steaks with a touch of basketball berry reduction?"

Having a world-class chef in the village had its benefits.

The chatter turned to happy meal prep, and Tiffany smiled widely as she watched the tight little community come together in a much happier environment than they had seen in some time.

Breakfast was fun. Randy was a bit of a comic, and he had his audience in the palm of his hands by the time they were cleaning up. Randy and Tiffany began packing "paperboy sacks" for their trip. Ann got busy stitching rudimentary sandals for them.

Randy and Penny began planning their adventure to the berry crop and laying out a stripping and drying strategy by the fire for when they returned.

I gained a new perspective on the Pass Camp at this time. Tiffany's soul-searching made me much more aware of the ramifications of our meeting later on. I also witnessed a dynamic between Randy and Penny that I wished I had known back then. I had witnessed a vital building block in Penny's foundation and growth in this world.

***

West to the Coast

The path to the top of the first falls was easy. Tiffany had made an internal vow to get to know Dan better, and the first leg of their journey was an eye-opener. She had resolved to open the conversation as direct but friendly to set the tone of their new relationship.

She stopped at an opening beside the shallow, widening river that was well covered from above, yet let the sunshine through. The result was a calm, inviting, little grassy bank over a dark back-eddy in the stream. She opened with a zinger.

"Dan, you're a good-looking, healthy man. I know living together without clothes is probably desensitizing to a point, but I've felt no sexual tension from you. I appreciate that because I'm not looking for that kind of relationship. Still, I get that vibe from Randy and even a certain amount from the ladies. I want to be open in our little village, so we are all clear about our intentions and keep the camp happy."

Dan looked at her, shocked for a moment, then with a slow grin, he sat on a moss-covered rock by the trail. With a shy, mischievous sigh, he said, "I was wonderin' when this subject was going to come up."

His smile grew wider, "Tiffany, you are drop-dead gorgeous. I understand why you would live with that vibe all around you. However, you're not my type. You are the first to know this, in my old life or the new: I am gay."

Dan's smile turned a little sad now, "I expect you and I have had some common influences in our background. I struggle around heterosexual men, too. Particularly the old-school, entitled white man who has had the mantle all their life."

Dan looked directly into Tiffany's eyes, perhaps for the first time. "They are a broken template of our society's image of a man."

Roger Haller

51 Pegasi - Sister Tiffany

Tiffany was awe-struck. This was not at all how she pictured this conversation going. The stunned leader took a moment to digest. Finally, she sat beside Dan, returned the look to his eyes, and told her full story. This time, it was Dan's turn to be awe-struck.

"Tiffany, I can now see how you became such an effective leader. The fires of hell have forged you. I promise that if you lead, I will follow. I feel safer in your hands than I've ever felt before."

Tiffany smiled, hugged the humble man, and said, "Let's go explore the Wild West, partner."

They chuckled at that and stepped back to their path. By late afternoon, they stood on a massive boulder at the top of a most impressive waterfall and gazed at a thin, horizontal line at the bottom of the sky but above the trees. Tiffany and Dan could see their first glimpse of the western sea.

Once the view sunk in, they hopped from rock to rock across the full width of the river in search of the best way down.

Tiffany called out. "Dan, come look at this. I think I see our path."

She pointed at a narrow animal trail leading over the edge on the far side of the river. The route featured a boulder-strewn pathway between fibrous shrubs, moss banks, and deciduous trees that resembled the willows back home. It dropped what looked like about sixty feet to the riverbed below. They could see their path continue out of sight to the West, along the riverbank.

Dan was excited but cautious. "It looks like our instant dusk is about to hit. Let's camp here tonight and test this climb in the sunlight tomorrow."

Tiffany nodded. "Good plan."

They found a suitable moss bed above the bank, laid out a dried meal, and found, with their shared lives, now in the open, they were happy to share body heat under a Chamois blanket, and both trekkers found some well-needed sleep.

By the time the full sunlight found the hikers in the deep canyon, they had reached the bottom of the falls. They were back on level ground now and onto the well-used trail. They noted mostly the little Humpback paw prints, but there were other small animals with cloven hooves, claws, and a couple of weathered human footprints.

"Ahh, the guys we met made it this far," Tiffany pointed at the clear track.

Later, they found the trail thrashed at one spot with sharp rake marks, scuffs, and gouges. Something big had happened there. They looked at each other but did not voice what crossed their minds. The trekkers quickened their pace.

By mid-afternoon, Dan stopped and held up his hand. Tiffany, following at this point, stopped to see what he was alerted to. He raised his hand to his ear.

Tiffany stepped up beside him on the narrow trail and listened. She heard it now, too.

"The second waterfall."

Again, they stepped up their pace and shortly stood over a smaller version of the falls they had cleared early that morning. They found the path over the edge on the same side as the climb on the upper falls.

Tiffany looked seriously at Dan. "I think we have enough day left to get down this set; what do you think?

Dan nodded. He was thinking of the scuff mark back up the trail, too. "Let's go."

They were on the lower level of their trail in plenty of light, so they put on another hour's worth of travel before looking for a camp. They could smell slight hints of sulfur in the air from time to time, and by mid-morning the next day, they were standing on the shale outcrop into the Western Ocean, with a host of natural bathtubs running where hot and cold streams of mineral and seawater mixed at their feet.

With a short amount of exploration, they found the most relaxing mineral baths they could remember enjoying in their former lives.

They were aware of the open sky above them, as they were now primed to watch and listen for Screamers, but there were none. A few small sea birds soared and skittered past. A flock of grey flamingo or snipe-shaped birds waded through the waters, but there seemed to be little to fear on this foaming shelf edge.

As the light of the day waned, they noted and enjoyed the pale blue phosphorescent cloud of light hovering over the waves.

This would be an amazing camp.

It was an amazing camp, and it had become one of my favorite places. Those mineral baths joined my reward for years of adventure in Bitter Waters.

***

Chapter 7

Bitter Waters

Early the next day, Tiffany and Dan noted that the land to the South of the massive delta they camped on was endless grasslands. To be sure, there seemed to be a mountain range far to the East that probably connected to the one they had just walked through.

To the South, they may have seen the tops of a hill or two, but it was clear they would not learn much from that land in the short time they planned to be on the coast. They agreed that the rise in elevation, flora, and fauna of the north side of the delta suggested the most diverse environment to explore.

Neither of them saw any sign of humans west of the lower falls. The coast seemed wild and beautiful. They found a slow grade increase north of the river delta to the base of a massive black cliff. Dan thought it looked like slate.

It was an old formation, and they noted an irregular base, with towering gaps of sandstone pockets washed out in the wall. Slabs of flat slate with broken sheets provided ready-made flagstones.

Roger Haller

Tiffany lifted one on end and spun it around to inspect both sides. "It's too bad these are so heavy. Can you imagine the floors they could make in our camp? Around the fires and even in the huts?"

Dan nodded. "Maybe we should move down here. I keep thinking of the hot and cold running mineral water baths over there." He pointed at the slate ledge they had enjoyed yesterday.

"That's a great idea," Tiffany agreed, "but we know what we have right now. We have some safety, an environment we are beginning to learn, and Chuckles and his band bring us Screamer meat, hides, and feathers."

Dan nodded. "Well, when we get back with our knowledge of this place, we have options if something should change. I don't want to get too far from that tower and the technology that comes with it until we understand it."

"Yes," Tiffany hugged Dan. "You are reading my thoughts. We must find a safe way to get back and forth to that tower and cabin as the first priority. Once we know how best to free our people from that horror and learn how to supply our own food, this place may be our first big step in this world."

"Okay, let's check out these caves. These may become important too." Dan was starting to get antsy about getting back to the Pass. It turned out that a few of the caves in the base of the slate cliff would be great dry storage.

They agreed the backs of the caves would even be safe from Screamers and Giants if they did come to the coast. The deeper caves showed a little small animal sign but were decidedly dry. There was more storage here than they had in the smaller caves in the Pass.

Bitter Waters

They stepped out and explored the gravel and sand beaches below the cliff and the lightly shrubbed highlands. Standing in the edge of the lapping surf, Tiffany picked up a handful of the black sand and marveled at the sparkle of tiny crystals shining through the black sand like stars in the night sky.

"Beautiful, it looks like you have a handful of diamonds." Dan's scientific curiosity was on high alert.

Tiffany looked closer at her handful, picked a couple of half-carat-sized crystals from the sand, and pulled them up to her face to look closer. "Maybe I do…"

She tucked the two crystals into her bag and investigated an umbrella-shaped tree providing a calm, breezy sanctuary from the tropical sun. Dan was studying an apple-shaped fruit with a dull, tan, leather-looking skin. He could peel the skin back from the stem to reveal a starchy white fruit with little effort. He took a small bite to roll around on his tongue before spitting it out.

"I'm not sure how to describe this, but I think I just tasted a tree potato."

They both laughed. "Well, if you don't die before we get back to the camp, you may have found another form of food for the crew."

To the North, they observed a slow, wooded rise in the land to a high headland overlooking the ocean. The land seemed to drop off in cliffs to the sea, but back from the rocky promontory, the tropical forest looked lush.

"What do you say? Do we spend the day checking out the rise to the North, then call it a day and head for home?" Dan readily agreed, and they followed the base of the slate cliff to a narrow animal trail rising from the promising campsite.

Roger Haller

Although narrow at the start, the trail opened up, and they could see a well-worn path. The padded feet of the little reptiles that supplied most of their protein seemed to keep it well-trod.

By late afternoon, the trekkers set up a camp by a string of small ponds that seemed to be sprinkled over a vast plateau, rising to craggy mountain tops in the East. They observed the silhouettes of tacking raptors far off over the peaks. From the plateau, they could hear the eerie screams from far off, sending shivers up their spines. It was easy to call this the end of their research for this trek.

The bonding pair sat comparing notes around an evening meal when Dan noticed a particular uniformity to the reeds growing at the edge of the nearest pond. He stepped over to the thin-stocked plants and tried to pull one from the soft soil. Surprisingly, the roots seemed to go very deep. He almost gave up. Then he attempted to break off one of the stalks, which snapped with a satisfying pop.

Tiffany went from chuckling at his troubled efforts to standing with a piqued interest before joining Dan in his quest.

Inspecting the stalk and experimenting with the joint between segments, they found they could snap straight arrow shafts out of the reeds perfectly.

With looks of disbelief, they grinned at each other with the epiphany striking both simultaneously.

The shafts could have been mistaken for fiberglass if they hadn't plucked the arrows themselves. Dan took the 3-foot section he was holding to the fire. He held the tip in the hot coals long enough to see the blackened end steam and sizzle as the tip hardened and solidified.

Bitter Waters

Tiffany picked the small Humpback tail they had just harvested with their dinner from her pack. She held it against the end of Dan's new arrow. "We've got some work to do."

Dan grinned. "All we need is a few breastbone feathers from a Screamer. These will work much better than the willow sticks we've been using."

He gathered another dozen shafts and tied them in a bundle with a bit of Humpback gut. Tiffany happily did the same.

Excited with their find and experiments, they worked on ideas for slotting the hardened ends and the best way to adapt the tail-barb to the shaft. With all they learned, Tiffany and Dan happily chatted until the twin moons joined the party and reminded them they had some serious miles to put in tomorrow.

The innovation these two applied to making arrows became the mainstay of our band of refugees, and with my background in archery, they became a foundation for the boot camps we ran all new citizens through over the years. These arrows became a part of my self-image and how I fit into this beautiful world.

***

51 Pegasi - Sister Tiffany

'Tomorrow' was bright and hot, far too soon. By the time they were well underway, the humid heat had them glad they were both carrying Humpback stomach bladders full of fresh mountain spring water from the plateau. Tiffany noted the sea breeze was blowing onshore and was thankful.

"Dan, this area would make a wonderful home. We do need to get the tribe down here to see this. Once we wean ourselves of Chuckle's support, I could be happy in a place like this."

Her revelation made Dan think. He said so. "Tiffany, until recently, I wanted to investigate that tower and cabin badly. My priority was to get back to my life. I loved the technical part of my life, and my personal goal was to be the best cellular network engineer on the planet.

Your comment made me think you may not want to return to your old life."

Tiffany walked a few steps before she looked over at Dan, walking beside her. She decided it was time to begin her new life and be truly happy. She would need to be fully open. As hard as it was, her bond with Dan was starting to work. She decided to expand on the brief history she had supplied him earlier.

"Dan, I told you I was a Catholic Sister working a mission in Africa. I told you a high-level version of my story, but I need to share it deeper so you can understand my goals. Bad people around me were perverting the mission. Two of my sisters and I were captured and defiled by these evil humans. I was nearly ready to die by my own hands when we woke up in the cages. I've already lost my sisters here. One was killed, and one was paired with a stranger and sent to a farm. When I escaped, my life began." She paused to let it sink in.

Bitter Waters

When Dan nodded, she continued, "My real mission began, and this world is where I will live for the rest of my life. With you and our camp, I see the beginning of a world I should have been born into. I will fight to free humans of captivity and from the evils of our former world."

It was Dan's turn to go silent for a while. Finally, he expanded with his new self-revelation. "Tiffany, I was married to my career. I didn't know that until today, but I wanted to return to what I knew, and it wasn't that healthy. I felt empowered by working 60 and 70-hour weeks. My self-image was my work. Today, I understood, for the first time, that I have never had friends like our tribe. I never wanted them. Because I was a closeted gay man, I couldn't confide in anyone.

The vice president of our organization and I had too much to drink one night, so we ended up at a hotel overnight. He was terrified I would tell someone. He confided he was married. He had children. What started as a great time coaxing me out into a happy, playful evening turned into a dark secret. I was sure no one would understand, and I didn't know how to be me in the light of day. You have helped me see me, and I like me. I'm with you, Buddy. I'm not going back. The Pass, or this place, would work fine for me."

They stopped and hugged.

Tiffany pointed down the trail. "Let's get back and free some more people… Starting with us."

The trail moved by faster now. The explorers camped against the slate cliff again late that night and, by morning, were heading back up the river trail. They found the blue mushrooms were thicker in the lower river valley but tended to be in bigger colonies. Although they found no stalks of the New World celery in the lower canyon, plenty grew near the slate cliff and up the trail to the pond plateau.

Roger Haller

51 Pegasi - Sister Tiffany

By mid-afternoon, they were at the base of the lower falls. Tiffany pointed at the crest of the falls where the busy river poured into the lush valley. "Let's camp up there tonight."

Dan thought that was a good idea and set the pace up the side of the falls. Bright heat welcomed them at the top, so they immediately started to look for shade. The South side of the river showed the most promise due to the shadow of the steep mountain slope. They started hopping from boulder to boulder toward the other side of the flow.

A piercing hiss followed by a bellowing roar North of the river, beyond where they had summited the falls, stopped them in their tracks. The wild alarm was challenged by a similar outburst and thrashing in the undergrowth. All of this action was beyond their vision, so instinctively, they headed over the rocks East of the falls. The slope to the South was far too steep for easy exit. North was where the problem lay.

West was away from their goal, so East was the natural goal for their fight-or-flight reaction.

Neither had to tell the other what they were thinking. Their hop-scotch path led them back to the North Shore, but East was the only choice their adrenaline would accept.

As dusk rolled over them, they were at the foot of the upper falls. Tiffany looked breathlessly at Dan and then up the climb. When she looked back at him, he was nodding and reaching for the first purchase on the rock accent.

By the time they reached the top, it was dark. They had only the soft blue glow of mushrooms to find their hand and foot holds. As they stepped up onto the large rock at the crest of the falls, the first moon broke over the canyon walls. They could now see their way to the south shore, where they sat to catch their breath.

Roger Haller

Bitter Waters

Even in the moon's light, the canyon's bottom was too dark to make good headway, so they decided to cold camp. They ate strips of dried humpback, mushrooms, and berries. There was no way they could sleep, so they talked quietly about their day, trek, and new world. When they ran out of words, they cuddled for body warmth and fell asleep just before dawn.

They didn't wake until warmed by the sun, but by early afternoon, they strode into their welcoming little village to hearty hugs and demands for stories.

These stories became the foundation for our expedition to Bitter Waters when we met Tiffany and her village.

***

Roger Haller

Chapter 8

Refugees

The little village spent a few weeks exploring the Southern hillside for a reasonable path back to the berry warren. The primary need now was to recover captives from the Tower Giants.

On one of his visits, Chuckles suggested there may be human-sized paths closer to his village through the higher valleys, but the Giants preferred a simple wade up and down the river to get back and forth.

At first, Tiffany struggled with Chuckle's ready advice. In human form, the conflict of interest made her feel another boot would fall. But the more she got to know Chuckles and the Giant's philosophy, the more comfortable she became with their live and let live rule. They didn't see conflict, only two different trains of logic.

Tiffany felt they should keep exploring closer routes before going further afield. She wanted to avoid Screamers in the higher valleys and any routes that may introduce them to more dangers.

Refugees

Chuckles also suggested there may be a path on the far side of the river, but he hadn't given it much thought yet due to the flock of Screamers guarding the Pass.

The Pass camp was self-sufficient now. They didn't need Chuckle's Pass Giants, but they did appreciate the regular supply of Screamer meat, hide, and feathers. Randy had perfected their drying and smoking process; even smoked berries had an attractive, sweet-and-savory signature. With Penny's help, Ann had a fully stocked hut of spare kilts and robes.

Dan, Kia, Tiffany, and Randy had improved the longbows with rawhide wraps. The new arrows were of professional quality.

Randy and Kia had also introduced them to local tea. They had tea for everyday use, to ease the stress before bed, and to relieve aches and pains after a long day. They all became experts in the gathering and steeping of dedicated blends of soothing tea.

Kia was the leader when it came to finding, testing, and preparing new types of plants. Her skills enhanced their meals, building supplies, and gear. Kia turned out to be a natural with the vines and fibers around them. Her weaving, braiding, and pleating skills enriched their camp more every day. Ann joined her with her sewing skills to enhance and improve their clothing.

Their basic needs were met, so their goal was to find a path back to the humans needing their help. The village naturally broke into two factions, where Ann and Penny took on support roles in the camp. The other faction was the scouts.

Tiffany, Dan, Kia, and Randy rotated through a pattern of exploration in the hills above the camp, looking for the southeast passage.

Roger Haller

Two of the scouts would stay near the camp, hunting and gathering. This rotation seemed to work well as a strong archer and explorer stayed near the camp while two scouts made a much better chance of both making it back to the camp. So far, they found several dead ends in clay-walled box canyons above camp and to the East. They continued to aim higher, feeling they would soon reach a pass that would get them over the cliffs.

Logic told them they would eventually find the path they needed. On their rotation, Dan and Randy finally found the high valley above their camp that seemed to run East and West. To the West, it quickly broke into a series of saddle-backs dropping toward the coast in the West and the South. The explorers finally reached a peak that overlooked a thin horizon over the ocean, where the sun disappeared into the sea while they made camp for the night. They rounded a peak in the morning to see a vast grass vista with rolling hills far to the South.

"I think we've seen what we need to see to the West and South, Randy. I think we have to follow this valley East now to see if we have our route back to the cages."

Randy agreed. "Ya, Dan, let's head down the hill tonight to check in with the camp and take the East path on the next run."

The case was settled, and by evening, they were sitting around the Pass Camp cooking fire and describing their discoveries with the tribe. Tiffany was excited now. She could feel the next stage of her personal quest on the horizon. She was thankful Dan and Kia were as keen to rescue humans and fight the human delivery chain.

Randy, Ann, and Penny seemed more driven by a future away from the Giants. She didn't mind. Tiffany understood the need for a variety of thought in the little tribe. She was afraid she could get tunnel vision if left to her own path too long.

Refugees

She and Kia would scout the eastern route in the valley above tomorrow. Tiffany could almost feel the breakthrough.

They started up the hill early and were looking East on the chosen valley floor by mid-day. They started trekking along a tiny stream that was going their way. The stream didn't last long, though. They filled their water bladders at the twist where the creek headed North toward the Clay cliffs below.

Satisfied they had what they needed for an overnight trip, they headed slightly downhill toward a set of diverging mountain tops in the distance. They made good progress toward those hills throughout the day but camped in the lush valley late in the afternoon. However, they hadn't gone more than a mile or two the following day before Chuckles and his mate came lumbering into their path.

Startled at first, they dove into the underbrush. When she self-consciously peeked out toward the trail, Tiffany waved an American Sign Language "Hi" to Chuckles and Mrs. Chuckles.

The Giants had already sat cross-legged on the trail, waiting for the humans to gain composure. Tiffany noted that they had gotten used to sitting to talk with her and her tribe. They still rose over 15 feet, seated, but she recognized the quiet grace they were capable of when addressing the much smaller humans. They had to understand how intimidating they must look to the tiny creatures.

Chuckles greeted them by name, as he had learned to do, making Tiffany aware of the distinction. He followed with, welcome to our home. She signed to Chuckles, saying that she had a name for him but not for his mate. The statement made him think for a minute. He signed back that she was simply known as his mate. Since their language was far more than vocal, he made a sign of two hands spooning, then pointed at his left, then right hand.

Roger Haller

Slowly, he signed that, in his tribe, he was known as the male mate, and she was known as the female mate, with mate substituting for his name. His name used to be Soft Brown, illustrated by rubbing his hand on his chest and pointing at a dull brown rock. He chuckled. Now, his tribe called him Chuckles… and he pointed at himself while chuckling harder.

Now, he made the spooning sign again and pointed at his mate. Now, she chuckled along with him.

Kia laughed. "We named him so well; his tribe adopted his name, and his wife is now Mrs. Chuckles."

Everyone was laughing now.

Suddenly, I was smiling too. Chuckles was teaching a valuable lesson. Giant's were not the enemy.

Misunderstanding and lack of insight were to blame for the conflict between species, like so many human failings. Everyone needed to be able to see through each other's eyes.

***

Refugees

Chuckles got quiet now. He signed, "I must speak."

Everyone was paying attention now. He told them that more humans had escaped and were coming to the Pass. Two of his tribe were on the way home from the Tower Giant's home when humans broke out but were captured and were now being used for sport. The Pass Giants had heard them planning to use the humans as bait for a Screamer hunt.

Chuckles told the two humans they should be in their camp because his Giants had seen them escape under a dead Screamer. The raptor was floating down the river toward the Pass. Chuckles explained that he could take them back to camp if they like.

Moments later, Kia and Tiffany swayed softly in a sash pocket twenty five-feet in the air. The human pair planned to spend the second night in the valley, but the ride home would have them in the camp by mid-day. Mrs. Chuckles returned to her brood, so only Chuckles escorted them home.

When they got to the village, Tiffany asked Kia to find out where Dan and Randy were so she could get them back to camp in time to help if help was needed.

Kia was happy to get off the Ferris wheel of fur, so she updated the village while Chuckles carried Tiffany upstream to be ready if they should find the escapees needing help. Chuckles didn't want a too big contingent in case Tower Giants were in pursuit. He wanted to avoid the obvious conflict of interest.

They began to hear excited Screamers up the canyon, so Chuckles deposited Tiffany safely on the shore, near cover, and continued upstream in deeper water. He was quickly out of sight, but the raging screams were not easing. As quickly as that thought entered her mind, it changed. Suddenly, the nature of the screams changed.

Roger Haller

One voice changed tone in surprise and stopped. Others seemed to move away. Still angry, but at some distance. Then more distance.

Suddenly, Chuckles appeared around the corner in the canyon wall, clutching four shocked humans. He gently dropped them at her feet and chortled his trademark glee.

"Greetings, Earthlings," she chuckled, "I'm Tiffany, and this is my Giant."

Tiffany gestured confidently at the Giant standing behind the worn travelers. The Giant stood with a silly grin. They both enjoyed the waves of mixed emotions running through the minds of the naked strangers. Particularly telling was the reaction to new views of their desperate vulnerability.

Tiffany took pity on the scared posse and opened with a genuine belly laugh at the sight. She asked the frightened escapees if anyone could speak English. The conversation began their deescalation, and the fear quickly changed to hope. She noted that the Black man appeared to be their leader, and he led the conversation from his team.

"Who are you?" Tiffany asked to no particular excited human.

The Black man took the lead. "I'm Mac. This is Willow, or Sharon. That is Jean and Shiv. He pointed at each in turn.

Soon, they were all asking questions. Tiffany answered a few, then looking at the still angry raptors circling far overhead, she asked them if they would like to move to her camp to continue introductions. She got no objections, so a few quick gestures with the Giant later, she was tucked into his sash pocket and on their way downriver.

Refugees

Tiffany noted that in their crew, Willow seemed a little amused yet apprehensive as she was tucked in one of Chuckle's massive hands beside the tattooed and heavily muscled bald man. She was sure there would be some interesting stories, but she needed to get to know this little tribe better before opening up too much.

A few minutes later, Chuckles deposited the captives at Tiffany's camp, and Chuckles waved goodbye and was off downstream. The Screamers hadn't followed, and dusk was beginning to settle in. After a few more minutes of vetting the new crew, Tiffany asked if they would like some clothing. The afternoon was still warm, but they could tell a cool Westerly wind would cool them off quickly. They all readily accepted.

Tiffany took them to one of the huts and introduced Screamer feather kilts and soft buckskin-styled robes. She informed them their clothing was courtesy of the massive raptors who had tried to eat them.

When she was confident the little band of runaways was as comfortable as they could be, she called in her camp.

Everyone went through introductions, shared their stories, and updated each other on what they had learned about this strange new world. Tiffany's village met Mac, Willow, Jean, and Shiv. Mac was a black man with a pleasant nature. Tiffany initially had a slight issue with him because he tended to interject and lead the conversation. The more she learned about him, the more she saw his natural leadership attributes and her internal bias.

The Frenchman Jean was a tall, handsome man who naturally took a back seat in the conversations. She wrote that off to his struggle to use English. Interestingly, the self-counseling Amazon didn't have a problem with him even when Mac and Shiv often called him Stud.

51 Pegasi - Sister Tiffany

She liked his personality right away. Noting the look on her face when he said it, Mac explained. "I should explain. When I was learning to communicate with the giants, they made it clear that he was a single male to be used for breading purposes. A stud. I tried to explain that to Jean, using the French word for stallion, Etalon. That was the first time I saw him smile. The nickname Stud, stuck."

Shiv was another story. He was blustery, full of himself, and coarse. He had trouble controlling his cursing and his forced machismo. Shiv didn't worry her, though. Tiffany saw through his facade and noted that his travel mates had already accepted him. In fact, he was a hero to them. He had saved them from the Giants and the Raptors.

Willow was still another story. She was intelligent, respectful, confident, and intuitive. Tiffany realized she was attracted to another human being for the first time she could remember. She even eluded to the fact when Shiv proposed that he stay and take care of her.

Tiffany calmly responded that she would rather Willow stay and comfort her. Suddenly, the Scandinavian Amazon ex-Nun realized she had just come out to her new world. No one batted an eyelash except for a disappointed Shiv, who asked if she had a straight sister.

Mac and Tiffany both agreed they were no longer on Earth. The others felt that was the case, but the gravity of not circling Sol anymore had not completely sunk in. It would take time for everyone to understand their new lives fully.

The two camps discussed Bitter Waters and the coast. Mac and his crew decided to continue on to the coast to set up a village there. Tiffany agreed, two camps would be better in the long run, for survival. They could visit back and forth to share knowledge and trade goods.

Refugees

Tiffany explained that she, Dan, and Kia in particular were determined to stay close enough to their captors to break prisoners out from the cages. She had developed a few tricks with the vines in the berry warren.

"The Giants have human help. Humans built those cages. The cage clasps and the hook on the roof, are both human-sized parts. We saw a giant steel tower and a cabin. A human sized cabin with a glass window. I don't know if they'd be friendly or if they are part of the reason we are here."

Mac was excited now. He interjected. "Folks, we've been in that cabin, and it is why we are here.

We were supplied to the Giants as food, by humans.

Humans from Earth."

He let that sink in a moment, then continued. "I'd think what I am about to tell you would be hard to believe, but our lives have been hard to believe for some time now. We have been transported to this planet with a simple little box containing technology we have only seen in science fiction. Think about Star Trek's transporter... Humans have been working on that goal for decades. They figured it out, and I have used it."

Jean confirmed. "Oui, Mac is gone, den he come back." Willow could only nod.

Mac continued. "I accidentally used the box to go to a lab on Earth. I found a folder full of papers that teach us how to configure the transporters. They use radio area network... Much like cell phones but much more advanced. To shorten a long story, I managed to scoop a few of the machines, including that one, reconfigure them, and we've hidden them in the berry warren."

Roger Haller

In the silence that followed, Mac added. " The bad news is, there are other Giant's camps, just like the one we have experienced. Primarily, one to the north, and one southeast. I found a map of these places so we have our work cut out for us. The good news, is we have captured some of these boxes and we can use them once set up, to make our travels much faster and safer once we have the coordinates. I've even used it to bounce around on Earth."

I gave one of these to my father and brother, who are working on the fine details. They think we can use it to freight supplies we need from Earth to our villages. The first box I get from the berry bush will be configured for a Seattle warehouse."

"Wait... You've been back to Earth, and you came back on purpose?" Penny was shocked. Dan and Kia were leaning into the story now and wanted to know more.

Mac looked softly at Penny, "I belong here."

He addressed Dan and Kia. "You two would understand the technology much better than I, but I plan to be back as soon as we get settled, to get those transporters and some human artifacts we managed to scoop. I should be back within a week.

I need to find a path back through the canyon so I can get back to the bramble berries." Mac just said the magic words.

Tiffany, Dan, and Kia all wanted to be involved. They planned for another raid on the cages while there. Dan, Kia, and Tiffany would follow up on the path through Chuckles Valley to be ready when Mac returned.

Tiffany was inspired by the news and promised collaboration, She had her new mission. Then brought the subject back to launching the new folks toward the coast.

Refugees

The result of the talks was that Randy and Stacey decided to go west with the escapees.

Now that I could see clearly, I could see Randy realized, for the first time that night, that he would never get the chance to have a relationship with the beautiful blonde. I could see how much he admired the camp leader from my vantage. He needed to refocus his goals.

Stacey also saw more opportunities with the new crew. She didn't mind Shiv's bluster at all.

Fate would shine on most of their decisions.

***

Chapter 9

New Trails – Chuckles Moves South

They found the high pass trail.

It was long and daunting, with steep climbs and descents on both ends, but Dan and Kia made it to the Cabin Mac had discussed and back without alerting Giants or Screamers. Empowered by their first trip, they did it again in a day less and captured a couple of packs filled with cooking utensils and a few pieces of clothing. The pair of trekkers spent an afternoon in the berry warren. They took the time to peek out at the cages and found the scene busy, but the Giants stopped what they were doing and several sniffed the air and looked to the thorn thicket. Kia and Dan sunk back into safety and headed out the way they came in.

They saw boot tracks. Clothed Humans had been in the warren.

With the activity in the cabin and human collaborators in the berries, this was no place to hang around.

New Trails – Chuckles Moves South

They left to the Southwest as soon as dusk settled. Dan and Kia reported that the Tower Giants and their human friends were on to them now, so trips back to the berry warren may be challenging.

Tiffany smiled. " I like a challenge."

However, they agreed that the next trip should include Mac if he returned in time so they could help him bring back his cache.

Chuckles and Mrs. Chuckles came to camp in the morning after the last trip back. They had been monitoring the human treks through their valley and had visits from the Tower Giants. The relationship began to sour because they suspected complicity since they found tracks headed straight for the Pass Giant's valley.

Chuckles was hesitant as he told them their village was about to migrate farther South. Under Giant Society policy, they were responsible for achieving transparent neutrality.

The village could see this saddened the friendly Yeti, but they understood as he bowed his head to look at his folded knees where he sat cross-legged in their camp.

Mrs. Chuckles reached out beside him, laying a massive hand on his shoulder. As she did, Tiffany noticed she had developed breasts. Lifting her arm, she pulled her chest fur aside enough to see her body developing for nursing. She grunted and rumbled softly from her chest.

Chuckles lightened up, and stood. He pointed to the cliff across the river and gestured to his sash pocket. Tiffany, Dan, and Kia all approached. Tiffany and Kia were scooped and deposited in his pocket, and Mrs. Chuckles reached for Dan. He grinned and happily accepted the ride as she upgraded her involvement in the relationship.

Roger Haller

After waving to those still on shore, the Giants waded downstream, nearly to the falls. They pointed out a wildlife trail on the far side of the river and followed it to the canyon wall. At the beginning of the clay walls, Mrs. Chuckles waded to the edge, pointed to where a ledge started at the water line, and slowly rose up the cliff face.

The ledge appeared to average about four feet wide, with a few narrow sections near three feet and some spread six or more feet from the cliff edge. When the ledge reached chest level on the Giants, Mrs. Chuckles coaxed Dan out of her pocket and deposited him on the ledge. At this point, he was about twenty feet above the river surface. With comically wide eyes, he first froze with his back to the cliff wall. After a few deep breaths, he tried a few steps up the trail and eased considerably. He sent the Okay sign back to the team.

Dan was a good choice for the first to test. He had experience with cell towers. Mrs. Chuckles coaxed him back into her sash pocket again, and the giants made much better time up the stream.

Against the North wall, the water seldom reached over their waists, but at times, the river bottom was slick and slightly sloped, so the journey was not completely without drama. Soon, they came to a section where Chuckles and Mrs. Chuckles were holding their nose. Chuckles pointed above the rising trail.

At the pinnacle of the ledge, he pointed at a large streak of guano flowing down the cliff, over the trail, from the lip at the canyon top. The humans shared in the daunting experience as the odor grew stronger.

Chuckles signed, "Nest".

New Trails – Chuckles Moves South

The Screamer's nest didn't appear occupied at the moment because the Giant's wading created splashing, and they continued to grunt and rumble with each other. Dan pointed out a shallow cave just East of the mess. Tiffany mentioned that the trail seemed to descend from that point. Chuckles nodded in agreement and continued upstream.

The fur tower tourists noted that the ledge path continued without a gap all through the canyon. It wasn't much longer that the tour reached where the river entered the canyon from the vast grasslands. From the vantage point of the Giant's chests, the humans could see the dark line of rainforest in the distance and the darker lump of berry thicket stretching West. They could see a network of small streams meandering toward them from several points East to combine into the substantial river at their feet.

In a business-like manner, Chuckles signed, "Enough?"

Tiffany nodded, and the Giants made double time with their charges as they waded downstream on the South side of the current. From the water level on the wading Giants, Tiffany could see the South side was much shallower than the North. It was still a mighty challenge for humans, but it was a wade in the park for the Giants.

Back in the camp, the Giants assumed the cross-legged position again to better communicate with the humans. Tiffany thanked the Giants for the insight on the North Side trail and apologized for the issues the Giants were now seeing from their cousins in the Tower tribe. She assured them that survival was their only goal.

Chuckles waved the issue off. He explained there were other politics involved that separated them before humans in their world. Although the high pass was an excellent location to raise families, the area they found in the South was even better.

Roger Haller

It provided a much bigger hunting ground, new sources of food, and a lower elevation that didn't include as much climbing. It would be a good whelping home.

Remembering the signs she had seen on Mrs. Chuckles, she signed to Chuckles if it would be all right to address a question to his mate. As she signed the request, Mrs. Chuckles chortled and signed yes. Surprised, Tiffany smiled and asked if she could approach her. The Giant happily nodded a universal agreement. Tiffany stepped up to her, tapped her own stomach with her open palm, then pointed at the Giant's midsection.

The towering female beckoned her closer and unfolded her legs on the ground, inviting her in. Tiffany stepped up and rubbed the expanding abdomen above her. The Giant was well along in her pregnancy. The bulge jumped as Tiffany rubbed it.

The females of two species, from two planets, from solar systems light years apart, smiled at each other in a sisterly bond. The act solidified that nature was universal.

Mrs. Chuckles proudly smoothed her fur aside on both sides of her chest to show the swelling breast tissue and growing nipples. She signed one more monsoon. Tiffany repeated the statement out loud. This was a new development. Kia repeated the statement and then added, "How long? We need to prepare."

Tiffany translated to the Giants. "How long till the monsoon? We need to prepare."

The Giants looked at each other briefly, and Chuckles replied, using his digits. He signed 24 Suns back to Tiffany. Everyone got it. Kia breathed, almost under her breath. "Three weeks, give or take."

New Trails – Chuckles Moves South

A shiver ran down my spine. Monsoons were still a trigger for me. I suppose the monsoon would always be the avatar for my removal from this planet.

***

Tiffany changed the subject without words. She stepped into the Giant's fur, her arms outstretched around the growing baby. Her face sunk into the luxurious fur, and she smiled. Mrs. Chuckles smiled widely, too, then softly cradled the striking blonde woman to her body.

Still smiling, Tiffany stepped back and signed, "Thank you". The rest of the camp repeated the sign and the Giants stood. It was easy to see they had mixed feelings. They were getting close to the little band of humans just as they had to say good-bye.

Chuckles signed. "We go now to our new home. When all is good, come South to visit. We will know you are there." Moments later, they were gone.

That evening, around the dinner fire, there were three hot topics. Dan submitted that they had to try out that North side trail immediately. He, Tiffany, and Kia planned the scouting mission. Dan and Kia would cover the trail while she took care of the move.

Tiffany also decided to stay in camp and prepare for their conversation with Mac. He was to be back in a few days. They had a lot to do, and they had to ensure Mac and his crew would be okay with that. She didn't think it would be a problem but wanted to have a plan-B ready. She remembered Dan and her trip to the plateau, North of the river, and thought there was much opportunity in that direction.

The third conversation of increased importance was about the monsoons and the time they had to make the trip to the East and migrate to the West. If they didn't hear from Mac this week, she would head for the coast to get things started.

The next day began with a surprise, however. Chuckles was back. Mrs. Chuckles was not with him this time, but he had two more humans in his pocket.

New Trails – Chuckles Moves South

First, he plucked a middle-aged man with thick, red-blonde hair from his pocket and deposited him gently on the camp landing. He was a small, medium-built man who clutched a pair of spectacles.

Then, the gentle Giant tried to pluck another human from his pocket, but the captive was elusive and seemed attached to the seam at the bottom. Finally, he removed his sash and carefully laid it at Tiffany's feet. She bent to peek into the fold and finally coaxed a young woman from the sash. The woman was petrified at the sights around her but sought safety behind the tall, powerful woman.

Chuckles announced they had smelled humans climbing the trail to their valley as they were leaving. He took the time to capture and get them to the Pass Camp but did not try to communicate with them. He said he had to hurry to catch up with his tribe, but he knew these two were in good hands.

Tiffany took the captives up to the cooking fire. Ann brought them robes, and Stacey brought tea. The little tribe learned they now had a doctor in their midst. Dr Tim Fletcher said his friends back home called him Dr. Tim.

He was not married; he had just lost his parents to an auto accident, and all other relatives were distant, both in relationship and geography. They were all in Europe. He had no siblings. The sad doctor explained the only thing he had to live for was the promotion to lead medical partner in the business he worked for. But another doctor hotly contested the position. The other doctor made his life miserable.

Sirih was another story. Priyasirih Vigaya Jones had married an American to speed up her green card application. Born Priyasirih Vigaya Ramachandaran, she had come from a small tribal village in India and had been working as a software tester.

51 Pegasi - Sister Tiffany

The trembling woman had friends in Kansas City, Missouri, but her husband saw that as a challenge and moved her to Indiana to break her connection to others. She was desperate to escape a cruel marriage, but she had no intention of going back to India. She loved technology and saw a future in America if she could break free.

Sirih rebelled and locked her husband out one evening, but a brick through her living room window was the last thing she witnessed before ending up in a cage. It took a lot to get her to open up, but clothing, tea, soft conversation, and empathy was better than she had experienced over the last few days.

Their escape came about when they were paired in the same cage with another couple. The cage they were transported in fell open, and the two dropped to the ground next to the berry warren. They escaped into the thorn bush, but the other two were still in the cage.

Dr. Tim acclimated quickly, but Sirih stayed in Tiffany's shadow for the next couple of days as the camp coaxed her slowly out of her shell. Two days later, Tiffany, Dan, and Kia were creeping up the trail on the North cliff face. They hadn't seen or heard Screamers for a few days, so they felt the time was right.

They made the pinnacle of the trail and inspected the slight convex in the clay wall that allowed them to tuck in off the trail. The bad part of the experience was the smell of the guano streak, which was a few feet east of the tiny cave. It seemed to be dried up, at least. Tiffany felt the smell could have been much worse.

The trio had seen enough for one day. The trail headed down now, and they had seen it from giant height, so they were confident they could use the trail, barring any Screamer activity. This trip wasn't bad.

New Trails – Chuckles Moves South

They had gone halfway, and it was still morning. As they reached the valley floor, Kia patted the top of a small tower of clay dust at the bottom of the wall.

"Hmm," she let her mind wander as they entered the forest-covered part of the trail. They looked across the river but saw none of their villagers.

"I suppose they don't expect us back just yet. I see smoke from the fire, but everyone must be busy." Tiffany thought about whistling but decided against it. There was no sense winding them up if it would be a couple of hours before they were back in camp. By the time the sun was directly overhead, they were hopping from boulder to boulder to cross the river above the falls.

They were back in camp within an hour and found the camp abuzz with a visitor. Mac was in camp.

Mac… How I wish I were walking into camp now, too. For now, he is happy. His Willow waits for him in Freedom. This path is critical to my history and the history of this small band of humans in this fantastic world.

***

Chapter 10

The Move to Freedom

Tiffany, Dan, and Kia whistled their arrival minutes after Mac had arrived. The timing was uncanny because everyone had news and was waiting for news. There was a lot to learn. The trekkers had looped around the bottom of the camp to the clearing where they all met. As they noticed Mac was in camp, they trotted into the fire circle to join as the second round of tea poured.

The questions started before they settled in. The first question was about the trip to Bitter Waters, the camp, and the health and welfare of the new villagers. Particularly pointed was the query on Randy and Stacey. The deluge ensured that Mac started the stories. He got to the bad news first.

"Randy didn't make the trip with us, folks. He was on point and disappeared at the top of the first falls." Mac dropped his head while he spoke. It was easy to see he struggled to keep his lip from quivering. "We heard a Screamer that was too close. We were tucked into the brush well, but we were worried about him then. When we finally caught up, we saw his tracks simply end in the sand between boulders."

The Move to Freedom

A brief silence fell on the camp. For a few moments, everyone was busy with their thoughts. A broken-hearted sigh broke the silence, followed by open weeping as Penny got up and strode toward her hut. Ann stood to take her elbow, and they stopped halfway to the hut in a quiet hug.

Mac saw an opportunity to break the mood and told the small camp how his crew had fallen in love with the base of the slate cliff at Bitter Waters and unanimously agreed their new home would be called Freedom. The cliffs protected some great sandstone caves. He told them that Stacey seemed to be getting close to Shiv. He felt they made a great team.

Hearing about the success of the new village, Ann led Penny back to the gathering. Penny smiled weakly through her tears. "Sorry, Randy and I were getting close. He was going to come back for me."

Tiffany wrapped an arm around her. "Don't worry, Penny. We all loved Randy in the short time we got to know him, but we knew he was even more special to you. Let's make our future on this planet wonderful in his name."

Penny nodded and tried to smile bigger. "Let's hear more, Mac."

He took his cue and told them about the discussion about naming the planet. The Pass village learned the Humans now called this planet "Aard." When they heard the naming story, no one had an issue with the name.

When she saw everyone absorbing the success of Freedom, Tiffany turned the tables. "Mac, could you use more citizens in Freedom?"

At first, he thought she was talking about sending more escapees his way and said, "Of course. That has always been the plan."

Roger Haller

She told him about the conversation with Chuckles. The Pass Camp had to move. There was no hesitation. "In a heart-beat. This pass is going to remain important, though. We need to continue raiding the Tower Giants and taking over the technology in that cabin. I hear you have a new trail out in the open."

Tiffany turned to point through the trees at the sheer clay cliff across the river. "Can you see the trail?"

"No... not really. I can imagine a few horizontal lines being ledges, but I can't imagine traveling across it in full view of Purple Raptors and Giants."

"Did you see us waving at you across the river as we returned down the trail?"

"No, but I was distracted by this great crew here."

"Okay, Kia has developed a great camouflage process.

I know there is always danger when we are out in the open, but you'd have to be looking for us to find us on that ledge covered in clay. Dan and Kia are planning another trip, so maybe now is the time if you were to join forces."

Mac was impressed. The Pass Tribe meant business. He agreed it would be the right time to join forces, and they quickly agreed to stage a new breakout and capture the cache he tucked away on his last trip to Berry Warren.

The rest of the day was spent with Dan and Kia relating their experience with the lab over the last two visits. Kia followed Mac's lead and was transported to the lab on Earth. The new technical team agreed they needed to set up their own connection to Earth before destroying this one. As they huddled to set up their excursion East, Tiffany and the rest of the Pass Tribe began preparations for Freedom.

The Move to Freedom

By the end of the day, they were ready to go their separate ways.

The morning started with hugs and even a few tears. Uncertainty was even stronger in this strange new world, as any trek could be the last, just as any trek could result in the beginning of something new and fascinating.

Dan, Kia, and Mac waved goodbye as they headed for the newly named 'Randy's Rock.' There, they would cross the river and head East to the Berry Warren. Tiffany and company took a little longer to pack what they could carry and to store and preserve what they had to leave behind for future use. By late morning, Tiffany and tribe were mobile.

Tiffany, Ann, Sirih, Dr. Tim, and Penny decided to take their time going West together. They had a new respect for Randy's Rock and wanted to spend the late afternoon tucked into the thick forest at the falls before making an early descent the next day. Tiffany had described the heavy drama the trail had seen between the falls. She related the story of the scuffing and scratching from something big that she and Dan had witnessed. They all wanted to be clear of the plateau between the falls in one well-lit day.

The first evening was somber, and the camp was quiet as the three original women remembered Randy. Penny scratched Randy's name in the colossal namesake and a simple RIP. Later, she confessed they had been closer than they let on and explained Randy to Sirih and Dr. Tim. As planned, the posse climbed down the falls to the plateau floor before the Sun was too hot. They made good time.

They did stop short, however, when they came to thrashed brush along the trail that ended the tracks of a cloven-hoofed animal. They heard a deep rumble like an awakening lion not far to the North.

Roger Haller

51 Pegasi - Sister Tiffany

No one had to urge them to move faster. The migration made double time for the next couple of hours and was soon at the top of the lower falls. Even though they heard or saw nothing but a few humpbacks and birds, they needed no reminder to get down the falls before dark.

Running out of time, they agreed to camp, which consisted of eating some dried Humpback, berries, and mushrooms. They then found a tall evergreen with a large pair of horizontal limbs branching out about twelve feet from the ground that they rigged into a small platform to huddle on for the night.

Feeling relatively safe, they kept one set of eyes open on two-hour shifts through the night.

I could feel the trekker's fear, but I could also feel their resolve as they launched a new chapter in this strange new land.

Tiffany was reconciling her past, her disdain for men, and perhaps her sexuality. She felt her guard slipping some with her new relationship with Mac and bonding with Dan. Still, the striking blonde felt more comfortable leading the ladies and reflected on her reaction to meeting me.

I noticed that Dr. Tim seemed neutral to her, focusing on the new environment. He was friendly but had the aura of a benevolent elder, even though he was less than ten years older than her. She remembered what she said when propositioned by the brash yet nonthreatening Shiv. She was asking herself if she would be more comfortable in a sapphic relationship.

Ann was also fearful but seemed to lean more on Dr. Tim during this trek. I could now see this relationship growing far before I noticed it in camp. In his turn, Dr. Tim didn't seem to be afraid. From him, I felt a deep fascination with his new world, and the mind of a scientist was at work. He seemed to be looking for the logic in everything new. For the most part, he was happy.

The Move to Freedom

Penny was on pins and needles. She was emotional and teary. The transplanted office worker overreacted easily and constantly looked at the sky. She was going to need some time and inspiration. I thought she would do well with some archery lessons. She was far from her office environment.

***

51 Pegasi - Sister Tiffany

The citizens of Freedom welcomed the immigrants into camp mid-afternoon. Their welcome became a celebration of inclusion as they were reunited with Stacey. There was a somber moment when Stacey mentioned Randy, but Tiffany made a mental note to talk to Penny about building a local memorial for Randy.

In Mac's absence, the new citizens were directed to Willow, so they held court on her porch, and she delegated. Tiffany needed to bond with the natural leaders growing in the village. Stud and Shiv showed her around and included her in exploration, scouting, defense, and hunting discussions.

Willow was impressed with the work Dan and Tiffany had done with the arrows, but took Dan aside to build his knowledge of archery mechanics. She started with Nocks and Nockpoints.

Stacey took Ann and Penny to the local foods and fibers we had collected and stored. She started leading them on foraging excursions. She was obviously in her element and had stepped into a leadership role in this regard. Penny was more interested in the archery class.

Willow took charge of Dr. Tim. She showed him the caves, and he chose a dry section in the back of one to store his growing stash of medicines, moss, and tools. Later, she took Penny aside, showed her where to find the arrow reeds, and began her archery lessons. She was a natural.

Tiffany updated the Freedomites on Mac, Kia, and Dan. She explained the new North Wall Trail and how it might speed up our guerrilla strikes on the Tower Giants. She also explained Kia's clay mud packs and how they helped trekkers blend in with the wall.

Tiffany added that the clay helped block the Sun's rays and made their skin feel soft and smooth when rinsed off.

The Move to Freedom

Tiffany took Stud and Shiv aside to trade some building techniques. She was especially helpful in identifying vines that could be stripped of fiber, rolled into rope, and dried. These fibrous ropes worked particularly well when lacing down thatch made from palm fronds.

The expanded village had gelled for a week, but nerves were on edge as Mac's expected return with Dan and Kia was due. There was no insight into their trip, but the air was getting muggy, and the season was ripe for the foreboding monsoon the Giants had forecast. The refugees knew their lives would change drastically as heavy rains hit and the mountain pass would become a vicious torrent.

The band was more fearful for the safety of their missing trekkers now, and Jean, Tiffany, and Shiv spent a good deal of time exploring the river bed to the falls for signs of their expected adventurers. No one could find any human sign on the trails.

The wind had started to get stronger onshore now, and it carried super-heated moisture. There was no comfort, so more villagers found an excuse to search the riverbed. They spent a lot of time in the surf and the mineral tubs, where the air was refreshing and sweet, mixed with the onshore breeze. Everyone kept looking inland at any noise. Still nothing after a week and a half.

The rain hit. The village watched the foreboding wall sweeping toward shore, and the world knew what was coming.

Small animals, birds, and even the vegetation were agitated and scrambling to address the onslaught.

The wind was powerful, and it was now wet. Darkness hit like a lead blanket. Just as the last light faded, they heard Tarzan from the East.

Roger Haller

51 Pegasi - Sister Tiffany

That would be Mac's signal that our people were incoming. The village come to life, and emotion rose through me as I watched the tribe rush out with pitch torches to welcome Mac, Kia, and Dan as a host of new citizens entered camp in a hero's procession. The crew hustled the travelers into the mouth of a cave where a large fire was maintained to fight the rain and howling wind. They carried transporters and sacks full of clothes and housewares.

The triumphant troop was banged up, to be sure. Mac had the most serious issue. A Latina, introduced as Maritza, had done an impressive job of bandaging Mac's shoulder. As the stories came out around the fire, it turned out there were a few more injuries and some death-defying stunts to escape the Giants, but all was well now in the little village of Freedom.

The valiant new immigrant, Jesus' plunge into the Rio de Libertade to save the life of Lawrence.

The man who despised Latinos, would be told over the community fire throughout the history of this fledgling village as long as humans lived on Aard. He never elaborated on the rescue, but Lawrence showed some humanity by telling the village how the wiry South American saved him. He had thought his life over when the strong brown hands pulled him ashore and made him breathe again.

The newcomers, Hilda, Julio, and Vera joined the camp along with Jesus, Maritza, and Lawrence.

My soul swelled with happiness and pride as I watched the exquisite beauty painted in the happiest time I had ever lived blossom in love.

The monsoon that would color our weeks ahead in muddy gray was no match for the beauty of this mighty band of survivors growing into thrivers.

Roger Haller

The Move to Freedom

I saw a new side of Jean as he looked smitten over the young German, Hilda. The newcomers would become cornerstones of this new society.

I think this was the first time I saw Tiffany smile with her eyes. As Freedom blossomed, so did she. In spite of herself, she was opening up to her village family. She was becoming fond of Mac, Jean, and even Shiv. She was also rather impressed with Jesus, the new recruit, who jumped 60 feet into a raging torrent to save a man who didn't like him.

Something was happening to these people. Each of them was becoming more than they were before, and when joining ranks, the village was becoming more than the sum of its people.

***

Roger Haller

Chapter 11

A Trail North and Biology

The Monsoon season had the villagers huddle and plan. Mac initiated town hall meetings where everyone was encouraged to give their opinion and listen to each other's views. Tiffany quietly paid a lot of attention to Mac. It was apparent he had been a leader before, and she noticed he was fair, if nothing else.

She felt he may have been trying to delegate too much, but he had everyone's attention, and his strategy seemed to work, so she decided to bide her time and see where it led.

He used a round-robin method to draw statements out of everyone. The contemplative warrior watched as she learned a great deal about the villagers. She felt she could trust any of them… but for one. She could not see herself trusting Lawrence, the lawyer. He reminded her of men who had ruined her view of the male of the species.

Most of these new citizens had been broken by people and events in their last life and were looking for direction. She knew she could help. Some were leaders and explorers.

Roger Haller

A Trail North and Biology

She would plan best with those ones because she was dedicated to building a team of warriors who would join her to free people from the cages. Her thoughts were interrupted when she heard Mac call her name. His question came into focus. "Tiffany, what should our priority be at this point?"

It took her a moment to form her answer as she had just heard others say they needed to recruit people with particular skills. She responded with, "We need people who want to be here. We need people who want a second chance and want to contribute to who we become. As we have all seen, it won't be easy, but our lives mean so much more here. Some arrived because someone decided we were no longer useful on Earth. Most of us found our calling here. We need to take the decision away from whoever is making it back on Earth and enable folks who have hit the end of their rope to find a new rope here."

Tiffany made a significant impression on everyone. They looked around the camp and saw people, just like who she called for. They related to her. Mac, in particular, was struck by her response. He recognized one of the new leaders of the camp, and he immediately knew what her calling was.

I caught a nuance I had missed before. Mac hesitated before he carried on. I now knew why. He balanced the needs and desires of the whole village but noted the strategies of those who showed leadership personalities. He knew one or more of these leaders would someday lead this society.

He continued the call-outs until everyone had a say. He called on Lawrence near the end of the circle, and I felt a sigh of relief from Tiffany as the snide lawyer said he wanted to leave. He wanted to go back to his life. Mac let him know his ticket to Earth was coming soon.

Tiffany closed her eyes briefly and sighed quietly again across the fire.

Roger Haller

The Monsoons cleared soon after, and the first transporter was built on a gentle hill beside a pond on the plateau to the North. It wasn't a far trek to the transporter pole, so the team got to know the trail well in the next few days. After a quick test from Mac, the new Landing Transporter was deemed ready, and Lawrence Hempler was sent home to Earth. No one else asked to leave.

Mac did go back to Earth to ensure Lawrence moved on and did not become a liability to the Transporter portal on Earth. Mac had big plans for this transportation, and he had the full attention of Dan, Kia, and Sirih,

The camp was excited about Mac's desire to import people.

They liked the idea of finding people who needed a new life but also had the skills the village needed. For now, Tiffany was much more interested in saving the people in the cages, but she agreed to focus on that effort while Mac focused on immigration.

Mac's movement gained more popularity when he set up freight delivery. His father and brother pulled through. The village began seeing some of the luxuries they had grown used to on Earth. They were deemed essentials in their last life but now were luxuries.

Knives, thread, textiles, paper, pencils, hammers, saws, and many simple tools that made life easier were suddenly available. Razors and scissors became some of the most popular imports.

Everyone seemed to fall into place in the new society. Tiffany, Jean, and Jesus stayed single and bonded as scouts and explorers, although Jean's relationship with Hilda was growing. Tiffany wasn't sure how long he would stay on the trail.

A Trail North and Biology

All three planned to hit the cages to save more people, while Mac worked on Earth more and more to disrupt the supply chain. This relationship worked well when Tiffany understood his need to shut the faucet off on Earth as the end goal. Shiv was more interested in building on the new planet.

The original plan called for Tiffany, Shiv, and Dan to go North and Jesus and Jean to get people from the Tower Giants back to Freedom. With all the changes happening so fast in Freedom, Tiffany, Jean, and Jesus were it.

They decided to make sure Freedom was not empty of firepower for too long, as we felt Larry or the humans who were supporting the Giants would be trouble.

Tiffany stayed behind as Jean and Jesus took a flash trip to the cages. Jean was back quickly with a bald young woman and a man. The scouts had split up on the way back and Jesus took an extra week on a southern path back. He had two more men. The village met Princess and Oliver as Jean, the Stud, brought home his two immigrants, but they had to wait a week more for Jesus to arrive with Mutt and Pete.

The next couple of Aardian months were spent building the village. This time was also a time for scouting for resources, hunting new game, learning about the coastal environment, and storing food.

Mac, Kia, Dan, and Sirih had the Transporter zoned in, and Mac imported Paul Sutler (Popeye), whom he had met in Seattle, while making sure Lawrence didn't stick around. Popeye was another middle-aged white guy who initially made Tiffany nervous, but the more she got to know him, the more she liked. Perhaps it was the fact he reached out to her as an expert when he needed to build the Landing Cabin. He seemed to be secure in his abilities but was unafraid to ask for help and treated her as a mentor, not a 'woman.'

Roger Haller

He listened with respect. He became a great asset to the village, so she had to admit that Mac's approach was not so bad... So far. The striking warrior needed to get to the cages, though. She felt things were good enough here, and it was time to save some people.

While Mac was busy, she spent some quality time with Dan and the transporter team, going over the maps of transporters they had nicked from the lab on Earth.

She brought Jean and Jesus into the discussion, and they began planning trips to the Northern cages. When they had that local clean, they would begin plans for the South East.

They started with a trip to the Tower Giants. They managed to get to the other side of the clay canyon without alerting the Screamers, then out into the rivulets that made the robust river that ran through the canyon. They got about halfway to the berry brambles when they noted that the berry warren was only half the size they had last experienced.

It had yet to grow out entirely from the burn the Giants did after the last raid. Traveling at night, they also noted lights on in the cabins. There were more cabins now, and they were occupied. Humans: These would be bad guys.

They stopped for a quiet discussion. Tiffany brought up the Giant's camp to the North. They had a rough idea of how to get there. They could skirt the Tower Giant's camp and head due North in the relative security of the rain forest jungle. Or, they could skirt the mountains to the west, staying near the vast grasslands but taking advantage of the scrub brushes and light forest. If they were to go through the Jungle, there would be a bigger chance of being detected by the Giants with their strong sense of smell. There would probably be well-used Giant trails between the Tower camp and the Giant's Northern camp.

A Trail North and Biology

Should they stay in the foothills, they were treading new ground. Territory that had not been mapped in the bad guy's lab.

I could easily see from my vantage point, that Tiffany was growing her passion for saving human prisoners.

She didn't have trouble convincing Jean and Jesus to join her mission. At heart, Tiffany was still a missionary. She needed to save those in peril. My love for this sapphic warrior grew stronger.

***

Roger Haller

51 Pegasi - Sister Tiffany

The freedom fighters opted for the Western path to the North. The team made good time back to the clay cliffs. They scouted the North route in the early dawn for a viable path. Jean found a way through the shrubs and small trees that seemed to stick to the shelter.

The predominant tracks were padded paws with thick, stubby claws. The tracks were about the size of a small dog with separate "finger" marks like poultry… but thicker.

Jesus pointed out some humpback tracks, but they were not as frequent as seen near the berry warren or out at Freedom. There was also a cloven hoof seen from time to time. This one seemed to come and go from the grasslands more than the bigger tracks, which seemed to stay in the hills. The thicker tracks provided passable trails through the foothills.

Tiffany was satisfied with the cover but would have liked more during the day, and the day was brightening. They could now hear distant Screamers, so she suggested they find shelter for the day as soon as possible.

It was beginning to get hot, and the Screamers were getting closer when Jesus found an entrance to a small dirt cave dug horizontally on the side of the hill. The hole seemed like a lair of the animals that left the bigger tracks. However, the tracks all seemed at least a few days old. All three set arrows to their bows and crouched to step into the dark. Once their eyes adjusted, the entrance was well-lit, but the den curved right for a few feet, then left again.

The explorers stepped into a cool cavern with a floor of dried grass. No one was home.

They had been up traveling a high, narrow ledge all night, treading against the flow in a creek until dawn, then diverted into the heat of a semi-desert day. This cave was what they needed.

A Trail North and Biology

Tiffany broke out a handful of dried Humpback, Berries, and Mushrooms. The guys followed her example and shared water from one of their Humpback bladders.

The tired troupe dozed comfortably for a few hours and rested to prepare for a moonlit trek when Alpha and Beta woke up. They took turns as they stepped out of the hole for bio breaks and to test their surroundings, with little to report.

Shortly after the sunset, there was a loud squeal at the entrance of the cave, a reply nearby, and a panicked scuffing as the homeowners found aliens in their home. The animals were gone before the intruders could respond.

Tiffany used the excitement as the launch for their trip North.

The explorers felt safe, although the light wasn't completely gone from the skies. They could hear no Purple Screamers, and the environment seemed still but for the regular movement of small birds or pollinators around them and the rustle of a humpback or two. Far to the East, they could see the dark line where the rain forest took over from the grasslands.

Soon, however, it faded with darkness. They got in a fair distance before the light left them entirely.

The travelers had to sit on the trail until Alpha showed up.

Jean noted that there weren't many mushrooms around. There were no Aardian night lights on this trail. Finally, Alpha showed up so the trail was now apparent again, so the journey continued, and soon they had Beta to help. Night travel was, by far, the best plan in this environment.

By dawn, Tiffany was happy they had put so much distance in with little trouble. They could no longer see the forest to the East, and the foothills seemed to wind northwest more.

Roger Haller

51 Pegasi - Sister Tiffany

The loss of forest horizon worried her as she knew they would need to move East at some point to get to the Northern Giant's cages.

She was pulled from her thoughts as Jesus pointed at a thick grove of evergreens up the hill several yards. The animal path split. One trail went up to the grove, and the other went down to the edge of the grasslands. Tiffany nodded, and the team went uphill to the green cover.

A trickling stream and a cool oasis of cover welcomed them. The haven even provided a patch of blue mushrooms and humpback tracks at the creek. Near the bottom of the grove was a welcoming little pool. Tiffany set her gear near the stream, stripped off her purple kilt, and sank into the refreshing pool.

Looking up at her partners, for the first time in a long time, she felt the hormonal vibe from her travel mates. The fleeting glances told the story in a micro-moment, and it was over. Jean grinned first, stripped, and climbed in to enjoy the pool.

Jesus took a minute or two longer as he prepared camp for breakfast. "Roca basaltica."

The happy camper pointed out a Basalt outcrop they could tuck under. He soon joined his tribe in the swirling pool. Tiffany recognized the gravity of the dynamics. Even though she wasn't interested, she knew her body was sending signals. The complicated warrior never felt safer, though. The considerable frame on Jean and the taunt muscle of Jesus' body should have been ringing her bell, too, but she knew that bell was broken. She had learned that these two men would give their lives for her. Not because she was a woman but because she was family.

Nothing was said, but everyone felt the biological message.

A Trail North and Biology

Jean moved the topic to the logistics of their safe little camp. He suggested they remember this camp. This trail was a great find so far. It could be a good choice for these raids as long as it connected with the Northern Giants.

Jesus agreed. Everyone was happy to change the internal conversations. Planning their night trek took their attention until their hunger drew them from the water. They diverted to the packs for food. Jean was able to pick off a curious Hump-back that was headed down the hill for the grain fields. They felt comfortable building a small cooking fire with dry sticks to cook their meal.

Very little smoke, no Screamers, comforting dips in the fresh pool, and rotated sleep shifts made for a strong team as the sun began to set.

I thought I knew Tiffany well by now, but the rest stop at the little hillside oasis made me think deeper. I suspected her evolution may not yet be complete. After today's insights, I felt Tiffany could go either way.

I felt the key to her future would be someone she has yet to meet. When Tiffany was broken from her life of service, a piece of the broken missionary was left missing.

I feel when she finds that piece, she will finally be able to heal her soul.

***

113

Chapter 12

Northern Rescue

It was hard to leave the little oasis, but the mission was calling. The Trio de Libertade had just enough confidence to feel they could deliver. Jesus named the group as they headed out in the dusk. Tiffany liked the term and hugged the grinning Columbian. Jean had to admit it had a nice ring. Just a touch more romantic than Trio Liberte. Tiffany hugged the big man around his waist, too, and the Trio de Libertade started down the moonlit trail like Dorothy, The Lion, and the Tin Man... Just missing the scarecrow and the sun. She felt sure that the scarecrow would join as the tribe grew.

As the hills veered West, so did the trail. At times, they were tempted to follow the cloven hoof prints down into the star-lit grasslands, but being caught away from the hillside cover come daybreak would not be wise. Jesus observed that the hoof print size suggested a deer or goat-sized animal.

Tiffany suggested an herbivore that size might make an excellent food source. She wondered if the tribe could domesticate or at least contain the animal. They had all eaten goat in their old lives. Jean and Jesus had regularly eaten venison.

Northern Rescue

"Let's try to catch sight of this beast. At the very least, we should report the find back to Freedom." Tiffany was excited about the possibility of an animal that could feed a larger village. Tiffany focused on saving people and growing human society on this planet. Through osmosis, back in the village, Jean, Jesus, and Shiv, had become more excited about her vision.

The trail took a sharp left turn into a ravine. The moonless night was beginning to show signs of Alpha's halo on the Eastern horizon, but the light was not quite enough to lighten the trail into the gully, and they could tell by the tinkle of water that they would be crossing a stream.

Carefully, they worked their way into the darkness. As their eyes adjusted, they could tell the point of the ravine sported a little waterfall in an oasis of tall, dry-land trees. There was a swatch of lighter ground as wide wildlife paths came down around the falls and joined at a small pool at the bottom. The explorers could see flickering points of starlight in the waterfall, the pool, and the small stream that continued down to the grasslands.

They could hear distant thunder.

Just as Alpha breached the far horizon to add features to the scene, Jean looked at his partners. "Mon du… Dat not thunder."

The rumble grew louder and more constant.

"Get into the trees." Tiffany bolted to the trees near the falls. She didn't stop at the tree. She climbed quickly as the ground shook. Jesus and Jean followed her lead without hesitation. The rumble became a roar as a flood of hoof-born animals stripped the little ravine of anything smaller than a tree. The trees they chose to climb were next to the falls, so the falls split the herd naturally.

51 Pegasi - Sister Tiffany

However, the torrent in the dark battered their sanctuaries violently as massive beasts plunged blindly around them. The dust was choking now as Beta arrived. The grainy cloud was too thick to get more than a vision of striped flesh and long, folded-back horns streaming by.

The animals were heavy and tall enough that the team had to scamper ever higher and hang on desperately as the trees took a beating. The stampede knocked Jesus out of his sanctuary, but he managed to squat at the leeward side of his tree and hold on.

As fast as the avalanche of hooves hit, it ended. The thunder moved East as the animals roared off. The cloud of dust emptied of beasts as the bouncing backs dissipated and continued down to the grasslands, leaving choking dust and flooding adrenaline.

Tiffany and Jean dropped from their perches to join Jesus on the ground. A deep thumping rumble made them huddle closer and strain to see through the dust. The new threat was deep, repetitive thumps that made the ground shake. They were more felt than heard. In moments, several furry Giants ran past in full pursuit of the herd. Several massive predators jumped off the small waterfall beside them and landed several yards toward the grasslands. None of them looked down.

Many others flashed by on either side. They do hunt at night...

Alpha and Beta shone through as the scene settled, and the action died off in the grasslands far to the East. The moon-light brightened to a battered ravine where an oasis had been, but now a muddy pit, broken tree limbs, and two dead beasts lay on the far side of the little stream.

Jean got up, hopped across the stream, and examined the beasts. Tiffany and Jean joined him.

Northern Rescue

In the growing light of the moons, they could see the animals had long, sectioned goat or sheep horns with delicate but strong hooks on the end. Their hides were the color of the dry grasslands with thin, darker, vertical stripes.

"A goat," Jean offered.

"Maybe, more like a horse." Countered Tiffany.

In all earnestness, Jesus, still trying to master English, added, "Ghorst."

The animal was named.

They examined the rather large body, like an elk or a horse, with long, thin legs, more like a shorter giraffe. The mouth was made for grazing, with tensile lips like a horse, and the legs ended on cloven hooves. The streamlined body suggested speed.

The explorers harvested enough meat for a few days on the trail but agreed this was no place to hang out.

By the time the moons were setting and light began to show on the eastern horizon, they had moved several miles North and were climbing into some well-treed foothills. Looking for a place to hide for the day, they stepped into a tall grove of trees on a riverbank.

Tiffany remarked that their new sanctuary looked much like their old home in the pass, but it was not nearly as steep. Their north-bearing trail met a clear East and West path against the river. Something traveled this way regularly. The path was too narrow for the Fur Giants, but they found several tracks of the 'Ghorst' they had encountered at the stampede. They found Humpback tracks and a few smaller padded tracks about the size of a large house cat.

Roger Haller

They also found they were back in Blue Mushroom territory. To be safe, they found a little high ground where they could tuck away with a good view of the intersection, access to the water, and enough shelter to build a small cooking fire. That night, they enjoyed some of the finest roast since arriving on Aard.

While drying and smoking the rest of the meat through the day, Tiffany, Jean, and Jesus discussed plans for the next day. They would be heading East. Leaving behind the psychological safety of the villagers on the coast, they would be striding into the home of the Northern Giants, a known delivery spot for human livestock, and the unknown environment they had to figure out or die in.

None of the dedicated rescuers held any assurance they could ever leave with their lives, but they all had confidence in themselves and each other, allowing them to plan an offensive on the cages. They were dedicated to humans they had yet to meet.

I was, again, impressed with the dedication Tiffany showed to rescuing humans from this terrifying supply chain.

Alongside her self-evaluation and drive to be a better friend to her followers grew her determination to break the human sacrifice to the Giants. Her commitment was contagious to Jean and Jesus.

***

Northern Rescue

In the early morning light, their water bladders were full. Their paperboy sacks were lighter now with dried meat, dried mushrooms, and a few stalks of Aardian celery. The crisp vegetable grew over six feet high in the sunny openings with any water source in these Northern hills.

The trail East was narrower with more forest overgrowth. It was well-trod and comfortable to travel. It rose slightly to the East and followed the river. The scouts could hear Screamers now. They seemed high and distant, but they skirted openings to stay hidden. They could travel during the day now but hadn't traveled a day when the territory began to change. The forest grew thicker, the adventurers had to cross several streams as they joined the river, and the environment turned into a rainforest.

In broken English, Jesus suggested they had been in a rain shadow along the eastern foothills, where the high mountains scraped off much of the lower rain. They were now approaching the same rainforest where the high rains gathered and fell. They had escaped from. A sweltering, tropical jungle, inland but wet. Jean and Tiffany agreed, the Northern Giant's seemed to live in the same environment as their Southern kin.

Abruptly, the jungle opened to a clear swath carved from the trees and vegetation. They approached carefully, being sure to stay undercover. The opening showed signs of regular traffic. Huge traffic. They had stumbled on a North-South highway. A highway for Giant Sasquatch. Tiffany convinced her companions to camp for the rest of the day and plan before moving farther.

Over a cold meal, they decided the road North was the direction of the Giant's settlement, and the South would be the highway to their original introduction to the planet. They noted that the sound of the Screamers seemed to keep its distance from the highway.

Roger Haller

51 Pegasi - Sister Tiffany

With the meal complete and a little daylight left, they started Scouting the perimeters of the Giant's path.

To their relief, they found the wildlife appeared to travel parallel to the highway. It seemed they didn't care to be out in the open. The little band of trekkers decided the West side of the trail would be their best bet and tucked in to see what the evening would bring. The evening brought Giants.

An earth-shaking march drove them into the under-growth. Luckily, the band of Giant's had bigger things on their mind. They were in a hurry to go North, and they carried a half dozen cages with pairs of humans. It seemed the North settle-ment may be a farm. A human farm.

The Giants disappeared as quickly as they arrived and were soon out of earshot as the ground ceased to shake. Jean turned to his friends. "We are close. North Giants live not far… No?"

Tiffany nodded as darkness dropped over the nervous scouts. The blue glow soon lit the narrow trail North, but it was too dark yet to travel safely. They waited for Alpha before heading North, and soon Beta joined, but the light was spotty.

They were now under a tall jungle canopy, and the moons lit their way, only where the trail neared the Giant's highway. The East-West orbit of the moons made them brightest when they passed overhead. So, the team made their best ground while Alpha and Beta were with them. They slowed down again when darkness took over, but the mushroom glow al-lowed them to continue, if much slower.

As the skies began to brighten, they could hear grunts and deep rumbles as the Giant's ahead communicated. They had a narrow window to pinpoint the camp and get hidden for the day to come. It didn't take long. The broken vegetation beside them opened into a huge settlement.

Northern Rescue

There were no fires, but a mass of Giants stood, sat, and milled around several cages hanging in the trees. The undergrowth was thick, so movement was strenuous, but the smaller trails through the dense vegetation were smooth and worn by Humpbacks and other jungle creatures. In the gathering light, they found shelter in a group of root balls beside the Giant's thoroughfare. They had mossy caverns under the massive root clumps that would work well. From their chosen sanctuary, they could watch the day unfold in the camp.

The camp was quietly mundane, food and water for the captives, and low grunts and gestures were the norm until a hunting party arrived with a pair of dead Screamers and three of the Ghorst animals. The Giants simply fed, and it was not a welcome sight to the trekkers. The Giants had little dining etiquette, and they ate raw.

After they had eaten, the Giant's left the farm. It seemed they had other places to spend the night. Tiffany and the team gathered vines from their surroundings, and by the time darkness was on them, they were ready to apply Tiffany's escape plan.

With quiet whispers, they got the attention of the captives and explained the plan. Just as she had done with Dan, Kia, Randy, Ann, and Penny, the rescuers strung vines up to the change caps and sprung one clasp at a time. They had ten people with them in a very short time as they headed back down the trail to the South. They reached the crossroads to the West just before dawn.

As the light was breaking, Tiffany stopped the trek and spoke to the escapees."Folks, we came from the coast to the West. The Giants don't seem to like the smell of the sea. We know the trail that goes South along the eastern slope of the coastal mountains, so we are going to take that route back home.

Roger Haller

However, this river gets stronger as it heads West, so I suspect there is a path to the coast that may be quicker. We simply haven't traveled it yet. I expect to explore that area as soon as I can, but we have been on this trek to free you for some time and need to get back home to check in before they send a search party."

A tall, redheaded woman said, "One thing I know is we cannot stay here. Those giant fur balls are going to come for us very soon. I want to get to the coast as soon as possible. I want to go straight West."

Tiffany nodded. "That's fair. If you want to lead a group West, it is probably a great idea to split up to make sure we have a better chance of confusing the Giants and getting to safety. Stay out of the open because the Purple Screamers want to eat us, too. Build your shelters in the trees." She took a moment to explain the Purple Screamers. Everyone who had been freed that night decided to go with the Redhead. The Scouts would head back empty-handed but happy for their successful quest. They made introductions all around. Tiffany convinced everyone to climb into the river to head West so the Giants would lose their tracks.

As they floated in the surging river, they heard a roar from the East. The Giants were aware of the breakout. The humans swam hard. Even as the day brightened, everyone swam west to the Junction with the East-side trail.

Rita, the redhead, showed remarkable leadership as she headed West with a full tribe. It was easy for me to see the people caged with her had learned to follow her lead. She had easy respect, and the rescuers could see it in the way they attended to everything she said and did.

I interfered for the first time. I led the striking redhead to the flowing stream, where she bent to pick out a shiny red gemstone from the stream bottom.

Northern Rescue

She picked it up and carefully snugged it into the paperboy sack Tiffany had given her.

Rita hugged Tiffany, Jean, and Jesus in the shallows, and said, "Come North as soon as you can to find us."

Tiffany nodded. "We will. Listen for a Tarzan Yodel. We will try not to surprise you so that call is our common introduction as we get close to each other."

She was on her way with her team, taking full advantage of the current in the water.

Tiffany, Jean, and Jesus headed South. There was a lot of noise behind them, so they scooted into the first Capybara hole they found and stayed for the day.

One resident giant rodent scampered past them and stood chirping outside the den as it paced back and forth between the hole in the ground and the North-South trail.

It quickly left when the Giants came thundering from the North. The Giants were on to the trail, and they heard them rage past three or four times. They weren't sure they could make out their small tracks or if they were working on smell, but they knew it wasn't safe to be seen today.

***

Roger Haller

Chapter 13

Home to Freedom and Adelphi

Thankful for the cover from the Capybara critter, the rescuers stayed huddled in the dark. The last Giants went North late in the afternoon and appeared to move out of earshot or ground tremor distance. When night fell, their world was silent again. Jesus peeked out of the hole to starlight and silence.

"Sin setas azules… sorry, no… blue mushrooms. No enough light."

Jean and Tiffany peeked out. Tiffany looked up at the foreign constellations, "Let's have something to eat and relax a little longer till Alpha shows up. Then we must make as much time as possible to the South. We also need to watch for action from the South. The Giants have probably notified the Tower Giants and possibly even gone there when they saw our tracks heading that way."

They were low on food now, so only one of their remaining sacks had anything left. They recognized they would not have time to hunt or prepare a meal now until they were well into the canyon pass. They didn't have long to wait.

Home to Freedom and Adelphi

Alpha soon rose, and they had enough light for the well-trod path. "Let's go." Tiffany didn't wait for an answer. The small band of scouts made good time through the night, but even with the speed they were able to muster when Beta joined the journey, dawn was breaking long before they got to the canyon.

Tiffany knew they would need to hide again, but this time, they all worried that the trail was going to get busy. There was no cover from above in the grasslands below, so they opted for a narrow, barely visible path sporting humpback tracks that started in a rocky volcanic slag above the trail. Above the slag, the trail wandered through grass clumps, woody shrubs, and blue-hued succulents.

In growing light, they heard far-off screams. They needed cover. A mile west and far above the trail, they found a mass of sandstone boulders in a hauntingly beautiful rock formation carved by wind and weather. In the crevasses, they found deep holes that many species had used for shelter over time.

The band of warriors had shelter, but it was hot. It was also noisy. The Screamers knew they were there. Although they were well out of reach, the scouts got a close-up and personal look at the size of the monstrous beaks and claws attached to the massive purple raptors. Then there was the sound. The shrieks and Screams were designed to flush their prey, and the volume alone could scramble a brain.

"Mon deu!" Jean was the only one to comment as they covered their ears in agony.

The cacophony was almost to the point where they were tempted to bolt when an unlikely rescue arrived with much more company, activity, and commotion. Giants arrived with arrows launched at hunting raptors. At the same time, Aardian Capybaras and other large animals, perhaps canine, began jettisoning from the crevasses around them.

Roger Haller

Two of the raptors grabbed prey and flew off. Two more died from well-placed arrows the size of fence rails. The remaining Purple Screamers left abruptly, and the wildlife scattered to other holes. One Capybara climbed in with them and didn't complain.

The Giants gathered their Screamers, scanned the scene for a few minutes, and left. When the vibrations of the massive pedestrians died off, the silence became as oppressive as the heat.

Tiffany poked her head out far enough to survey the scene. It was hard to tell if anything had happened around them. She did note a small trickle of water from a bathtub-sized crater above them, so she ducked back into their hole to fetch her humpback stomach and announce her discovery. "We have some fresh water."

She filled the stomach from the coursing little rivulet and offered her friends a well-needed drink. When they had drunk their fill, she folded the vessel open and offered the water to the scared rodent. It was trembling in fear but recognized the water and needed it as badly as they did.

"Tak some, Cappy…" Jesus encouraged the scared animal in a cooing voice that may have helped. A few moments studying its benefactor gave way to need, and the Aardian Capybara drank.

"Good job, Mon Ami," Jean was impressed. "Ma-bee you baby-sit mon firs-born in dis new world; oui?"

This prompted a chuckle from everyone, with the exception, perhaps, of the scared rodent. There was no more sign of the raptors or Sasquatch Giants, so, in turn, the scouts got to know their unique surroundings. The little stream ran Southeast through more crevasses and cracks to a trickle steeply downhill.

Home to Freedom and Adelphi

A humpback trail closely followed the rivulet. The new path promised water and, perhaps, food for the trip back to the canyon entrance.

"Let's try this trail out in the moonlight, guys." Tiffany received affirmative nods, and the team tried to doze in the suppressive heat. By nightfall, the scouts were fully rested, the hunger pangs were softened with half of the remaining dried food, and all were anxious to be moving. Jean peeked out at the waning light. "Once we get pass de clay ledge in de dark, we know where is da food; oui?"

His partners chuckled as he voiced everyone's thoughts.

As Alpha broke the horizon, Tiffany stepped out of the lit sanctuary, and in moments, the trio were moving quickly but carefully along the tiny stream. By the time Beta crested, the fast-moving trekkers were against the grasslands and within sight of the beginning of the clay-ledge trail.

The trekkers stripped down, stowed their loincloths in their sacks, and patted down in Kia's clay makeup. They made short work of the low reaches of the trail but slowed for exact footing as they climbed to the peak of the trail and the stomach-churning smell of the Screamer nest above. They could hear slight activity above them but no alarm.

Silently, they continued the trail through the descent to the riverbed across from the deserted Canyon Pass camp. In the darkness, they could see no detail across the river, but they smiled at each other as Jesus pointed at the blue glow to the riverbank and whispered, "Ba-loo much-room." At river level, much of the moonlight was lost, and treading through the shallows became an issue, so the small band climbed onto the northern bank in the shelter of the forest and camped.

Berry bushes and mushrooms were nearby, and with a little patience and luck, they would soon have a Humpback.

Roger Haller

Their complaining stomachs were comforted before they felt the need to hunt. While they ate, Jesus opened up on a thought he had on the clay ledge. "Me pregunto por las Screamer no nos olio en la cornisa… ah, ingles…," He caught himself thinking out loud in Spanish. "Why no Screamer Smell… Me…You?"

Tiffany looked up from the small fire. "I was thinking the same. I don't know, but perhaps the smell of the nest is so strong it hides other smells." Before considering his comment, Jean added, "Ma-bee der is human sent in da nest…"

The trekkers grew silent. Jean had just said the silent part out loud. None of their brains wanted to consider that point any deeper. He quickly changed the subject.

"Tomorrow, we go down da falls?"

All the scouts were deep in their own thoughts for the evening. So was I. The upper falls on Rivier de Libertade would always send a shiver through me as the place my corporal adventure on Aard ended.

***

Home to Freedom and Adelphi

All were deeply intent on their overall mission. Jesus broke the silence in flawless English. "We must go quick."

Tiffany nodded, "Yes. We need to get back into the berry warren and find out what those people are doing there. It will be dangerous. We also need to make sure Rita and her folks made it to the coast. Tomorrow, I want to clear upper and lower falls. I don't like what is between the falls."

Jean agreed. "It is important we let Giant's cool off for a little while. Let berries grow more, but we come back soon to know what humans do."

Tiffany responded, "Let's get back to report to Freedom and let everyone know what we have learned. They need to know we have new people in the North, and our village needs to know there are many humans in the cabin at the tower. That does not feel good."

Her comment caught me by surprise. I felt she could feel what I felt. With the freedom to travel during the day and full bellies, the scouts made record time over the falls with no interruptions. They harvested a Humpback for a late-night dinner at the bottom of the second set of falls.

By the end of the second day, as Pegasi was setting over the sea, Tiffany yodeled her Tarzan yell, and they strode into a happy camp, celebrating their return. Tiffany hugged Jean and Jesus tightly, then sat at the village fire to begin their adventure stories.

With Jean being closely attended to by Hilda and Jesus in animated conversation with Julio, the guys sat back while Tiffany updated the village on the new neighbors to the North, the human menace at the Tower Cabin, and the fast-growing rebirth of the berry warren. She also laid out the urgent reasons for future raids on the Giant's compounds.

Roger Haller

Dan and Shiv wanted to join the trek next time. Dan wanted more details from the cabin and perhaps the lab, depending on what access they could gain with humans in the cabin.

Shiv wanted to get first-hand knowledge of the trail north and possibly make a visit to the Northern Giants. A lot had happened while Tiffany and team were on the trail. The village had news for the scouts, too. It seems Popeye Paul, a new addition and another named Jewels, along with Willow, and Mac, had been busy with the transporter. Dan, Kia and Sirih were also deep in the technology of transporting.

A new recruit from Greece was due at any time. A young woman named Adelphi, a friend of Mac's father. At first, Mac had gone to visit her using the transporters, but she wasn't ready to leave her family yet then Paul and Jewels had visited her to set up her books, tools, and inventory for immigration. All four seemed smitten with this young lady.

Tiffany was a bit dubious when she heard this was a favor for Mac's father, but after hearing more of her story, she was excited to know the woman in question was an expert in natural foods and medicines from nature.

She wasn't sure how this would translate to Aardian flora and fauna, but she was interested enough to be curious. For now, she simply wanted to prepare for a trip North to see how Rita and company were doing.

Shiv mentioned building a village to the South, and she liked the idea. Perhaps a related village to the North would fit her well. The trekkers found their beds early in the evening as the constant adrenaline, once removed, allowed their bodies and minds to crash. They got much-needed rest. It didn't take long for the new immigrant plot to thicken. Mid-morning the next day, Jewels trotted into camp. It seems Adelphi had arrived at the transporter landing but freaked when she didn't have her dress.

Home to Freedom and Adelphi

Apparently, she had no problem arriving naked; her problem was her dress was far more than a garment. She promised to be back tomorrow at the same time if they could recalibrate and bring the dress. Kia had made the necessary adjustments to include the one piece of clothing, complete with dried herbs, minerals, and liquids described by the immigrant.

The problem was that no one could tell what 'Tomorrow at the same time' would mean to the transporter. Someone would need to stand by for twenty-four hours until she arrived.

Mac went with Jewels to help with the welcoming committee. It wasn't until the next evening when the immigration team showed up with a dramatic circus. Adelphi was, indeed, beautiful. Stud and Willow trotted up to meet them on the trail. Willow welcomed her like a long-lost daughter. What made this a circus, however, was a man included in the immigration, introduced as the man that had just tried to rape the new camp darling.

They all looked at the creep simultaneously, and he physically shrunk from the disapproving stares. Mac quickly led him to a tent to get him out of sight, and it was easy to see he welcomed the chance to hide. Ann took him a bowl of soup while Dr. Tim stood guard with a spear.

Mac said something to Jean, and he came running to get Tiffany, Shiv, and Julio for a chat on Willow's porch. Julio was pulled into his old occupation as a Judge in Ecuador, and asked for a little one-on-one time with Adelphi. They strode off for a few minutes, and when they returned, Julio nodded to Adelphi. Tiffany stood with her mouth open as she listened to the most beautiful woman she had ever met. Adelphi said she would need to be the interpreter for her attacker.

She was the only one who spoke his language. The olive-skinned beauty offered to translate everything said so everyone would understand the conversation, the logic.

Roger Haller

51 Pegasi - Sister Tiffany

The resulting decision on the fate of the disgusting man. With this, Tiffany found her voice. "Adelphi, please come stay in my hut tonight while you decide what you want for this village. You will be safe and comfortable."

Adelphi gazed at the tall Scandinavian warrior, and a new look spread over her face. For the first time since arriving, Adelphi smiled wide. She accepted the offer and, with no more said, walked arm-in-arm with Tiffany to her hut.

The village gathered around Mac and Willow's hut, looked at each other in stunned silence, smiled, and went about their business.

Freedom had just witnessed two women's metamorphosis in the blink of an eye. The two women I had known became someone else, and the combined effect was far greater than the sum of their lives. I remembered the backhanded offer she made to me when Shiv proposed to Tiffany. I knew now that her soul was really waiting for Adelphi... Or someone.

***

Chapter 14

Danger From the Sky, Sea, & Land

As morning dawned, the fate of the sulking, dismal Greek perpetrator began to roll out. Julio called the camp to Mac and Willow's cabin porch, which had become the de facto town hall.

Talking about Willow in the third person feels surreal, but the Willow that lived on Aard was her own entity. She was unique to all worlds, including my reality. Mac asked Adelphi how she felt the village should deal with the man who had accosted her.

"Please, let me talk to him in our native tongue." With a bare top and robe secured around her waist, she walked alone to where the skulking Greek hid his eyes behind his long black hair. He stood a head taller than her and was, by any definition, very fit, but she showed no fear. Adelphi was silent at first, but when she spoke, her tone was much like a business meeting. She talked directly, looking him in the eyes.

She lifted her arms to flex her biceps and pointed at the ground. She released her pose, never leaving eye contact, and slipped a small pouch from her robe belt.

Roger Haller

51 Pegasi - Sister Tiffany

Opening the small sack, she tapped a small amount of shiny green powder into the palm of her hand. She offered it to the downcast man. He looked past her hand at the ground for a moment, nodded, and licked the powder from her hand in one quick gesture. Everyone in the camp was stunned to silence.

His eyes widened, and he bolted for the undergrowth of the delta, retching as he went. The sounds were not pleasant as he lost all content from his body, from both ends, and the sound didn't stop till he reached the ocean. Adelphi padded back to the awed group at Willow's porch.

"Julio, Mac, when that man returns, his name will be Marus.

He will put every effort into learning English and demand that you work him hard so he can again build up his proud Greek honor. He will no longer be a threat, and I forgive him."

Planning drove the next few weeks.

Mac voiced Tiffany's desire to return to the North Giant's camp for a new rescue. She wanted to follow the river they had found to the coast and catch up with Rita and the group of humans who decided to settle there.

Mac also called on Dan to explain how he discovered a vast diamond source on an island off the coast of Bitter Waters. The lab documents he had captured mentioned the diamonds as a pressing goal for the bad guys.

It would make several multi-millionaires on Earth. There was also a great deal made of a flower that grew on the island that bled a potent compound that appeared to stop bleeding and reverse age-related illnesses. Perhaps even regenerate sick organs in humans. This news captured Adelphi's and Dr. Tim's attention.

Danger From the Sky, Sea, & Land

Jean volunteered to build and pilot the raft that would take them there; it seemed Marus came from a ship-building family and was quick to volunteer to design the raft and help Jean sail it to and from the island. Hilda would not allow Jean to go on the next adventure without her.

She begged Adelphi to teach her what she needed to know to collect the samples she wanted, and the motivated 'Junge Frau' convinced Stacey to teach her what she should look for regarding food candidates.

Kia was the last volunteer. She wanted to set up a transporter on the island. She wanted a quick way to return to the island if the flower was viable. It seemed strange to think transporting would be simpler and safer than sailing, but that had become a reality for this band of survivors.

She was also determined to redeploy the transporter the initial humans used to return to the island. Dan had coordinates for them to use, except for the location of the island site.

With the crew sorted out, Tiffany and Shiv held off their next explorations to help the Aardian Mariners build and sail the first attempt at ocean travel on this new planet. It was not long until the nervous villagers waved off the brave crew, who had no guarantee they would ever see Freedom again. There were tears mixed with the nervous laughter at the celebratory launch.

Monsoons were due in less than a month and a half, so the village had much to do. With so little time before the rains hit, Tiffany and Adelphi decided to hold their trip North till after the monsoon. Tiffany led the village in thatched hut building.

As the hut building wound down, Mac and Willow headed off to visit Mac's brother, who had taken up homesteading in Aard's polar zone. Mac wanted to discuss expanding imported tools and supplies the village would need from Earth.

Roger Haller

51 Pegasi - Sister Tiffany

On the way back, they were to stop at the Tower Cabin to scavenge anything more they could find. The explorers were not prepared for what they did find. The cabin was now a command center with barracks, and they found a folder with a hand-written plan to wipe out the village of Freedom at the end of the monsoon.

A man named Howard Thom was leading the attack, and true to their fears, Lawrence was listed in the plans as a guide. They planned to hit just as the monsoon ended to catch the vermin off guard and unfocused from the rains. They also noticed the berry warren was ablaze. They had no time or opportunity to rescue people from the cages. Mac and Willow bolted West in the creek and headed for the high canyon pass on the North side of Rio de Libertade.

They made great speed over the high ledge trail, and everything seemed to be working out by the time they reached Randy's Rock at the top of the first falls. The sadness over losing Randy was ominous.

Love took over as they bonded again over the bittersweet paradox of beauty and tragedy they found in this world. The lovers talked about what they had lost and gained since they met and agreed they were where they belonged. Right now, they had to get back in time to warn Freedom.

Arm in arm, they looked toward the sea and found only the black wall of the monsoon bearing down on the horizon. Behind them, to the East, rolled a luminescent green waving sky.

Mac feared they were about to witness a war of nature. His memory of the small cave behind the waterfall came back. "Willow, there is a small cave behind the waterfall. I discovered it on my last trip up the falls. I think we can get into it while this initial blast hits. We must continue in the torrent of the rains when we can see again."

Danger From the Sky, Sea, & Land

Willow nodded. "It's getting dark fast, but we can get part way down the falls." They headed over the crest of the falls trail as the first moon showed up to help them see. The moonlight didn't last.

As they got to the ledge leading to the cave behind the falls, the black wall swallowed the moon, lightning flashed around them, and a torrent of water hit instantly after.

It still seems strange to talk about Willow in the third person, but I understand now. We were on the ledge, and I had to let go of Mac's hand and use both hands and feet to find my way. We would be safe in a moment, and I could see Mac just ahead in the distant flashes.

He disappeared behind the sheet of falling water the moment my life on Aard ended.

There was sudden peace and light, then a growing ache for the devastated lover I had to leave behind. I ached for the suffering he went through in the moments, hours, days, and months following, but the ache eased as full understanding settled in, and I knew my purpose… and his.

***

51 Pegasi - Sister Tiffany

Mac quickly discovered I was gone along with the ledge we had been crossing as the lightning bolt ensured the pinnacle of his grief was spent trapped in the small cave behind the falls. In the morning, he committed a selfless act of heroism or suicide. A distinction even he could not discern as he dove through the swelling waterfall to the rocky riverbed below.

As luck or fate would have it, eons of water wear had carved the pool deep at the bottom of the falls, and the rising river made it deeper. Still, Mac was banged up in the act, and it would take the heroics of his friends downstream to save him. They would also retrieve what was left of my cocoon from the rock shore at the bottom of the falls.

Tiffany and Shiv had been increasingly panicked as the monsoon rolled in. Mac had promised to be back before the rains hit. When the weather arrived before Mac and Willow, they headed upriver. Several others wanted to come with them, but the monsoons meant too much work to spare more than the two experienced scouts.

The night Mac spent crying in the cave, Tiffany and Shiv huddled together for warmth in a sturdy tree to stay out of the reach of the wildlife. With little rest, they climbed the lower falls in the morning and headed upstream. The scouts noted that the river was rising quickly, so they understood that time was critical.

About the middle of the short day, Shiv excused himself for a bio break, and Tiffany scoured the shoreline. She found the badly beaten Mac and screamed for Shiv. Mac lived, but he was battered and cold. He was unconscious but breathing.

Tiffany rotated his shoulder back into its socket, and together, She and Shiv put traction on and splinted a broken left arm. His broken nose could wait for Dr. Tim.

Danger From the Sky, Sea, & Land

Mac was showing signs of hypothermia, so Tiffany pulled him into her robe with her and laid on a little high ground on the trail.

Shiv built a fire to warm them, built a basic lean-to with moss for cover, and searched for Willow.

The warmth began to revive Mac, and through sobs, he told them what had happened to Willow and where he thought she was.

Shiv grabbed his weapons and bolted for the upper falls. In the fog and driving rain, he found two Rainbow colored lizards fighting for the right to dig Willow's body from the rubble of the exploded ledge.

They were the size of alligators but luminescent in the colors of the rainbow.

The battle raged, so he let them decide who he would have to fight. It didn't take long, and one lizard was dispatched. Shiv had time to prepare, so his first arrow was the only one he needed. He was now free to recover the body of the woman he had learned to admire so much. Willow had a massive burn from left shoulder to heel. She had not felt the end of her life.

Once freed, he cried all the way back to Tiffany and Mac with her broken, lifeless body on his back. Together, the friends cried over the sad cargo, but they got Mac fed and nursed back to his feet.

They couldn't stay between the falls.

Tiffany and Shiv made a quick trip back to the upper falls to grab Willow's pack in the ledge rubble, and they found Mac's bobbing against a rock in the stream.

Roger Haller

51 Pegasi - Sister Tiffany

Mac insisted on carrying his pack on his right side, as Tiffany and Shiv shared the precious cargo and Willow's pack. They managed to get down the lower falls with Screamer hide and rope, then tackled the misery of driving in the rain and wind. Just before dark, they made it back to calling distance of Freedom.

Tiffany let out her Tarzan yell, which was answered before the echo died. Soon, the exhausted trekkers were surrounded and relieved of their burdens. Adelphi, Ann, and Maritza took possession of Willow's body and carried her to her hut. While Dr. Tim set, splinted and put Mac's arm in a sling, Adelphi talked with Mac. She took over the preparations, and Mac spoke to his friends. "I want to bury her at the Landing. She loved that little pool at the bottom of the knoll."

Mac then asked to have a village meeting in the mouth of the cave where the village had built their dry cooking fire. He told them what he and Willow had learned at the Tower cabin. They would be under attack by humans near the end of the monsoon season. Lawrence would be guiding them. The Freedomites would need to spread their warriors out to ensure they weren't found huddled in Freedom.

"Folks, we need to diversify. We need to spread out so we can't all be attacked at once. Shiv, you've been talking about a site to the South that you and Jean found, and Tiffany, you've been talking about a river to the North. We have options, and it may be time."

A small voice came from the back of the cave. "We must wait for Jean, Marus, Kia, and Hilda to return," Vera spoke for everyone.

Mac agreed. "Of course, Vera. I was hoping they would be back by now. We should begin the migration process either North, South, or a combination, but keep a rotation of folks moving up and down the coast for signs of our mariners.

Danger From the Sky, Sea, & Land

Then, when we get them safely home, we can quickly make Freedom look deserted and let the rains clear our tracks."

Adelphi interrupted to say Willow was ready, and Mac went to their hut to be with her. With Adelphi leading, the village prepared for a funeral march to the Landing in the morning, and by mid-morning, the whole village was on the move to see Popeye and Jewels at the Landing. Of course, Popeye and Jewels were devastated by the visit, but they had to find a way to share good news amongst the tears.

Surprisingly, they were excited to hear the news of the move. They had another option, and they wanted to show the village. They had found cathedral-vaulted caves overlooking the ocean but hidden to eyes on land. The caves had fresh air, shelter, fresh water, and very defendable entrances.

My funeral led to the revelation of these caves and all the benefits they provided. Once my shell was put to rest in my favorite spot on the planet, the village of Freedom found new hope in 'Willow's Cathedral'.

***

Chapter 15

Sailors Return, and So Does Larry

With the safe haven of Willow's Cathedral now chosen as the short-term goal, Mac still pressed to plan for the tribe's dispersion. He was spooked by the plans he learned about at the Tower Camp. It was agreed that they would begin their explorations North and South while constantly searching the shoreline for the overdue sailors.

The village now had all the creature comforts they had at Freedom in the chambers of Willow's Cathedral. Even more useful as there was much more dry room during the rains. Internal fires were well-vented far to the East, in the woods of the plateau. Masonry, Rock-work, and tiling were new skill sets in the builder's teams. Now that Freedom was clear, most travel North and South was done from the beaches and shoreline. Although the Monsoon rains were refreshing, the rain was heating up. This was a clear sign that the rains were ending, and the search along the shoreline became an everyday task.

Tiffany and Adelphi were glued together. One hardly saw one without the other. It was easy to see that their love for each other was blooming.

Sailors Return, and So Does Larry

Tiffany and Adelphi were particularly focused on the shores of Bitter Water, as their quest for Northern opportunities depended on the fate of the mariners.

Today the searchers finally found their sailors. The news wasn't all good.

Some of the searchers had headed North, and some had gone south along the shores of Bitter Waters. Some used the trails down off the plateau since the constant rain wiped them clean in hours, and some used the shoreline. Adelphi and Tiffany had used the shoreline. Mac had followed them slowly but caught up at the tubs.

Tiffany spotted the raft first. It was upside down on the bathtub rocks. Jean was spotted first, unsuccessfully fumbling to untie the frayed, stiffened rope secured around his waist. As Tiffany ran to his aid, he looked up and smiled through tears.

"We made it…"

Mac also responded and took over his task with the rope with surprising dexterity, using his good hand and adrenaline. Tiffany bolted for the upturned raft and dove under. There, she found Hilda unconscious but breathing. She untied her from her tether and pulled her gently out in the open. Adelphi took over and pulled Hilda into her robe. The sight of Hilda coming out from under the raft changed Jean's silent tears to sobs.

"Hilda!" His relief was his first emotion, but he quickly followed with directions to find Marus in the broken cabin and reported that important cargo was secured there with him. Again, Tiffany took the lead and pulled him free with strength she didn't know she had. Marus was in bad shape. He was severely burned, but he was breathing.

Mac looked at Stud. "Kia?"

Stud's tears started again, and he could only shake his head. Kia had been lost.

Adelphi had been warming Hilda against her bare body. "She just needs to warm up." She directed her comment to Mac, who, still with an arm in a sling, took over, warming the hypothermia young woman in his robe as Adelphi took over the task of administering to Marus.

Popeye, Jewels, Vera, and Mutt, who had been searching North, arrived on the run. They had seen the activity at the Bitter Water hot springs from a distance. Jewels and Popeye took over for Mac, who struggled to keep Hilda covered.

Hilda started to come to as she warmed in Mac's robed embrace, calling for Jean. He found his feet and stumbled over. They both wept as she returned to official business and asked that Adelphi be notified that they had harvested the valuable 'blood' from the 'bleeding flowers'.

Jean reached in to hug her. "Le Faille…, she have it."

At Vera's panicked search of the scene, Mac had to tell her Kia hadn't returned. It suddenly became evident how much Vera's fragile emotions depended on her relationship with Kia. She had finally found her destiny, and it was ripped away. On seeing this, Mac had his epiphany. He and Vera were in exactly the same emotional loss. Vera looked into his eyes, understood, and hugged him deeply, and they wept together.

Adelphi told the tribe they needed a litter to take Marus to Dr. Tim. Princess stood from her tasks, stripped off her robe for Adelphi, and said, "I'll run to get Dr. Tim and Maritza to prepare." She was off in a sprint. The villagers headed back up the trail to the plateau with Marus on the litter. Mac spent the trip updating Jean and Hilda on the news of Willow. "Take care of Hilda, my friend. There is nothing more important than love."

Sailors Return, and So Does Larry

With Mutt, now holding Vera close as they walked directly behind, there were many more tears on the trail. Popeye, Jewels, Adelphi, and Tiffany managed the handles of the litter. Farther up the trail, Pete, Mutt, Ann, Stacey, Penny, Oliver, and even Vera took turns.

Shiv and Jesus were hunting, and Julio prepared the caverns for the returning rescuers.

Dr. Tim was ready for Marus with a dose of Digoxin, which was very similar to what Adelphi had given him as punishment when he first arrived.

The drug would inspire his heart to pump harder.

Shiv and Jesus arrived while the group was heading up the trail. Hunting hadn't been fruitful in the driving rain, so when Jean mentioned the cargo still at the raft, they happily trotted back to the bathtubs to capture the goods.

The next few days were spent making the scene look deserted and planning quick departures to the North and South. Some stayed in the caverns, feeling they would remain much safer than out in the open.

The larders were quickly stocked for a long siege, a stockpile of arrows and water was secured from multiple sources. This including a comfortable little stream-fed pool near an outflow high on the cliff wall. They even had a pockmarked 'toilet' channel with a constant flush of ebbs and flows provided by the twin tides. Much like the Bitter Water hot tubs, although communal, there was an opportunity for some privacy in the nooks and crannies of the channel.

The old Landing, now Willow, Randy, and Kia's memorial, was scrubbed of signs, so Willow's grave was indistinguishable from the natural environment. Of course, the huts and landing pole were gone.

Roger Haller

51 Pegasi - Sister Tiffany

Traitor Larry's information would be useless.

I was surprised at how emotional I was, as the evidence of my people was being removed from this beautiful land. Still, I was warmed by the comfort and 'home' feeling the village was getting from the caverns in my cathedral namesake. I suppose I was a little surprised and relieved that the love of this community still meant so much to me. This terrifying and beautiful land was still home to my soul.

The village packed and prepared to split up. Shiv, Stacey, Sirih, and Pete headed South to homestead the site Shiv and Jean had found in the foothills. Tiffany, Adelphi, Jesus, and Princess decided to be more nomadic. They wanted to share all the villages, but their first move would be a trek North. Tiffany and Adelphi decided to soak again in the hot tubs before heading out, but they were all packed. As they left, Mac said, "We have a great lookout above Willow's Cathedral now, so I'll try to keep an eye on you ladies. I'll try to warn you if I see anything happening."

They swam naked around the pillar guarding the South entrance to the cathedral and strolled arm in arm in the shallows south to the tubs. The weather was easing, so Mac was concerned but did not press the point. He had learned that life in this environment did demand some downtime, stress relief, and even some fun. He did, however, have a lookout site at the head of one of the vent tunnels and a high-end set of binoculars that came in on one of the first freight shipments.

A natural formation of stones on top of the south-facing cliff provided a rock seat behind a small outcrop, which allowed for comfortable scouting of the old village site and Bitter Waters. One could see the entrance from the village to the East, past the slate cliffs and a good view of most of the delta. It even had a great view of the hot tubs.

***

Sailors Return, and So Does Larry

Something was off.

As soon as Mac got set up, he noticed the tides were in simultaneous ebb and out farther than he had ever seen them. He noticed the ladies, startled as they observed the same thing. Adelphi pointed outward and screamed. She turned to run inland.

Tiffany, who was further out, looking for a place to dip, followed her point and turned to run, too. As they started to run, Mac heard the delayed alarm in her scream. The breakers were swelling and rushing at the shore. There was no way the ladies were going to outrun the surge.

As the wall of water hit the tubs, Tiffany turned and dove into the first slope as she saw the marine life doing. Farther ashore, Adelphi headed up a leaning tree. Mac watched the surge take her and the tree into the thicket of delta trees far up the river channel. Tiffany popped up many yards out in the sea and started swimming hard for shore. She managed to catch a wave wall and tried to surf it like a dolphin, but the ebb drove her back to sea with a wall of debris full of squirming and panicked small animals.

Mac could hear her screaming for Adelphi. He noticed movement to his east and watched Mutt and Stud run for the bottom of the trail. They had been busy sweeping tracks off the trail.

Tiffany tried a new strategy: she swam north of the delta and then in. The current wasn't as strong here, and she finally reached shore. She ran to where she had last seen her lover, and with the surge and ebbs subsiding, the Scandinavian Amazon dove into the chore of ripping debris aside in the search for Adelphi. Mac watched helplessly as he heard her frightened calls, but he did not see Sean and Mutt again after they disappeared around the end of the slate cliff.

51 Pegasi - Sister Tiffany

He wondered why they hadn't reached Tiffany yet or appeared in the delta where he last saw Adelphi. Suddenly, Tiffany stopped casting and dove at a pile of loose brush at the bottom of a sand-trapped log. She had found her mate and was franticly digging in the sandy mud at the base of the felled tree at the edge of the tsunami's reach.

Mac felt helpless as she dug, but he soon saw an arm, then a leg. Soon after, he watched as Tiffany pulled Adelphi from the mud and collapsed over her in tears. He couldn't tell if she was alive at that time. He noted he had never seen Tiffany emotional before. Her armor was down as she rocked her soul-mate in her arms.

Suddenly, she started and sat upright. Adelphi was re-sponding. The tall blonde woman cried even more as she rubbed the offending mud from her woman and checked her arms, legs, and torso for damage. Mac saw the attack first and almost screamed but held his voice to a grunt as a buried net swept out of the delta's sand, powered by a bent sapling. The women were snared in a common game net.

Two of the Giants stepped out of the forest, chirping and signing with glee. Thom celebrated the perfection as the tsunami had played their prey into their hands. The Giants had been dubious about the human's plan to flush some escapees into the trap. The human voice that joined the chirps, however, was not dubious. Howard Thom was delighted and confident.

He greeted the trapped women with pure evil bubbling up in his laugh. He could reach them as they hung near the ground. He poked at them through the net as he chided them. He laughed as he signed to the Giants as another human and four more Sasquatches joined and unfolded a familiar collaps-ible cage.

The second human wore camouflage with a high collar and a wide-brimmed hat pulled low.

Sailors Return, and So Does Larry

They deposited the women in the cage and hung it in a tree, just low enough for Thom to continue his torment.

The rain had stopped, but night was falling, so the two humans built a fire. The second man then approached the cage. Mac had the glasses trained on Tiffany, and although he could not hear what she said through her snarl, He read her lips and knew that Lawrence was back.

He dropped his head to his hands for a moment. Regret overtook him as he realized ownership of the mistake. He felt it was his fault Lawrence was back. He should have planned a different path for 'Larry.'

Mac lifted his head back to his field glasses. There was little he could think of that he could change without becoming more like Lawrence or Howard. He realized he could not operate like they did. Still, he felt there must have been a better way of dealing with a human, guided by a different moral compass. His logic told him he could not change who he was, but that thought didn't ease his regret.

A long night began for the villagers of Freedom. The evening air brought a chill to the naked women. Ann supplied Mac with a blanket but knew getting him to come into a fire for the night was useless.

Mac noticed the men using American Sign Language to discuss their plans over the fire. He didn't think Lawrence ever heard that Tiffany knew ASL, too, and used it to communicate with Chuckles. Although Mac's language skills weren't as smooth as Tiffany's, he learned that Lawrence had convinced Thom that the village was deserted. He pointed at the wrecked raft. Lawrence's experience at Freedom and the wreck made the bad guys conclude that the village had moved South. He had heard Shiv and Jean discussing scouting the South, although he wasn't around when they found the foothills site.

Roger Haller

149

51 Pegasi - Sister Tiffany

I now knew how confident Howard Thom felt about his mission. He had no doubt he could get easy information from the women in the cage, and he was more confident than ever that the survivors would be easy to clean out. They didn't look like they were faring too well.

***

Chapter 16

Survivors to Warriors

When night fell, the scene grew dark. The captors rolled out their sleeping bags and settled in for the night. As the twin moons rose, the women, who were quietly whispering, started from a sound. They both looked to the East to see a pair of pale faces and a waving hand. They knew they were not alone with the bad guys and their pets.

The night was long for Tiffany and Adelphi. It dragged on for the villagers watching from the dark as well. The women spooned at the back of the cage, changing places occasionally to warm up other parts of their bodies.

No one slept for more than a few minutes except for Larry, Howard, and perhaps the Giants. Even then, the two captors sat up to check on them periodically, and the Giants seemed to grumble and grunt from the darkness occasionally.

Howard Thom even got up to investigate a sound and relieved himself on a log near where the villagers had appeared. He was satisfied that the scene was quiet, so he went back to his bed-roll

Roger Haller

51 Pegasi - Sister Tiffany

As dawn began to seep through the marine layer of wispy fog, Tiffany and Adelphi were quietly searching for flaws in the cage. They had been silently working that task in the light of the twin moons much of the night.

They were about to simultaneously pull on the latches on two sides of the cover that held them suspended over the delta floor. To do that, they had to climb the bars to the roof, reach out through the bars with one hand while holding on with the other, and then pull on the latches simultaneously.

The first attempt to climb the bars to test the plan resulted in a swaying cage and rustling of tree limbs. The sleeping enemy awoke. They sat up to see the chilled captives reaching for each other and embracing. They sank to the floor in their embrace, and sleep finally found them.

The captors started their day by huddling over their re-awakened fire and quietly planning their next step. After eating a jerky breakfast, they strode to the cage to taunt the captives and call out to the Giants. The women woke, startled, to a rock banging against their cage.

It seemed events were poised to escalate.

The noise woke Mac, far up on the headlands, too. He woke to see the angry confrontation happening between cage bars below.

The conversation was moving too fast for him to make out the words, but he could see the taunting glee on Howard and Larry's faces and the rage on the faces of the captured lovers.

Howard signed to the Giants, who were now with them, and the shaggy monsters lowered the cage to the ground. One of them removed the cage lid, and another plucked Adelphi from Tiffany's grasping arms. The first placed the lid back on the cage, keeping Tiffany inside.

Roger Haller

Survivors to Warriors

Adelphi was delivered to Larry, and it held her from running, with two huge fingers pinching her long hair. Larry threw her to the ground, straddled her, and held her arms to the ground with his knees. Even from a distance, it was apparent how much he enjoyed his task.

Adelphi stopped struggling as Thom stepped over to the cage to discuss his demands with Tiffany. She answered with rage, so Howard Thom walked back to where Adelphi was pinned to the ground. As he walked, he pulled garden shears from his belt holster and cut off her left little finger at the top knuckle.

Both women screamed, and Tiffany pleaded to be allowed to help her mate. She gave the men the information they had been looking for, and it confirmed their assumption that the tribe had moved South.

Thom was pleased with his plan and agreed to have the Giant bring Tiffany to her mate. She quickly reached under the gloating Larry and grabbed Adelphi's finger and squeezed to stop the blood flow.

Both men laughed with glee as Larry still sat astride the struggling Adelphi. The glee was interrupted by the deadly sound of an arrow in flight, a dull 'thock', and Larry rolled off Adelphi with an arrow threaded between both front and back ribs. Larry died without objection.

One of the Giants roared while swiping at a weighted arrow embedded in his neck. The camp broke as Giants and Thom headed East on the run. A sapling saved Howard as another arrow was stopped just short of his escape. The humans all carried the weighted arrows designed for large adversaries.

The whole village ran for the delta to help Mutt and Jean, who were at war with the reason they were all here. Even Tiffany and Adelphi were in full pursuit. They were headed for the lower falls.

Upon finding Jean, they asked where Mutt had gone.

"I am following Thom and one of the Giants. Mutt caught the attention of the other Giants and headed across the delta to the southern pass. I showed him that pass when I brought him to Freedom."

He dropped his head. "Mutt has no plan beyond leading the Giants astray."

Penny, Princess, and Popeye headed after the wounded Thom and wounded Giant; some headed for Willow's Cathedral with Adelphi to get her to Dr. Tim.

Tiffany and Jean went after Mutt and the Giants. Tiffany had to stretch, as they ran, to match her stride with the robust Frenchman. Momentarily, she was distracted as she noticed the flex of his strapping body gracefully speeding along slightly ahead of her. The time she had spent bonding with the big man known as Stud had made her look at him through a different lens.

Even though she was smitten with the beautiful Adelphi and noted Jean's relationship growing with Hilda, she was slightly embarrassed by how this running vision made her feel inside.

Jean jolted her out of her straying thoughts as he spoke. "I tink Mutt, he is headed for da little opening on da hill where we fought Screamers before. I tink he can hide der."

He didn't wait for her answer, and she didn't offer one as he picked up more speed. Soon enough, they heard the raging Giants. That meant Mutt was probably still alive. Jean pointed at an opening o n the hillside to their left, where the prairie met the forested hill. Grass and low shrubs climbed into the trees a few hundred feet ahead.

Jean moved over to the edge of the trees and slowed his pace to stay quiet and catch his breath. Tiffany followed, thankful for the chance to breathe. They arrived just in time. Mutt had eliminated one of them, but three more were trampling the body of the dead or dying Giant to get to him.

Tiffany pointed to the Giant to the right of Mutt and said, "Mine".

Jean nodded, set an arrow, and focused on the Giant to the left. In unison, they launched heavy arrows from full draw. The warriors re-strung as the Giants swung around to address them. The wounded Giants received two more deadly arrows and dropped while staggering downhill. Distracted by the plight of his brothers, the last Giant took Mutt's next arrow to his side. It bolted past Jean and Tiffany before they could set their next arrows and fled to the East.

Tiffany jumped up to help Mutt as he scrambled down a log leaning against the rock face he had scaled, and Jean joined her once he ensured the bodies of the Giants were no longer a threat. Their rest was short-lived, though, as a panicked roar from the bottom of the hill broke their relief. The Giant that had fled with one arrow returned with two more arrows deep in its chest.

As the beast died at their feet, Shiv strode into the clearing. Seeing the result, he whistled, and the Southern tribe soon joined the survivors in hugs.

"We were still on the prairie and were flushed inland by the tsunami. We're all okay, but we figured we had better come back and see if Freedom was alright. Although we knew we would need to deal with Thom and the Giants at some point, we weren't expecting to see this war so soon."

51 Pegasi - Sister Tiffany

Tiffany replied, "It seemed like the tsunami was working for Thom. We were sitting ducks. We have to get back."

She reminded the warriors that the rest were after Thom and at least one other Giant.

I felt the desperation in her soul to get back to Adelphi, which pushed aside the relief at the successful end of this battle.

***

Survivors to Warriors

Tiffany and Jean updated Shiv and his crew while returning to the village. Tiffany was in a hurry as she needed to know how her lover responded to her lost finger. When they got back to the delta, all was quiet. The lack of action made them head for Willow's Cathedral, where they knew Adelphi was being treated.

Half of Adelphi's little finger could not be saved, but she was sleeping peacefully through the effects of her own anesthesia. Dr Tim had done a great job with the stub. Tiffany took a stool beside her sleeping beauty. Jean curled up in a corner with Hilda. Both looked like they were about to fall asleep.

Jewels was trying to stay busy with the teleporter landing room. She was scared for Popeye. The last she had seen him, he was climbing the lower falls to run after the escaping Howard Thom with Penny and Princess. She knew they were all more than capable, but she also knew how powerful Howard was, even though he was wounded.

The story of the Tsunami, Thom, and Larry set the team in action. Shiv and Mutt headed for the delta to deal with Larry's body. They decided to build a travois to take him to the south side of the delta to bury him in the grasslands. Armed with a shovel, an axe, and vine rope, they headed for Larry. They would do a service for Larry that no one would have expected he'd do for them.

Mac announced that the time had come for him to return to Earth to sort out his future direction. He would wait for Popeye and the hunters to get back with a report on Thom, but everyone felt that would be the last of him for a while, at least.

Tiffany nudged Jean. "Hey, Jean, would you like to help me bring Popeye and the girls home?"

Stud grinned, nodded, and they loaded up and left.

Roger Haller

They met the subdued warriors as they climbed down the path beside the lower falls. It seems they managed to dispatch the last Giant at the foot of the lower falls, and Howard took an arrow to the arm as he sneered over the top of the falls. They climbed after him but noted he left a heavy trail of blood toward the upper falls. They didn't have to finish the job. The rainbow lizards welcomed Howard Thom with excitement at the smell of his blood. The roars were heard long before the warriors witnessed the grizzly sight, but as they turned to get out of range, there was no doubt Howard Thom would not be back.

It was a somber but thankful team that headed back to the safety of the caverns that now protected the village. The melancholy feeling stuck with the village as Adelphi woke to Tiffany's arms. The village prepared a meal, and they discussed the next steps. Mac led the discussion with his vision for those steps. "Family, I guess I'm feeling the need to go be with my memories long enough to picture a life after Willow."

He looked around the cavern chamber. "Tiffany, you have Adelphi and plan to expand our family to the North. Shiv, you have Stacey and plan to lead a migration to the South."

Then he called on Julio. "Amigo, As the mayor of Libertad, you have a good handle on Freedom and the Cathedral. Dr. Tim, you have the resources and help to look after the village."

He waved his hand over the tribe. "Most of you have found your tribe roles and mentors. You have matured from survivors to thrivers."

"Vera, you are the one I worry most about because, like me, you have lost your best friend and mate. I need some time to talk to myself. How about you?"

Vera didn't answer for a moment, and a hush fell across the room that would echo a whisper.

Roger Haller

Survivors to Warriors

The mood grew heavy before she answered. "Mac, I spent my life talking to myself. For me, that was not healthy. Here, I found action broke my old habits and freed me of my self-built prison. Kia gave me a gift I will carry for the rest of my life. I miss her every minute. I will love her memory until I die... and with Julio's help, I will meet her again one day... But I have reason to be here now. My Aardian family believes in me, I have purpose beyond myself, and I can lead when I want to. I am where I belong."

There weren't many dry eyes in the Cathedral, but they were soothed by smiles of pride in the shy girl from Canada. Mac hugged her tight. "As long as Willow rests at the landing pond above, this will always be my home so that I will be back. It doesn't matter how long it takes me to figure out what I need for my future because I have the transporter. I will be back before you miss me."

After pointing at the transporter room, he directed his comments back to the village. "We are about to be in trouble... again... very soon. The Giants have lost some of their brothers and sisters to our arrows. I know enough about them now to know they feel the same kind of pain we do. They will want to wipe us out. I want to be here when they come, but I suspect if we spread out, the core village will be safe in Willow's Cathedral, and transporters can be set up for easy transport to and from the North and South villages."

Tiffany took a leadership step. "We are thrivers. We've got this."

It felt strange at this time, but the village was releasing Mac to heal. I knew I could help. I knew what he needed. I had someone for him to meet.

***

Chapter 17

War and Immigration

Mac was gone in the morning. The village began to prepare. Although natural leaders were well known, everyone turned into a leader. They knew the hammer was about to fall, but no one was devastated that Mac was missing. The difference was confidence.

The humidity was oppressive, but the scouts were busy. Jean reported that the giant's body was missing from the bottom of the Falls. Even with the giant's strength, the feat was hard to imagine. Mutt and Jesus also reported the bodies had been removed from the clearing on the hill south of the delta.

The Giants were here.

The village shuttled the last supplies into the cathedral caves from Freedom, and the Aardian pioneers braced for the attack.

They cleared tracks and stuck to the water entrances when they needed to go out or come back in. They didn't have to wait long.

War and Immigration

Shiv and Pete raised the alarm as they swam in from the south side of the cliffs. Giants had flooded across the delta and were thrashing the ruins of Freedom, looking for evidence of the human prey.

The citizens doused the fires; meals consisted of dried meat, vegetables, and fruit. They drank only water or cold, steeped tea. Oliver was a genius with these meals and teas, so the cool caverns did not have much hardship.

Sentries at the vent holes at the tops of the cliff could see large clouds of smoke to the south. The Giants were burning the grasslands to hide any cover. The scouts witnessed the massive bipeds trampling all over the plateau, but they saw no evidence of Willow's memorial, the pond huts, or the old landing pole. The Giants spent a lot of time sniffing the headlands, but when they were near, the village spent as much time as possible near the ocean vents at the bottom to mix their scent with the ocean breezes.

The attempted flush lasted for an Aardian month, but the oppressive, muggy heat on the plateau and the sulfur from the hot springs at the Bitter Water tubs wore heavy on the massive natives. They began to wear out, and most were gone when they found nothing of value. With little trace, the giant's human partners must have thought there were not many survivors. The wrecked raft, the villagers hoped, led them to believe the escapees had tried to move out over water.

Finally, they were all gone, with the local vegetation stripped back and thrashed. Thankfully for the village, Tropical Aard regenerated spectacularly. New berry bush sprouts were a foot long before they left.

The Humpbacks were back to normal when the last thud of a heavy foot was gone. The Aardvarks and Capybaras in the foothills hardly noticed the disturbance. However, the Screamers were quieter for a few days.

Roger Haller

The leaders began planning for the tribe's distribution to the North and South and the configuration of the tribe staying behind at Freedom and Willow's Cathedral. Shiv and Popeye called a meeting in the main hall to coordinate.

Shiv's tribe was heading South with him, Tracey, Pete, and Mutt. Originally, Sirih and Vera were to go with them, but they decided to stay back and help Julio rebuild Freedom.

Tiffany and Adelphi recruited Jesus to go North with them, and Princess joined them. She had an eye for Jesus. The timing was uncanny. Mac strode into the back of the meeting and commented on how the center hall was so 'fixed up.'

"Spreading out, are you?" He continued.

Laugher rang out through the cavern as several people offered to take him outside to see the changes. Through the laughter and din of excitement, he asked to have a moment with Popeye and Jewels. "I have a task for you."

They walked back into the teleporter landing room for a few minutes.

He told them about an impressionable young lady… maybe two—who would be landing, and they would need a most empathetic female guide.

He asked Popeye to help him rebuild the old Landing Hut near the pond and Willow.

They returned to the meeting to announce a new immigrant or two and requested a couple women to help Jewels with the teleporter chores while he and Popeye went to work at the old landing. After the mysterious immigration news, Mac sat through debriefing on the fruitless war of the Giants and the plans for spreading out.

War and Immigration

At the end of the debrief, he asked for a little one-on-one time with Jewels and with Shiv to explain. He asked Shiv to hold his trek for a few days since he felt the new immigrants would be best served on his team.

Once those two were up to speed, he asked for a few days' patience, as Willow had charged him with a significant task. Mac, Popeye, and a small crew of builders headed for the old landing with tools and materials for a new hut and a proper memorial for Willow, Kia, and Randy.

Mac had recruited a young adult version of Popeye Paul's daughter, Kelsey and probably her friend, Sylvia to come live on Aard. These two young ladies had been working as ladies of the night in downtown Seattle. Reintroducing his innocent 4-year-old to Paul as a street-hardened young woman would not be easy.

This task would be delicate and could prove to be dangerous. Mac knew it but was convinced the benefit far outweighed the cost. Jewels sold the plan to go south to the two new immigrants. A decompression time while Popeye Paul learned his daughter was on Aard would be a smart move.

Shiv and Stacey introduced them to the rest of the Southern Tribe, and they headed South as soon as the landed young ladies understood the plan. While they were rebuilding the old landing cabin, Mac sat Paul down and, with the help of Jewels, explained the new additions to Aard and their assignment to Shiv and his village. It didn't go well.

Paul broke Mac's nose, driving him, ass-over-tea-kettle, over a newly repaired bench. It got delicate in the landing camp, but Jewels got Paul thinking again. Once the adrenaline wore off, they all hugged and made up. Mac then explained the plan to Popeye Paul, and the plan was hatched to set up their meeting as soon as both were ready.

Roger Haller

51 Pegasi - Sister Tiffany

This event wouldn't be a typical father-daughter reunion. This family had traveled some broken roads, so the vision had to be much clearer before meeting on equal terms.

Mac had to drop one more bombshell before he ran off to catch Shiv. He let Jewels know he was her uncle. During his elaborate recruitment to save Popeye's young lover from a malignant tumor in her brain, Mac found out Jewels was the daughter of a step-sister he had never known.

This unlikely news brought another round of tears all around. The story of how and why she was recruited warmed their hearts, and the drama was replaced by love and hope for a bonded future.

Neither Dan nor Sirih desired to leave Freedom. Dan had a life with Oliver, and Sirih wanted to introduce a hybrid of technology and nature into the new life she found in Aard.

Secretly, the technologist also felt she might find a husband quicker if she lived near the hub of this colony. Sirih hadn't seen the combination that would be a gentle soulmate and inspiration. By now, however, she knew this would be where he would show up.

Mac had an idea who might gravitate to the transporter, though, and it couldn't be a better fit if he could convince her. I felt his plan would work in many ways. Now that I was seeing Mac from this angle, I was more sure than ever that he was the catalyst that would make human life on Aard a success beyond the dreams of anyone who had yet to leave Mother Earth's protection.

Word had come back from Shiv's camp that they named their village Moon Bridge. I knew why.

***

War and Immigration

The time had finally come for the nomadic scouts to hit the trail. Adelphi decided to stay back for this first trek, as Marus still needed her help to heal, and she had work to do on the 'blood of the flower' that Kia had gathered for her. The alchemist felt she owed it to Kia to make the best of her sacrifice.

Tiffany reluctantly agreed but was torn by the thought of leaving her behind. The lovers decided that this focused trip would be over soon, and they would be free to spend the rest of their lives together soon enough.

Tiffany, Jesus, and Princess headed north from the Landing Pond. At first, travel was slow and careful because the Giants had beaten the small trees and shrubbery flat on the plateau. There was little cover from the Screamers, and the scouts could hear them every day. The rage on the hillside had disrupted the Screamers' usual prey, so the hunt was constant and vicious throughout the days. Until they reached good cover, the danger was high.

Learning from their last venture, Tiffany and Jesus easily convinced Princess of the value of night trekking with the help of Alpha and Beta.

Toward the end of the first night, scouts were still in trashed vegetation, with no sufficient cover. They had been scanning the vista at a greater distance as the dawn lifted over the Eastern mountain crags. Nothing seemed sufficient.

"We are inland too far to be protected by the Screamer's aversion to the sea, so if you see anything we can fit in, we had better get out of sight." Tiffany pointed ahead.

Jesus put more effort into searching their surroundings, but Princess followed Tiffany's outstretched arm and pointed at what might have been a pile of rubble to the East but slightly ahead. "Do you think we can make that rock pile?"

Far-off screams answered her. They couldn't see the floating specks over the mountain tops yet, but could hear them.

"We had better reach them and hope there is some cover because there won't be time for a plan 'B.'" Tiffany's voice reflected her concern.

In the distance, to the North, they could see the wall of undisturbed trees, but they had no hope of reaching that far before the Screamers would be on them. The distance to the rocky boulder pile was closer, but it wasn't a sure bet either.

As they ran, Jesus moaned a warning and pointed at the eastern sky. The flecks of danger were now visible in a formation headed West. The scrambling scouts now knew they were prey. Princess, with the longest legs, was now leading the sprint. Her breathless voice flowed back, "How can they see us from that far?"

Jesus, running full stride in the back, answered, "Pueden Olernos… dey smell…"

The screams were getting loud. The boulders were close, but the three sprinters didn't look up. Their focus was shelter amongst the rocks. Heavy shadows swooped over the trio as Princess and Tiffany dove through a gap in two huge boulders. Amid a spine tingling scream, Jesus joined them, although a hesitation interrupted his entrance while he shrugged out of his ripping toga. Massive talons swept his robe into the air.

The screams grew in volume and urgency as smaller boulders were knocked from the mound of glacier sweepings, but the trekkers were now deeper in the shadows.

Princess gasped as they piled into a darkened crevasse. A reptilian tongue flickered at her from between luminescent eyes. Along with a threatening hiss, other eyes became visible.

War and Immigration

Every living entity in the rock pile was startled and every sense was aware and concerned over the din in the open, above ground. Jesus and the lead set of eyes in the darkness took point. Jesus squeezed by Tiffany and Princess as they retreated as far as they could before serving themselves to the raptors. Jesus had lost his weapons to the attack outside the shelter but found no resistance when he reached for Princess's spear.

The reptile turned out to be a serpent as it slithered out of the den, but it presented small feet on each side of its torso, that helped it push past the rock walls. As it closed the distance, Jesus faced it with the tip of the spear. It kept slowly inching forward, raising its head nearly to the ceiling of their shared rockery. It was now looking down on the defensive warrior.

As it reared back to strike, Jesus drove the tip of the spear into the throat of the challenging beast, just below its chin.

A wild thrashing ensued. The reptile retreated, wounded, but was replaced by another, moving faster. It snapped the spear shaft as Jesus pulled it from the wounded creature and reached for the struggling man. Princess let fly an arrow, and this snake recoiled back into the den.

The screaming and thrashing above the rocks increased as the Screamers sensed the drama inside.

Another snake launched forward before Tiffany could launch an arrow, and Jesus was grabbed by the arm. With a powerful flip, it wrapped a coil around the fighting human, then another and another while rolling upward, past Jesus's struggling companions. The enormous serpent was outside in moments, wrapped nearly completely around the hapless warrior. Moments later, it was high in the air, secured in the talons of a ferocious Screamer.

Several other limbed serpents bolted past the humans and spread quickly over the landscape. The raptors attacked. Many were now airborne.

Tiffany and Princess watched helplessly from the entrance to the rocks, looking for a chance to protect Jesus.

The multi-legged constrictor attacked the screamer, and the fight raged in uncontrolled flight, often bouncing on the ground and soaring skyward.

The remaining raptors swung wildly at the locked battle, contributing to the chaos. About twenty feet from the ground, the reptile lost its grip on Jesus, and he tumbled to the ground. A Screamer dove for Jesus but dropped to the ground, dying, with two arrows draining its lifeblood.

Jesus made it back to his team and the rock sanctuary before another raptor could reach him. The war of the Titans roared around them as the legged serpents had little defense against the raging raptors. Within an hour, the humans were forgotten as the Screamers soared away with the spoils of the war.

The newly found nest of legged snakes was extinct.

I took a moment to reflect on each of the survivors. Tiffany had let others lead. Even though she naturally led, she had learned from Mac to inspire everyone to lead in their moments.

Princess had stepped up as a warrior. Her speed was an asset, and those around her recognized her advantage.

Jesus had sacrificed himself for his friends. Without hesitation, he stepped in front of danger. This trait reinforced his legacy after the selfless actions when Larry had fallen into the river.

War and Immigration

These three counted on each other as a team and would always stand up for each other. Their bond was growing stronger every day.

Even from my vantage point, I felt spent by the drama that had just ensued, and I showered my friends with my love. It was not yet their time.

***

Chapter 18

Shangri-La

The battered scouts spent the rest of the day tending to Jesus's wounds and thanking their personal gods and luck that they were again safe for now. With relative safety, the team relaxed, ate and drank from their kits, and restored their strength.

Jesus would be all right. The bites were not poisonous, but they did need attention to clean and stop the blood flow.

Princess found Jesus' weapons near the rock pile, and although much worse for wear, he found his toga robe. The belt with tools was still hanging to it through a belt loop. Tiffany used some of the shreds from his torn tunic to bandage his wounded arm. She found a little of the orange moss on the north side of the rock pile to pad under the bandage. He was soon patched and healing.

The exhausted scouts spent the rest of the day in the little rock hill, snacking and sleeping to refresh their spent energy.

The night trek to the Northern woods would be the next unknown challenge.

Shangri-La

Princess reflected quietly, "You know, months ago, when I landed on this planet, I was convinced I had only days or weeks to live. Nothing mattered much. Now that I've been through boot camp, hunting trips against creatures far bigger and stronger than I am, and scouting treks with you, it feels like years."

The bald head of the pale, slender woman who first arrived in Freedom had morphed into an attractive, blonde woman with defined muscle. Princess was now one of the village's able scouts and most intimidating warriors.

"Tiffany, I have modeled my growth after yours. I have always admired how you stepped out of the image society had for a beautiful woman to become a force to reckon with. Jesus, you and the Frenchman have done the same. Neither of you are judgmental, and you lead with actions, not words."

Uncharacteristically, she leaned into her trek-mates and hugged them both close. Tiffany smiled, returned the hug, and said, "Princess, you are becoming a role model we can all learn from. I'd follow you into battle just as easily as follow you into a hug."

Jesus copied Tiffany's hug and said, "Eres familia… me fam-illy."

I got a deeper insight into Princess as I watched her study the emotion in her teammate.

Princess noticed what looked like the start of tears in the corner of his eyes. It was hard to tell in the dim light of the rockery, but his eyes betrayed him as one of the eyes leaked his emotion down his cheek. She took note of this and looked at Jesus differently.

He accepted her for who she was, not who he thought she should be… This intrigued the sturdy young woman.

Roger Haller

51 Pegasi - Sister Tiffany

He was only a few years older than her but seemed the most mature man she had known. Perhaps it was the strength of his silence.

Tiffany broke the train of her thoughts. "We will be in the forest by morning, safe from eagle eyes, but as we found in this rock pile, perhaps we will meet new friends or foes. We can't rest easy till we find Rita and her village, so let's get some well-deserved rest."

She received nods in return, and everyone found a comfortable spot to nap. It surprised no one that they all found the best comfort when snuggled with each other. As she fell asleep, Tiffany marveled at her expanding personal horizon. Perhaps there was a higher power who cared, after all…

The twin moons guided the trio of trekkers to the deep wood without further issue. As they entered the tall, evergreen cover, they also noted that the blue glow of their mushroom staple was more abundant here than on the plateau. However, the trail became more challenging.

The moonlight was screened out much of the way, and the new trail was faint in some places. This environment was much like the canyon pass below Randy's Rock.

The path was now much more vertical, too. The trio were now in the foothills of a mountain range. Their direction had been mostly North but slightly East as they followed a natural web of wildlife trails. Since the rock pile, the most prominent path leaned to the Northwest and the coastline. This was a relief as East meant Screamers.

As daylight spread in the morning, they could see mountain peaks ahead, but there seemed to be a gap to the Northwest. Daylight also brought the Screams of the Raptors. They were much closer than they liked. But the thick canopy of the forest appeared to be more than sufficient to keep them safe.

Roger Haller

Shangri-La

The light of day made travel easier, but finding the right path became tougher. They spent most of the day trying trails toward the mountain gap, only to find them twisting back or dead-ending along bluffs and shale cliffs.

At a point where a promising trail took them back to a place they recognized from two hours ago, Tiffany pulled a small notebook and pencil from her pack and drew a map. She received confirmation from Princess and Jesus, so they avoided circling and backtracking. The rest of the day was trial and error, and by evening, they had a grid mapped out with a web of Humpback trails.

She laid a darker line through the middle, leading to the Northwest gap in the mountains ahead. Time and daylight ran out, so they camped with a fire for the first time.

They refueled on Humpback, mushrooms, a relative of the asparagus fern with small, red berries and slightly woody stalks that softened nicely in the boiling water of the Humpback stomach.

Over the evening fire, Tiffany reflected while watching the growing bond between herself, Princess, and Jesus. Although she had bonded well with Jean, she recognized a common thread around the campfire centered on three common goals. The three trekkers were all drawn by the life on the trail, discovery, and adventure. All three were dedicated to breaking the supply line of human freight, and they loved each other enough to give their lives for each other.

This revelation made the Blonde Amazon Sister of the Catholic Church think deeply about her future. She loved Adelphi deeply, in a raw, endless passion. Tiffany loved Jean physically, too, but that connection was complicated by the remnants of her distrust of the male gender and his smitten-ness with Hilda.

Roger Haller

51 Pegasi - Sister Tiffany

Adelphi had now backed out of two treks because of a passionate desire to serve the villages. Jean was also, by heart, a villager. The three sitting around the fire with her now were bound to motion. They would probably always be scouts and adventurers.

Tiffany fell asleep through silent tears. She had just lost the vision of settling down with Adelphi. This epiphany was painful, but the saddened scout had accepted the reality by morning. She would always love Adelphi, but they were not destined to be arm in arm on the trail it seemed.

With their morning tea, the little team planned their day. Yesterday's only productive result was a map that showed all their failed trails. It seemed each hopeful start yesterday had ended against a cliff or rock slide at the bottom of an unforgiving climb. This morning, they reviewed the rock wall they had camped against without much optimism. They planned to spread in both directions for the day to investigate the west and the East of the impasse, then meet back at the camp before dusk to compare notes.

First, however, Jesus wanted to explore the small cave they camped near to see if it would be handy in the future. He suggested he could catch up with Princess, who was heading east, after a quick look.

This was a critical milestone in expanding human settlement on Aard. This cave would be a centerpoint on Tiffany's map.

***

Shangri-La

With that, the ladies headed in opposite directions, and Jesus stepped into the dark to see how far he could go without a torch. He wasn't out of sight of the entrance when surprised to see what seemed light in the cavern's depths.

It was light. Jesus used the light as a guide as he passed several caverns to his side. As he drew near the brightening opening, he found a massive cavern to his left. It was stocked with dry goods. He recognized a well-organized stock room built by humans.

The excited explorer stepped lightly past the stockroom into a breathtaking mountain pastoral vista. A small river ran through the grasslands of a wide valley and far off granite canyon to the East, then curved slightly north at the west end of the valley, below the wooded hills Jesus peered down from. Although he couldn't see smoke, Jesus could smell a cooking fire nearby.

Excited, he turned and bolted back through the tunnel to the southern glow of the cave he had entered. Trotting into the clearing, he sounded the 'Tarzan call' Tiffany had introduced. Jesus was too inspired to decide if he would follow the original plan, run after Princess, charge after Tiffany, or stay put.

The grinning Columbian Scout heard answering calls from both sides, so his dilemma was solved. He could stay put. Staying put was a task, though. He wanted to get through the tunnel to explore the vista he had just experienced.

To burn off his adrenaline rush, he thoroughly explored the cave entrance to note the gate's dimensions and pros and cons for security purposes. It may be handy in the future, at some time, to be able to defend the entrance.

His lost life in Columbia drove some survival lessons to the front of his mind.

Roger Haller

51 Pegasi - Sister Tiffany

Princess was back first, so he explained what he had found and offered to stay behind to wait for Tiffany. She declined, suggesting she wanted to experience the tunnel with her complete band of scouts. Jesus tried to explain the caverns, the stockroom, and the valley on the other side, but he struggled to keep his thoughts in English, so by the time Tiffany sprinted into camp, Princess still didn't have a full picture.

Instead of starting over, Jesus picked up his weapons and pack and stepped into the tunnel. He slowed down enough to point at the cavern entrances in the dark but made haste to the other end, where the growing light illuminated the well-thought stockroom. Moments later, the three scouts stood at the edge of the vision he had seen less than an hour before.

Jesus said, "Smell."

They could all now smell the cooking fire.

Tiffany lifted her chin and cupped her mouth with her hands. Her yodel rang out.

Quickly, it was answered. Moments later, the scouts were surrounded by happy humans, led by the striking redhead. Rita had done well.

"Welcome to Shangri-La!"

The hugs quickly enveloped Tiffany and Jesus and, among introductions, extended to Princess. The overwhelming welcome made it clear they were happy Tiffany and her team had finally made the connection.

Far-off screams interrupted the happy greeting, and Rita suggested they get to the shelter. The band of humans retreated west along the rock ledge to another cave entrance with a low-ceiling, that opened into a much bigger cavern.

Shangri-La

The cooking fire they had smelled stood sentry outside the cave entrance.

The dimly lit sanctuary had beds tucked against the rough walls. Benches and tables were in the center of the room, with storage in the corners. The cave was safe, secure, and dry, but not much for comfort or light. There was no good place for a fire or running water, so water had to be carried in Humpback stomaches, and cooking had to be done outside.

Rita pointed down to the tree line at the edge of the valley grass. "We tried to build shelters inside the tree line, but the Screamers destroyed them. We lost Patty, Jim, and Leslie on the day the Screamers figured out our huts. We have been in the caverns ever since."

This news saddened the scouts, but Tiffany responded. "Rita, I'm so sorry. We can help you because we were able to build shelters in the past that kept the Screamers at bay. Do you have any builders we can work with?"

"Yes, Bill and Les are handy with wood and vines. Matt and Ann have been leaders in beds and furniture, but we don't have any tools, so the cave has been our best bet so far."

"We mas tool... More tool… for you. We set transporter buen…" Jesus was already planning.

Princess joined. "Yes, I have a transporter to install, and we can get you the tools you need to make huts that the Screamers don't recognize, camouflaged huts in places they don't see well. Who can you point me to, to learn about the transporter and who can maintain it for your village?"

Tiffany smiled wide. Princess had an opportunity to lead here and would make a considerable difference for this Northern tribe. "Rita, things are about to get much easier for you folks. Princess will connect you with Popeye and Jewels.

Roger Haller

They know the perfect resources to help you build a safe haven that will be secure, comfortable, and home."

Rita hugged her beautiful inspiration and called Jen to introduce her to Princess.

Soon, Jesus and Tiffany were working with Bill and Les to identify locations deep in the evergreens and high in the valley, close to the storage cave and tunnel, for hidden huts that would blend in with the forest canopy. Tiffany was making a list of hardware needs Princess and Jen could send to Popeye and Jewels. By evening, Princess and Jen had transported to and from Willow's Cathedral. With guidance from Princess, Jen planned and prepared the first freight shipment.

Matt and Ann were leading the design for the first hut. They had longed for the privacy a hut could bring, and Tiffany was helping Les and Bill plan the materials.

Over the evening meal, the Shangri-La tribe was planning the village layout. Popeye, Jewels, and Vera visited, and Tiffany, Jesus, and Princess prepared for the next leg of their journey.

They were heading for the Northern Giant's camp with the light of Alpha and Beta tomorrow night.

I noted three significant milestones that happened that day. Shangri-La and Freedom were connected. The trio of scouts were gelling as a rescue team. And, in the cooking firelight, I noticed Rita's heart-shaped red gem was now a pendant displayed deep in her freckled cleavage.

***

Chapter 19

Buzz, Stuart, and Friction

Their first night on the path East led the scout trio to a narrow canyon Rita had told them about. Rita and her band of escapees had a harrowing passage through the canyon in the river. They were all battered in the rapids, but unlike the Rio de Libertade, this river had a gentle drop to the West. The river wasn't as big as the river the rescuers had navigated to the South, but it had its challenges.

This canyon was littered with boulders, with a looser canyon wall depositing granite rubble in the path of the westbound stream. The boulders and rocks made the river wind more, but the hikers could scramble from perch to perch along its banks. The granite canyon was much lower than the clay canyons to the south, making it more visible to sky-borne eyes.

Tiffany, Princess, and Jesus found suitable dens among the boulders to hide for the day.

It was a good thing, too, because the raptors knew they were there. There was a lot of screaming above the roar of the rapids, but as long as they stayed still in the crevices, the Screamers couldn't pinpoint the humans.

Roger Haller

51 Pegasi - Sister Tiffany

The current of heated air, following the current of water, made it hard for the monstrous birds, so they flew up and down the canyon for most of the day. The scouts rested, ate, and planned their approach. Things may be different at the Giant's camp now, but it had been some time since their last raid. They were playing with a new set of circumstances.

"Let's take only the essentials past here, team. We will need to travel very light when we return with refugees. We will all need to swim downstream, so think about what we can pack in our pockets." They all wore short tunics with pockets for bud knives and steel blades hung on their belts. "I think we can live without the artillery until we get back here."

They stashed their weapons. None of the three were worried. The trekkers knew why they were here, and they knew the consequences of failure. They also knew what the humans trapped in the pipeline were going through. Their determination was not blind. It was careful.

From the path described by Rita and her village, they knew they would have to fight the rocky canyon for at least the next night, and they'd need clear skies. There were no blue nightlights through this open canyon, and one mistake in the darkness could end it all.

The granite rocks kept them challenged all night as clouds moved across the moon's surface much of the time. But, as they hunkered down the next day, they could see the jungle canopy in the distance, and the canyon walls were much lower.

The following evening made for better travel, and the trio of scouts were now in familiar territory. It looked much like the top of the Eastern trail, and they fully expected to see the familiar crossroads at any time. They didn't find it that day, but they had good jungle cover near the stream. They even harvested a fresh Humpback and picked some Aardian celery. Fresh food was a nice change.

Roger Haller

Buzz, Stuart, and Friction

The scouts did find their crossroads the next evening. The clouds had cleared, and the moons were on constant duty. The jungle was getting thicker, however, so travel was slow. They camped one more night at the crossroads to research the environment, look for changes, and plan their escape route. They decided to return the way they came, following the success of Rita and her village in the last escape.

"It may be important to get back to the Teleporter with fresh escapees. The quicker we get them away from the Giants, the better it is for those who don't know what they are up against." Tiffany had full agreement from her partners.

By morning, they were within striking distance and camped within sight of the Giant's North-South Highway. They felt it wise to cross that highway at night, but they had to hope the camp was where it was the last time they were here. Success would be much easier if they could count on their landmarks.

The camp was not where they had raided last time, but the Giants were too big to hide their trail. The highway now ran East from the old camp. Evidence of the old camp was everywhere, including a stack of discarded cage walls, floors, caps, and a couple with important clues. Latch guards on the newer cages prevented human arms and hands from getting to the latches from inside the cages. The Giants and their human partners assumed the latches were pulled from the inside.

"The Giants think the escapes have been inside jobs…" Tiffany's thought didn't finish in her sentence.

"Si…"

"Ya… we…"

They all stopped and looked at each other.

Roger Haller

Tiffany continued. "They don't know we have been freeing the captives. They don't suspect that we would come back to our cages if we were still alive…"

All three were absorbed with the new train of thought. Princess finally expanded on the topic. "Humans built those latch guards. They also think escapees would not come back to rescue people from the cages. They assume everyone transported is a loser." Jesus was listening with his eyebrows cocked. "Larry no nos delato… Larry do not tell about uz… Si?"

The three looked at each other in a new understanding, and Tiffany and Jesus followed Princess' gaze as she searched the canopy for vines. They were everywhere. The environment was the same as the Southern Giant's camp.

Tiffany smiled. "Business as usual. Let's find us some humans."

It didn't take long. Before the moons set, they found hanging cages farther down the Giant's highway trail. Since it was close to dawn, they pulled well off the path and circled to the South. They stayed far enough back to stay out of sight but got close enough so their scent mingled with the cages' humans.

"I don't think they can differentiate between humans, so they will smell us and think we are part of their farm if we stay close. Let's collect some vine and stay quiet through the day." Tiffany was smiling while she spoke. This was what she was meant to do. Jesus and Princess were mirrors of that emotion.

Soon, the camp was active. From their shelter, the scouts could see three cages holding couples and another cage holding a group. They counted twelve frightened humans. They heard them communicating with each other. Some spoke English, they thought another couple spoke German or Dutch, and Tiffany felt the group cage appeared to speak Arabic or a Northern African language.

Buzz, Stuart, and Friction

This would be a large rescue, making it more complicated than usual. Escape could be especially tricky if there may be some language barriers. By evening, they found that the European-sounding cage held a German-speaking woman and a Scot. The Scot could speak some German. The English-speaking cage seemed to sport an American accent and perhaps a French Canadian or Canadian Maritime accent.

The group cage sounded more Arabic but seemed to host some extra tension. None of the rescuers could speak Arabic, but Tiffany had been around the language back in Africa and could understand snippets.

The rescuer's plan did not change. The Giants could smell the escapees, so distance was the best option. The river West would provide no footprints and the fastest exit. This route may mean some travel during daylight, so the gap between jungle cover and granite boulders would be the second biggest challenge. The angry swarm of Giants would be the first.

I was most impressed with Tiffany's plan. So were her partners. She was an easy leader to follow. They all knew there was never a foolproof plan, and there was always the unexpected to expect. Jesus and Princess knew the plan before it was voiced. It fit their way of thinking, too. The only bad plan was one without action… That was just a dream.

***

Roger Haller

51 Pegasi - Sister Tiffany

When the Giants were far enough away for the cages to begin their evening chatter, the scouts jumped into action. They spoke English, made shushing gestures, and held their hands up with palms forward in a sign to get attention to their actions.

Princess threw a vine up, starting with the English speakers, and the man in the cage caught it. He handed it to the woman, who he then lifted to his shoulders, and she tied it to the inner cage loop with a double knot and pulled it tight. The Man tested the pliant vine for strength and started tying knots for foot holds for climbing down.

Princess threw a vine to the Scot, and he and his partner did the same. By now, the Arabic cage understood the assignment and followed the template. The first cage dropped their vine through the bars, and Princess scampered up to climb the cage frame.

In moments, the shock of the first latch release was over. The occupants had been warned. Except for gasps from all cages, everyone followed the process as if they had been doing it all along. No one declined to escape. They had all seen their future, and the prospect made it easy for them to accept some danger.

Within a half hour, all were racing Westward along the Giant's Highway. They headed South on a well-worn Giant's trail when they reached the North-South route. Tiffany led them past their Eastern exit to lay a trail to the South but turned back within an hour. They broke through the trail edge into the river that was streaming West.

The stream was small here, but she urged the escapees to get down in the water and swim along while pushing with their hands and feet. Experience told her they would travel faster in the current than splashing in the water at varying heights from their knees to their waist.

Buzz, Stuart, and Friction

A couple of tributaries later, they could swim most of the time. Even the non-swimmers could swim in this natural environment with their lives as motive. With the help of the current, they could see dim light at the edge of the Jungle. There would be a short time between the jungle and the granite boulders, where they would be vulnerable.

By the time they reached the opening skies, dawn was upon them. Tiffany stopped momentarily to explain the dangers; Granite boulders, Giants, and airborne raptors could all threaten their life and limb. The only actions available would be to flee or to hide. To hide before the granite boulders would leave them vulnerable to the Giants, who would be sure to follow if they could tell they took the river West.

By now, she had learned to respect their intelligence.

To stay in the open would make them vulnerable to Giants and Screamers. The only plausible choice would be to bolt for the rocks in the canyon using the river for power.

The English speakers got it. The Scot translated for the German, so they were in, but the Arabic group didn't understand what pointing back and at the skies meant.

They were hesitant to leave the cover of the Jungle.

The scouts spent a few more minutes trying to convince them, but far to the East, the Giant's roared. Upon their roar, Screamers could be heard. Everyone was alerted now, so Tiffany dove back into the steam and swam hard to the center of the current. Everyone followed. Even the hesitant Arabic group followed now. They kept looking back at what they had left with fear, though, so they were not as quick to surge ahead.

Although the Giants appeared to be slowed by the false trail, their roars were soon closing distance. Faster than them, however, the Screamers were approaching.

Roger Haller

Tiffany wondered; It seemed Screamers were attracted by Giant's roaring. It may be a sign of mutual prey. She remembered the Ghorse hunt from a former adventure.

The granite cliffs were in sight now, but not close enough. A new, muddy tributary joined before the canyon, and the water was silty. The silt was uncomfortable to swim in, but Jesus remembered how the Raptors couldn't see swimmers underwater in that environment.

He yelled at those following, "If da Eagle come, dive down. Swim to side." He demonstrated.

Tiffany and Princess understood his strategy and followed suit. The English speakers began doing the same to different levels of success. The German woman got it and watched Jesus carefully. The Middle Easterners, some new to swimming, were confused and didn't attempt the maneuver to begin with.

The Screamers arrived as the swimmers approached the first boulders. The last swimmer was grasped from the water and screamed skyward in a purple raptor's talons.

Most of the swimmers understood the maneuver now, and they spent as much time as they could underwater. However, another hapless swimmer was lost before the swimmers found refuge in the crevices between the boulders near the shore. Now partly hidden in the rocky rubble, one more raptor scream drove the escapees deeper into the boulders. Most of them stayed submerged in water-filled crevices but for their heads for breathing.

The Giant's arrived, wading down the river. The war now broke out between the Screamers and Giants. Purple Screamers dropped from the skies with massive arrows silencing their screams. The battle of the giant predators lasted well into the heat of the day, but the surviving humans quietly pruned in the murky water.

Roger Haller

Buzz, Stuart, and Friction

The Giants witnessed the end of two of their escapees but having arrived late to the party, had no idea how many more were lost. They took their frustration out on the winged raptors and took many of them home as they ended their hunt.

The screaming raptors lost interest once they found no more opportunity and dusk arrived.

This had been a costly fight for their flock. A smaller, spent formation finally flew off to the East.

No one moved until the Pegasi sun set.

Tiffany finally climbed out of the water, staying close to a cavity she could scramble into. Princess joined her when she called out, and soon, Jesus stepped out and scrambled back over the rocks to join them. The German woman followed but pulled closer to Tiffany. She sensed the tall woman was their leader.

The rest of the Americans and Europeans peered out of the crevices but were slow to emerge in the dusk. The remaining Middle Eastern refugees weren't yet ready to join. Once Alpha arrived, Tiffany called again, "We must move now. We need to get through the canyon as soon as we can."

This call got more movement. The English speakers joined the scouts on a house-sized boulder, and the Arabic escapees began to join. The American said, "We have a lot to thank you for. I am Buzz. I hail from Oregon." He pointed to a dark-haired woman hiding behind him to cover her nudity. "This is Charlotte. She's from Eastern Quebec. She has some English, as most French Canadians do, but she has a way to go before she gets comfortable. My little bit of French is slowly getting better as I try to talk with her."

Charlotte nodded and held his elbow.

Roger Haller

51 Pegasi - Sister Tiffany

The fair-skinned Scot stepped up. "I'm Stuart. It seems I ha' been paired wi dis German Lady. She is Anikka."

He pointed at the worried woman standing beside Tiffany. "She's kinda fine, but not me type." He reached to put a hand on the middle-aged woman's shoulder. She shuddered and stepped away from him.

"Aye, don' tink she understands what the fuzzy Yettis wanted."

The frightened woman said, "Bring mich weg von ihm.." She pointed at Stuart and stepped up to take Tiffany's elbow.

"I know where we can get her a translator and support." Tiffany pointed at herself, "Tiffany." She then pointed at the German. "Hallo…Du?

The woman's fear eased, and she said, "Ich bin Anikka."

"Hello Anikka, …Kommen.

Anikka smiled a little at her new leader, who patted her hand on her arm. By now, the Middle Eastern folks were gathered and listening. Tiffany extended an open hand to them. "I'm going to try this, but my memory and skill is lacking… Marhaban… bikam. Taeal…"

Most of them smiled and nodded.

I watched with interest as they headed West over the boulders. I caught myself smiling as the trek was interrupted momentarily when the boulder field lit up. For the first time, the rescued learned that they were traveling under two moons. Welcome to Aard, immigrants. Most of you will love it here.

***

Chapter 20

Inclusion or Exception

Trekking West through the canyon boulders was much slower than the eastern journey. The new folks struggled with footing. When the hint of dawn illuminated the sliver of sky on the eastern horizon, Tiffany pulled up, and Princess and Jesus dug a little dry tinder from between the rocks. Princess lit the fire, and Jesus harvested a Humpback from the darkened recesses near the timber above.

Tiffany explained the process and next steps to those who could understand. She used hand signals and even tried some American Sign Language in case some of the foreign folks would understand. Several Escapees had issues eating fresh Humpback over the evening fire. They had eaten the meat since they had been in cages, but they had not known what the creature looked like.

Buzz, Charlotte, and Anikka were okay with it, but Stuart only accepted a bit of jerky. He was satisfied that it was cured, at least. The trekkers, who could not understand, settled for the last dried berry and celery sticks left from the trek. It wasn't much.

51 Pegasi - Sister Tiffany

Through gestures and body language, Princess conveyed the expectation of a village in one more day. Princess and Tiffany were concerned that the new folks may have thought 'village" meant civilization. It was hard to convey that there would be no indoor plumbing and refrigerators.

Jesus wondered aloud why the four remaining Middle Easterners were naturally separated into a pair of men, a single man, and a single woman. They would not mingle if they could help it.

The group had lost a man and a woman to the Purple Screamers, but in flight, it had been impossible to say which faction they would have gravitated to, if any.

Interestingly, to the protest of the two united men and the disappointment of the single man, the woman approached Jesus and bowed before him before reaching for his arms and looking into his eyes. Jesus looked up at the protesting men, then to the disappointed solitary man, and pulled her into an embrace. She never left his side for the rest of the journey to Shangri-La.

He tried to share his meal, but she silently shook her head. She did, however, tug gently at his loincloth. She needed the remnants of his clothing from the original trek to Shangri-La. The gentle Latin understood her need with that nervous gesture. He removed his covering and helped her belt it around her slim waist.

She seemed much relieved and held his hand while she knelt at his feet. Jesus gently pulled her to her feet, helped her tuck into a gap between boulders, and climbed in beside her to wait out the bright sunlight that would soon be on them. Tiffany and Princess did the same, including Anikka in their sanctuary. Buzz and Charlotte followed the example. Then, when the distant screams from the mountaintops began, the Arabic speakers joined them in the dark crevices for the day.

Inclusion or Exception

The Purple Screamers returned refreshed, and they knew immediately where to look. The new citizens learned first-hand the power of the screams. By mid-afternoon, Buzz had to pull Charlotte back into their hole as she was driven to the point of running. She cried against him in the dark as the unrelenting torment continued until dusk.

The single Arabic man almost made a dash for the timber but settled back in as Princess presented herself to the Raptors long enough for them to attack her sanctuary. The vicious attack convinced the single man to stay in his hole.

Tiffany noted that despite the distrust, the new citizens, who could not understand, were learning from examples. She thought they must learn to accelerate their understanding if they were to survive. This environment was not kind to those who could not learn.

They hadn't made as much progress as they'd hoped, so the trekkers began to doubt they could make it back to their weapons cache before the next dawn. Tiffany began to formulate a plan with Princess.

"Princess, we are out of food the new Aardians will eat. One of us must run ahead and dig out our cached weapons tonight. We need to harvest a Screamer while still on the rocks."

Princess looked at the tall blonde warrior quizzically. "What do we gain by sending someone early? We can all make it through a day without food, and it will probably take all of us to keep the new folks going through the night."

Tiffany expected some pushback. "I'm just thinking that action speaks louder than words, particularly to someone who doesn't understand our words. These people are all still thinking like they are on Earth. The ones who don't understand us expect civilization at this trek's end."

Roger Haller

51 Pegasi - Sister Tiffany

The light was coming on for Princess. "Hmm."

Tiffany continued. "These people need to see us provide food, and they need to see us defend ourselves. It may seem dramatic, but they will begin to see what they need to survive. We could accomplish the goal tomorrow, but by the time we get to the end of the boulders, it will be dark, and we will have missed the chance to harvest a predator and turn it into food, clothing, and tools."

"I get it now. The timing is the key.

Someone has to go ahead and get dinner ready."

Tiffany smiled and nodded. "You are our best hunter and the only one of us who has brought home a Screamer."

Princess lit up now. She knew Tiffany was presenting the best option. She knew it was dangerous to travel alone at night without weapons, and she knew she was best equipped to take the task. Her stomach growled, and she nodded her head.

Finally, evening fell, and the Screamers retreated.

As they climbed from the cracks in their world, Tiffany explained the plan to those who could understand. She dealt with the objections. Jesus offered to take the task, but Tiffany simply pointed to the quivering young woman at his elbow. Buzz offered to go with Princess, but she shook her head. "She who goes alone travels fastest." Princess modified the line from Rudyard Kipling or Merl Haggard, depending on your background.

Stuart saw an opportunity and insisted he was fast and agile. He insisted Princess needed a man to protect her. His comment didn't even get an answer, although it received several notable glances from the rescuers.

Inclusion or Exception

Princess shook her head with a grimace.

Stuart was agitated. "You are going to let a girl run off by herself? To get weapons? I'm a crack shot. I was the top sharpshooter in The Royal Scottish Regiment."

This guy would be a challenge. "Tiffany said, "Our weapons are long bows and spears."

Stuart was silent for a moment but wasn't about to let his chance to be alone with Princess slip by. "Okay, I get it. Still, two are better than one in a dark trek."

Again, the scouts shook their heads in unison. At last, Stuart decided to bide his time.

The sun was down, and the screaming in the distance had stopped. Before more could be discussed, Princess sprinted over the boulders and was quickly out of sight around the next bend in the river. Tiffany and Jesus advised everyone to get a drink from the river. The silt had long settled, and the water was clear and tempting for the humans that had sweltered in the granite ovens.

The new folks marveled at the soft blue glow from the fungus between the rocks and noticed that the scouts had no problem snacking on the fresh mushroom caps. After asking about them, those who understood tasted them. Buzz and Charlotte ate a few bites, and the Arabic speakers even tasted them. Hunger is a powerful motivator to experiment.

Beginning with the young woman who clung to Jesus, Tiffany, and Jesus tried to convey the plan with gestures. The simple message that transpired was that humans and food were ahead.

I was beginning to see shades of Larry in Stuart.

Roger Haller

51 Pegasi - Sister Tiffany

I was also worried about the differences between the Arab speakers, even though I knew where each had come from. Beirut was a melting pot and the center of the proxy war oxymoron that changed its identity with every conflict.

New to Aard were elements from Sunni, Shia, and Christian peoples who had all claimed the state to be their sacred home. This immigration could be an excellent new start for scared people or a devastating disruption from the biases on Earth. My Aardians had their work cut out for them.

***

Inclusion or Exception

Tiffany and Jesus soon followed Princess with their struggling charges. Although their progress was painfully slow, when they began to see the Eastern sky warm the horizon, they could also see the heavy evergreen forest beckoning from the West.

At this time of year, the moons traveled farther to the South, so the light they provided didn't last as long. This path also meant a longer stretch of starlight at the beginning and end of the night. Thankfully, there were few clouds in this season, so the night lights did their duty. The dim sliver of Beta still hung over the mountains as the Eastern light rose.

They could not see Princess ahead, but Tiffany and Jesus knew she would be planted in a shelter, allowing good access to the East. They didn't think they would hear or see anything from her until the Screamers were about to leave. On cue, the far-off screams grew louder, and soon, they were accosted by purple fury. This time, everyone sheltered quickly and smoothly, and the humans in the holes did not complain. However, anticipation made the wait longer.

Jesus made good use of the time, building communication with his refugee. He found her name was Basma. As much as she tried to pronounce his name, she finally settled on Hafiz. He later discovered that the name meant Keeper, Guardian, or Preserver in her language. She smiled when she addressed him with it, and her relief made the smile contagious.

Buzz and Charlotte continued to lean on each other on this excursion. They met the same way Mac and Willow met, so this trip to the sanctuary was similar. They spent the hot days learning about each other and napping in a supportive embrace.

Anikka remained silent, but she watched Tiffany and the other rescuers' every move and listened to every word.

Roger Haller

51 Pegasi - Sister Tiffany

Stuart and the lone Arabic speaker's hibernation worked opposite to the bonding. Alone, they were left to overthink their fate, and the time turned negative. The two men who sequestered together were already bonded. They had known each other from Beirut, and their conversations were quiet but constant.

Without the ability to communicate and collaborate with the rescuers, they had their theories and were biding time till they could find their kind or strike off on their own.

At this point, all escapees had been nude for weeks, so the initial shock was wearing off. No one was comfortable with the vulnerability, but there had been no opportunity to cover up during the escape drama. The proximity of screaming beaks and probing claws kept everyone at attention, but the relief was like a wave of cool air as the raptors began to back off.

Suddenly, the screaming raged again, and a Screamer lay amongst them, draining blood and life from a very long arrow. Another raptor screamed but flew awkwardly out of site to the East. As quick dusk sank over the scene, the rest of the Screamers followed the first, and silence fell over the body of the massive purple predator.

Jesus stepped out to ensure the raptor was finished and cleaned the beast with a bud knife and a practiced flair. Tiffany joined him in the chore as Princess arrived with three long bows, three full quivers, and a few chamois paperboy sacks.

She laid down her load and asked Buzz, Charlotte, and Stuart to help gather wood for a fire. Reluctantly, Stuart joined as the rest began their chore, and seeing this, Anikka and the Arabic people joined the effort.

That evening, over a cooking fire, everyone ate.

Stuart couldn't take his eyes off Princess.

Roger Haller

Inclusion or Exception

He asked if he could look at the weapons. Nodding over her meal, she watched him inspect the binding, the sinew string, and the specialized arrows. Some short, some long, and he asked what the curved wooden handle laid by the sack was for.

The Arabians watched the interaction closely.

"That's an atlatl."

He struggled to say the word, but she chuckled and said, "It's an ancient spear launcher."

Stuart quietly inspected the weapons through his meal, and Princess helped him understand. "You're not in Kansas anymore, Stuart… or maybe you're not in Edinburgh anymore. You are now on Pegasi d. We like to call this planet Aard." He looked to where Beta had disappeared. Then he looked at the stars. Princess followed his gaze. "Recognize any constellations?"

An understanding was settling over his face as he looked skyward. "Ohhh."

Everyone was following his gaze now. Even the Arabic speakers were beginning to get the point. Princess stood up. She crouched and then jumped high. She could have been a superstar in the NBA. "Try it."

Slowly, Stuart stood, crouched, and jumped. His eyes lit up, and he smiled for the first time. "I'm going to enjoy this place!"

Moments later, the Arabs were jumping up and down. They understood. They also pointed at the novel constellations and talked excitedly to each other. They weren't as happy as Stuart. This changed everything.

51 Pegasi - Sister Tiffany

Basma teared up and sobbed quietly onto Jesus' chest. Princess took notice but respected Jesus' new role enough to let the young Indian lean on her rock.

Buzz pulled Charlotte close as they looked at the stars floating above the fire sparks. "What is that large star to the North? It almost looks like another moon." Charlotte didn't make a big deal of it but stood up to stretch as a less obvious way of leaving Buzz's embrace.

Tiffany offered, "I think that is Pegasi b, the first planet circling another star that humans were able to identify. It doesn't rise and set like Alpha and Beta but seems to move around our sky with the seasons."

Learning from Larry, I wondered how many new folks may want a ticket back to Earth.

I'd like to know how many needed a ticket before they knew more about my happy place. I hope Popeye, Jewels, and the other leaders of Aard have thought more about the immigration policy.

Relationships would be gelling now, not all the way they envisioned, as I see with Buzz and Charlotte.

Here, we are at a crossroads. Can humans find the happy medium between inclusion and exception? Is there one?

***

Chapter 21

Refugee Distribution

The escaping humans were in the deep woods before the Screamers were heard. They were packing fresh feathers and raw Screamer hide for chamois. They had sinew, fresh meat, and talons. Even the recruits made good travel time now that they were off the granite. The wildlife trails were plentiful, and the path had been easy. Now, however, Tiffany led them into the undergrowth.

Stuart didn't like this. When the Screamers didn't appear to follow them into the woods, he vented his frustration at the need to tramp through ferns, berry bushes, and moss when the trails seemed so safe.

Jesus tried to reason with him. "Da Screamer, he watch da trail. He use to hunt da trail. He look at trail…"

"We're just heading West to the top of that valley ahead. Right?" Stuart was confident in his abilities. He'd hit the undergrowth if needed, but if he got to the village before everyone else, his status as a brave leader would be established, and he could have more choice than a simple follower. This was his chance to stand out.

Roger Haller

51 Pegasi - Sister Tiffany

"Si, but trail not safe."

"If the birds get close, I'll jump into the brush. I'm getting the hell out of here. I'll see you at the village."

Before anyone could answer, he bolted for the trail and scampered West, out of sight. The Screamers immediately changed tone. The purple raptors saw him, and Stuart had no idea how fast they flew. Tiffany, Jesus, and Princess dove deeper into the undergrowth and found shelter under ridge overhangs. The remaining escapees quickly joined them.

They all grew silent as they listened to the rage in the forest ahead. A short, panicked scream joined the rest, then the thrashing increased, and one panicked voice stopped. The action stopped abruptly after a few minutes, and Screamers headed northeast to the mountain peaks.

The wary trekkers sat still for an hour, then slowly worked through the scrub brush along the bottom of the mountainside to the village at the head of the valley. They had to pick their way quickly through the thrashed underbrush where Stuart ended. In their rush to get back under cover, some of them discovered with dismay they carried dried blood on their legs.

Rita and her scouts met them just short of the new Shangri-La huts. The returning rescuers were escorted into camp, where they met a quiet man from Morocco named Omar working on hides. One side of his hut featured a tightly strung Screamer hide with a detailed copy of a map of Shangri-La and the surrounding valley.

His map included a trail South to Willow's Cathedral, with a route supplied by Tiffany. Princess turned her raptor hide over to the smiling man, and he handed her back two tunic robes. She promptly gave one to Jesus, who was completely out of clothing.

Refugee Distribution

Tiffany introduced Omar to the Arabic speakers, and he sat them down to talk. The discussion became heated at times when the two males, identified as Shiites, Tamir, and Emran, demanded the woman, clothes, and supplies as they were going off to start their own community. They were honest with Omar. They felt they would lose their heritage and culture if they lived with the Kafirs and Infidels.

The single man, Samman, was a Sunni. He also wanted the woman but looked forward to living in the village and learning from Omar. He loved Omar's map and explained to his new friend that he was a cartographer and would love to map this new world. Basma was Christian. She wanted no part of the Arabic men and wanted to stay with Jesus.

Negotiations began with Tiffany and Rita talking privately first. They then called Omar into the conversation. The three decided not to explain transportation to the Arabs before they knew more about them. When Omar had left them, Rita spoke with Tiffany, "Tiffany, I just received a note from the Transporter. Mac is heading out for a tour of Aard. He wants to start here and needs directions."

Tiffany grinned. "I've got a map." She stepped into the storage cavern and sent him the map she had drawn on her way to Shangri-La. She told him to watch for the tunnel.

Omar went back to the conversation with the Arabic speakers. He called Jesus over and asked him to take Basma to meet with Rita. She had a place for Basma until she could be thoroughly interviewed and could be part of her new direction.

Tamir and Emran negotiated robes, dried food, and some tools from Omar. They now had longbows, an axe, knives, a pair of survival kits that had landed from Freedom a few days earlier, and a couple of blankets.

Roger Haller

Without ceremony, the two said they would be back for the woman when she learned what it would be like surrounded by infidels. They suggested they would become good trading partners and headed North without a map.

Samman asked if he could stay with Omar until he could build his hut. He had been a street vendor specializing in maps in a village near Cairo in Egypt. He saw a lot of opportunity in Shangri-La. Omar liked that idea and began helping Samman get to know the camp. He also suggested Samman talk to Tiffany about her map.

Rita had called on Jen and Vera to house Basma for now. Rita also asked Vera if any German speakers lived in Freedom or Moon Bridge. Vera confirmed that Hilda was German. Rita explained Anikka and Vera headed for the transporter to contact Hilda.

Jen, who had landed in the first wave of immigrants, had built a tight friendship with Vera, who had helped Sirih set up the Shangri-La transporter in the impressive storage cavern. A mighty copper vein streaking through the cavern's ceiling and walls was a perfect antenna.

Vera joined the village when she saw how her hunting prowess was needed, and she met and befriended Jen. Jen was a tiny woman, and she adored the striking Canadian hunter. Vera wasn't ready for more than a platonic relationship, but she felt needed and wanted and was happy with her newfound role as a mentor. Adding Basma to their large hut was easy, and Basma was thrilled to have a haven from men. She found it easy to explore her new village with her new friends as long as she had her sanctuary. The three ladies spent quality time with Omar and Samman, learning Arabic and English.

Buzz and Charlotte gravitated to Matt and Ann. The two Aardian couples bonded over the evening fires after working together during the day to build huts for the immigrants.

Refugee Distribution

Charlotte, however, was not fully bonded with Buzz. Now that she had a choice, she kept it platonic.

Rita pulled Tiffany aside to talk about Shangri-La. She pointed out how much they needed her in the village. Her hut design worked well but needed to be adjusted to the terrain and available materials. They needed to build more with rock and evergreen branches as palm fronds were not available. Rita made it clear she needed Tiffany's help.

Tiffany told her that Jean, and Shiv had been leading a lot of rock building since the tribe located against the shale cliffs at Freedom, then grew their skills in Willow's Cathedral. Pete also turned into a natural mason and led a lot of the rock work now. She sent a teleporter message to those villages and Pete agreed to come and mentor folks at Shangri-La.

I felt her pain as Tiffany didn't sleep well that night. She was worried, and for the first time, she longed to talk to Mac or maybe Julio about her dilemma. It had been a long time since confession, but for the first time since escaping the evil from Northern Uganda, and particularly from within her church. I felt the change as she realized that she needed to pray.

This night, she prayed to god for direction. She hadn't thought about her god or religion much since waking up on Aard, but what could it hurt? As she prayed, I watched as much of what led her to her faith and service, overwhelmed her with tears. Tiffany remembered the beauty of her faith and the pain that expelled her. She had no idea whether she could return to her church, go back to the overwhelming love for Adelphi, whether men may be an option in her future, or who she wanted to be.

Tiffany was adrift and needed a life raft.

***

51 Pegasi - Sister Tiffany

Tiffany began to feel it was time to visit Freedom. Everyone seemed to be growing from the trauma of the escape; the village was coupling up, and Vera reported that Hilda was primed and ready for Anikka.

She missed Adelphi and was worried that perhaps Adelphi didn't miss her as much. The pair-bonding around her took her thoughts back to the different paths Adelphi and her were drawn to.

Tiffany took a walk with Rita to talk privately. Rita listened quietly, as the troubled scout explained her need. She promised to return. The tall blonde felt at home and wanted to help build the village. She felt she could help once Pete started to train some folks.. She also wanted to be closer to the Northern Giant cages till they were no longer a threat. Tiffany explained that she would likely live on the trail in the future but wanted to call this northern village home.

She had to go back and convince Adelphi to come along… or not. Rita was supportive and without any judgment, assured Tiffany she would be most welcome in any capacity.

Tiffany thought about her next steps as she walked toward the hut construction against the rock wall. First, she would have a chat with Mac. She was looking forward to seeing him again. Maybe a simple conversation with an old friend would help the struggling scout settle her mind and find her path.

Tiffany didn't have to wait long. Later that afternoon, Rita strode happily into the camp while the striking scout was helping with a hut design. As she looked up from her work, grinning widely, Mac stepped out from behind the fiery redhead and enveloped her in a warm hug.

Emotion rose in her eyes as Tiffany hugged back, perhaps tighter than she planned. Mac misted up some, too.

Roger Haller

Refugee Distribution

They both pulled back to look into each other's eyes.

"My friend, you look like I feel. Willow's Spirit has been kicking my butt to step out and get to know our new home. I could be a while, but I will spend some time looking at this beautiful planet."

Tiffany smiled through her mist. "I know what you mean, Mac. I've been spending a lot of time on the trails, but I haven't had time to look at it. Frankly, I need to take some time off to look at me. I need to see Adelphi and figure out how we will live."

"That's a good idea, my friend. I've been doing the same."

They heard a slight sigh beside them and looked up at the smiling redhead.

"I'm sorry, Rita, we got a bit carried away." Tiffany smiled.

"That's quite alright, you two. I love happy reunions… Mac, I can't help but notice your beautiful locket."

Mac looked down to his chest and lifted the polished red gem to look closer. The hardened rawhide windings held it securely to the toughened cord that hung from his neck. "Just a treasure I keep close to my heart."

Mac looked up to see Rita holding an identical stone that hung in a similar locket around her neck.

"I know what you mean, Mac. Something made me pick this out of the stream-bed when I first started this adventure."

The three leaders looked incredulously back and forth between lockets and shook their heads in disbelief.

"Wow!" Tiffany started giggling.

Roger Haller

Mac reached gently to touch Rita's stone. "Do you mind?"

Rita shook her head, smiling. It was the same size, same shape, and looked like the same stone. "I pulled mine from the edge of the pond back home." Before thinking about his next words, he said, "Willow made me pick it up."

Rita smiled softly at him but had nothing more to say. Tiffany had explained Mac and Willow. Tiffany changed the subject.

"I'm getting a crew ready to transport to Willow's Cathedral tomorrow. Come meet them, Mac."

Rita took the opportunity to find a chore, so Tiffany and Mac walked together to talk a little more about her uncertainty with her relationship with Adelphi. Mac thought for a few moments, then said, "Relationships are complicated sometimes, my friend. Willow struggled with me being on the trail all the time, too. My biggest regret was that I convinced her to come with me on the last trip.

Hindsight tells me I should have settled down and stayed in Freedom with her, but you know as well as I that would not have worked. I would have felt curtailed, and she would have felt guilty. I can't tell you how you and Adelphi feel or how you should resolve your different paths, but even now, I can tell you that you must be true to your heart. She must, too. If you compromise past what you can do for the rest of your lives, it can't work."

Tiffany smiled sadly. "Thanks, Mac… I guess I knew that. That's why I'm struggling. One good thing is Adelphi is straight up. Blunt even. She can communicate over emotions."

The friends walked silently until they reached the hut the two couples were working on. Introductions and visits continued throughout the afternoon.

Roger Haller

Refugee Distribution

Princess, Jesus, and Vera offered to guide Mac through the granite pass before turning him loose to travel the east side of the mountains alone. They had a few days to kill while Tiffany and Rita set up distribution details for the migrants.

Mac found an empty cot to nap in. They would be on their way in the morning. Traveling with a few scouts turned out to be a good idea.

They met another pair of stragglers working their way West. Marcel and Patrick escaped as the Giants closed down their human breeding program. The few remaining humans had been turned loose to be hunted. In a blind panic, these two found the river and swam downstream at night.

These tiny bipeds were becoming too much trouble. They had even proven to be dangerous. The Giants to the South had convinced them the escapes weren't worth the effort. Purple Screamer farming was becoming popular. With this new information, the Scouts returned with the latest immigrants, and Mac headed down the Giant's highway.

The scouts were nervous about the new escapees, though. They seemed to stick to themselves and talked quietly on the way to Shangri-La. Once back, they warned Rita and Tiffany of their gut feelings.

With their return, Tiffany was ready to move. The troubled Amazon scout stood at the evening cooking fire and announced she would be transporting to Willow's Cathedral in the morning. She asked those who wanted to move to the cathedral or Freedom to chat with her. She pointed out Anikka and suggested there would be a German speaking woman waiting to answer her questions, translate and explain, and serve her needs until she decided what she wanted to do.

Buzz and Charlotte stepped up.

Roger Haller

51 Pegasi - Sister Tiffany

They wanted to see the rest of the settlements before deciding on a home, and Tiffany explained to Charlotte that Jean would be a French speaker who could help her understand her new world.

Matt and Ann also wanted to see more of the landed immigrant environment before settling down, but they felt they loved Shangri-La and would probably want to return. The small band transported to Willow's Cathedral in the morning, one at a time.

Tiffany led the process, instructing each to step away from their landing as soon as possible. When the transporter was clear, Jewels would send a message for the next arrival. An excited crowd received the migrants. Jewels handed out fresh robes and Purple Screamer kilts for those who wanted them.

I couldn't tell how I felt with the crossroads I had witnessed over the last few days. Aard was growing, and not without growing pains.

The Islamic friends striking out to build their own society based on religious reasons worried me that humans might be building on mistakes they made on Earth.

My old friend, Buzz, was heading for Freedom. He and Charlotte had the chance to create what I had started building with Mac. I wasn't sure how Charlotte was feeling about it though.

Matt and Ann were doing the same, and Vera had a new chance at life on Aard.

Tiffany was internally struggling with her identity, church, and Aardian-born romance. Humans, after all, are complicated. Mac's advice was on point. He truly understood how I felt while he was off saving the human race. All his decisions were correct based on everything he knew.

Refugee Distribution

However, the biggest whirlwind in my soul right now was seeing the seeds I had planted in two small heart-shaped gems and finding fertile ground to germinate. After all, Aard is the world of second chances. If Mac and Rita had met on Earth, I may have never had mine.

***

Roger Haller

Chapter 22

Heart to Heart

Adelphi wasn't at Willow's Cathedral. She wasn't in Freedom, either. Julio explained that Adelphi had been working with Oliver and Hilda at Freedom to produce new foods and working with Dr. Tim and Maritza on medications. She was excited about the discoveries of new benefits from the flower blood Hilda had brought back from the island of the bleeding flower. However, currently, she was working with Sylvia and Stacey at Moon Bridge. Adelphi had found her calling.

On the one hand, Tiffany was proud of her talented girl-friend, but on the other, she knew they would be going in different directions most of the time. Adelphi had already decided she didn't want to make the Southern trek they had planned. This was expected, and Princess stepped up to join. She was particularly thrilled to be going on another adventure with Jesus.

Tiffany was feeling third-wheel syndrome. She bit the bul-let. The Southern tour was official after a brief chat with Jesus and Princess. They would start the trek with a stop at Moon Bridge to catch up, and Tiffany felt she could finally get some time with Adelphi to plan the next steps.

Roger Haller

Heart to Heart

She wasn't looking forward to the conversation. They headed south across the Bitter Waters delta.

The scouting trio traveled by the light of the twin moons to avoid the far-off raptor eyes and the highly sensitive olfactory organs of the Aardian Giants. The trekkers were thankful for the cloudless skies to start the journey because they knew monsoon season was coming soon and the moons would not serve them through the deluge.

The sea breezes were comforting in the evening heat, but the story would differ south of Moon Bridge. The scouts were looking forward to some local rain gear the southern village had perfected from grassland Hoop Horn stomachs. The worn-out Humpback stomaches had been a great rain poncho, but they were tight and split easily. The new, bigger version worked through full monsoon seasons with ease.

Before dawn's light and the final moon setting, Princess pointed out the bottom of the nut tree forest that rolled over the top of the foothills above. Before sunrise, the team was safely in the trees, and Tiffany announced their approach with her famous Tarzan yell. A happy surge of villagers crested the hilltop and gathered the travelers. At their forefront were Adelphi, Stacey, and Sylvia. Breakfast was a feast and family reunion around the cooking fire. Everyone needed full details from the latest adventure.

When the festivities died, Tiffany walked arm in arm with Adelphi to the hut she was living in while Princess and Jesus spent quality time with Shiv and Stacey. On the way to the hut, Adelphi turned to look Tiffany in the eyes and said, "Life is far too complicated, isn't it my love."

Tiffany was relieved to see the love in her eyes and that she was ready for the conversation. The lovers sat at a small table looking out over the lake and the beautiful vista of the mountain peak behind.

Roger Haller

"I listened to your heart while you were away, Sweetheart. I know what makes your heart heavy and I feel it, too." Adelphi was leading the conversation. She knew, in this matter, she was stronger than the warrior.

"Tiffany, your heart lives on the trails, and your mission is to break the human cargo line. You are driven to help humans survive. You are not able to live in a village."

Tiffany's eyes welled up and spilled over. She nodded through her tears.

Adelphi continued, "You also know I must stay in the villages as my mission is to help the people thrive."

Tiffany continued to nod. She was not yet ready to use her voice. Adelphi stood from her chair, stepped around the small table, pulled her mate up, and folded a warm hug around the trembling woman.

"It's okay, my warrior. Because we will live separate lives most of the time, our love doesn't have to die. We will need other people to be close in our daily lives, but we will always love each other and embrace like this when we can."

Finally, Tiffany was able to pull her voice through tightened vocal chords. "I love you, Adelphi."

The weeping Greek medicine woman pulled her head back from the embrace to look into Tiffany's eyes again. "I love you too. Let's have a nap."

The two women snuggled tightly on a single-width bed and fell asleep in each other's arms. Nothing had changed in their deep love and respect, but their lives changed dramatically. They woke in the afternoon sweaty. Their arms and legs were tingling from lack of blood flow, and their tear-dried faces were dry and red.

Heart to Heart

The ladies walked down to the lake, near the outflow creek, and dipped into the cooling water. By dinner, they were fresh, happy, and full of life as they mingled with old friends and met new ones. Their new relationship was tighter than ever.

By evening, Tiffany, Jesus, and Princess were fully provisioned and headed down the south slope of Moon Bridge hill, which is covered from the northeast by well-forested hills. By the time the moons arrived to escort them south, they had put in a good afternoon's launch. The rolling plains were muggy and close. Even though their path often ran near or in sight of the western sea, the sea breezes did little to freshen the air.

"Soon, we will have a monsoon." Jesus' simple statement wasn't necessary, but it opened the travelers' minds.

While talking about the rainy season, they were startling large herds of the Hoop Horn grazers munching in the dark. The reflections from their eyes made it clear they were comfortable in the moon's glow. Their zebra-like stripes in tan and brown made them invisible in the tall grass if they were still in the day. Their long, curling horns were much like a mountain sheep ram but were more slender, and rather than curled in, the outer tips looked more like tusks at each side of their jaw.

They showed no sign of fear of the humans, so they had not yet associated the deadly arrows of Shiv's hunters with the newly introduced bipeds. Their eyes rode high on their heads, with a clear view of the skies. Princess pointed out that these animals seemed shaggy compared to the hides being worked at Moon-bridge.

"They may be preparing for Monsoon," Tiffany said, as all three had become sensitive to the environment around them. The need to survive was maturing into a talent for thriving on this remarkable planet.

Roger Haller

51 Pegasi - Sister Tiffany

A few days in this pattern brought them into a tropical forest. Travel was much easier on the coast. They even had to cross a few smaller rivers winding to the sea. The Screamers seemed to be less evident at this point, but they did hear them to the East from time to time.

On the fourth day south of Moon Bridge, they noticed a small tower of smoke far out to sea. As they studied the discovery, they began to see the tip of the mountaintop beneath it. A volcano.

"I wonder if that is the Island of the Bleeding Flower?" Princess said.

Tiffany replied. "It may be, but it seems quite a ways south compared with the description Mac and the transporter crew got from the Tower Cabin."

"Maybe many islands. Maybe another land." Jesus was thinking hard as well.

Now, in the trees, the trekkers were comfortable enough to cook over a fire. They could also travel during the day, which was handy because the wind was shifting.

I noticed the team dynamics were changing now, too. Tiffany found she needed some time alone and would step out of camp to hunt, explore, and document the flora and fauna as Princess and Jesus' relationship was evolving.

At the beginning of their partnership, they all huddled while sleeping. Now, Tiffany preferred to roll in a hide by herself. I understood as Tiffany was feeling very alone. This would change again as the rain and wind arrived.

***

Heart to Heart

The scouts pulled out their new Hoop Horn stomach ponchos as the black wall of weather grew on the western horizon. The team was camped against a small river. As the rain hit, they found as much shelter as possible in the forest canopy, but it wasn't an ideal setting for Monsoon. The river was too robust to cross at this point, so their only options were to head back or go upriver to find a crossing.

Tiffany pulled her friends together. "I'm going to scout for a crossing, team. Would you like to come along or maybe try to find a place for us to wait out the worst of the storms?"

Jesus answered, "I'm tink we fine cave in da hills, Tiff'ny. Maybe no mas big cliff…"

"I'll help Jesus, Tiffany. But if we can get across, maybe we can find a little highland away from the water soon. We should split and cover as much territory as we can today, and talk it over tonight."

"Agreed."

Tiffany headed east along the river, but Jesus and Princess hesitated before splitting off on their searches. Princess caught Jesus by the sleeve of his robe hanging below his poncho.

"Jesus, we need to pull Tiffany into our bed. She has split from Adelphi now, and has no one to hold. I feel her loneliness all the time."

"Si, I feel it too… but dis is strange. I wan you in my bed, no mas."

"Let's think this through. When we need our romance, we take it out of camp. When we sleep, we sleep… and we include Tiffany."

"Still feel strange but entiendo… I try."

Roger Haller

51 Pegasi - Sister Tiffany

They searched all day without better luck. That evening, Tiffany told them about a boulder field half a day to the east. "We can hop from boulder to boulder. I tried, crossed quickly, then crossed back to get you. The hills get steeper on the far side, but it was too dark to see out of the river valley."

Princess and Jesus had strung a hide between trees and built a fire at the lee side. The wind pushed most of the smoke away from the cover and some warmth. The radiant heat helped, though. The rain was warm, but evaporation was cooling, so they felt the chill of the sea wind.

After their meal, Tiffany started to prepare another cover, but Princess tugged her shoulder. "We sleep together, my friend. We learn from the Giants. We are family."

Jesus nodded, and Tiffany teared up as she wrapped herself into a Jesus sandwich near the fire. They did get across the river the next day but didn't find any better shelter. After a brief discussion, they decided to keep moving. Their only consideration was finding as dry a shelter as possible with as much protection as possible from the lightning that rolled in with the warring weather fronts. It wasn't long, and everything they had was wet.

Hiking was challenging due to wet, heavy clothing. The only comfortable time of the day was when they shared their new sleeping arrangement. It became their favorite time of day… or night.

After a couple more weeks of the constant damp trek, they noticed the rain easing. Some days became warm, with open skies populated by puffed white clouds. They were now making reasonable distances, documenting interesting landmarks, and enjoying the trek. Tiffany was transported to the bonding experience she had with Jesus and Jean a lifetime ago on the eastern side of the mountains.

Heart to Heart

The hike was full of laughter, friendship, and bonding. Princess seemed to lead the new closeness with jokes, stories of the past, silly one-liners, and hugs. She had become more tactile. Tiffany marveled at how far she had come from the sickly, bald girl waiting to die.

Their bed had become more playful, with hugging, pinching, tickling, and caressing. No one seemed to plan or discuss anything, but the physical bonding took the trio deeper into their relationship.

Tiffany stayed platonic, and no one said anything. Their growth was organic. The hikers were happy when they arrived at the large southern river. Far to their east, over the forest, they could see mountains rising to the north, with a broad valley stretching over the river as far as they could see to the Eastern horizon.

Across the river, they saw only low forest—no hills or mountains. The forest here, however, was shorter. It seemed weather may have been a factor because many trees and shrubs were low and bent. The environment was tropical, yet more arid.

With no easy crossing of this vast delta, the little band headed east. "This may be the path to the Southern Giants and the cell tower we learned about." Tiffany was excited about the possibilities.

The river led them slightly North, toward the towering mountains to their left, and a day or two into this direction, they began to hear Screamers in the distance again. Luckily, the river valley, though broad, was well forested, so cover from the Screamers was available. Though the moon track overhead was lower on the northern horizon and shorter, it provided a better option for travel in Screamer territory. The band of hikers became nocturnal again and spent the sweltering days quiet in the deep shadows.

Roger Haller

51 Pegasi - Sister Tiffany

The scouting party worked well together, but I could see the conflict in the tall Swedish Amazon. I could see her taking some thinking time on her own little treks.

Tiffany spent more of her days in this valley, exploring the darker corners of this environment, using this as an excuse to keep Jesus and Princess private. She needed some solitude to counsel with an old role model. I felt her search was as much internal as external.

***

Chapter 23

Spiritual Epiphany

Tiffany found her serenity escape deep in the coolness under a massive root ball. A windfall in the lower valley offered Tiffany a quiet sanctuary to put in a call to her creator. She had been struggling with her religion, her past, and her identity since before she arrived on Aard. Something in her gut told her she was lonely because she was missing the deeper answer to why she was there.

For the second time on Aard, she reached out in prayer. She utilized the prayer model she had spent most of her adult life using and teaching others to use, but it wasn't working. The damage to her soul through her expulsion from Earth had damaged the connection. In frustration, she looked up at the resounding blue of the Aardian skies through the scrambled roots silhouetted in dark contrast above her.

She spoke out loud. "Why am I…" She wanted to finish with 'here' but stopped the query at 'I.'

Julian of Norwich came to mind.

Roger Haller

51 Pegasi - Sister Tiffany

The random thought took Tiffany back to her studies at Marquette, the Catholic university that had launched her life of service. Some of her favorite readings had been the Revelations of Divine Love. The shorter version impressed her so much that she researched and found the more extended version.

Although the shorter version was written in the thirteenth century, the more detailed version she loved was written long after Julian's death, in the sixteen hundreds.

Still, Tiffany's message now synced with the female or maternal view of God. Under the root ball, the point that resonated with her now was the religion of the gut rather than the church. Julian of Norwich had refused to assign gender to God. She insisted God was much bigger than gender and had qualities of both.

This epiphany resolved the conflicts between a male-driven church, the males who had done her wrong, and the spiritual needs of her soul. Suddenly, the conflicted Scandinavian Amazon had clarity. She didn't need the structure of the church she grew through. She needed only the church of her gut. Her gut told her Mac, Jean, Jesus, and most of the men she met on Aard had meant her no harm. Many, in fact, would give their life for her.

Tiffany smiled softly, looked up, and thanked the bright blue sky. God would approve of whoever she loved.

Given what she felt was ample time for privacy, Tiffany crept back through the undergrowth to the hiker's camp with a smile and a notebook full of notes and sketches of her findings. She whistled softly as she approached but found the pair preparing an early dinner for the evening trek.

"What's for dinner, folks?" her playful question brought an interesting response.

Spiritual Epiphany

"Miniature dinosaurs." Princess pointed to the scaly creature with a beak and long legs. Beside it was another specimen that Jesus had prepared for the spit, which looked very much like a chicken with great drumsticks. Dinner was particularly pleasant and matched Tiffany's new persona.

The hike through the night was challenging. The river wandered back and forth in the shallow valley, and the forest was thick. The wildlife trails were thick but local. There didn't seem to be a solid transient path along the river. The shelter was good, the food was plentiful, and the weather held, but progress was slow. However, a week of slogging paid off, and the valley took them higher, leading to less undergrowth and less climbing.

The Screamers had noticed them, so they had to avoid the flying purple scouts. Finding good sanctuary wasn't hard, but they had to travel at night. This worked well until Chuckles found them.

He, Mrs. Chuckles, and another friend pushed the canopy aside and sat down in their camp while they were hiding from the heat. Chuckles signed 'Hi' in American Sign Language. Abject terror quickly morphed into giggles of delight as Tiffany ran to hug as much of the furry giant as she could reach.

It took Jesus and Princess a bit longer to warm up, but it was soon apparent this was the Chuckles of camp stories and lore. Soon, Tiffany was translating as she signed. Introductions were made, and the conversation was warm until Tiffany explained their goal.

Chuckles updated the scouts on what was happening in the Giant's camps. The human delivery system had been broken. Humans had become far too much hassle, and Screamer pens had replaced pet humans. The bang for the buck was much richer, and although Screamers were more dangerous, they also provided much more food with less effort.

Roger Haller

51 Pegasi - Sister Tiffany

Humans were now vermin.

Mrs. Chuckles looked worried. She grunted at Chuckles, waved at the humans, and added a short line of squeaks and groans accompanied by complicated gestures and facial signals. The friendly Giant acknowledged with a palm gesture and signed to Tiffany.

"There is too much danger and too little reward to go farther East. Past the mountains, there is nothing but sand, the hunting ground for running humans."

Tiffany translated, then asked if there were any humans she could collect and lead to safety. The Giant Sasquatch thought for a moment and then suggested they could pack Tiffany and crew as in the old days to do a quick survey of the edge of the desert, then bring any survivors back to the river to head west with the scouts.

Everyone thought that was a good idea, so the humans were quickly loaded and carried east. They were closer to the sands than they thought. Within an hour, they were surveying a vast sweep of dunes as far as they could see. Behind them, cliffs and high banks glittered with silica. The rescuing humans had never seen any visa so striking on this planet. The high sun made the walls sparkle and dance. At the bottom of the closest one, huddled three surprised humans.

The scouts were lowered to the ground, and the Giants backed off. Two women and a man quaked as Tiffany explained they were there to help. It quickly became apparent that the escaped humans were too weak to do anything but accept their fate. Within a half hour, the new refugees surrendered their lives to the rescuers' will and rode west with the scouts.

Chuckles and family carefully dropped the humans near the last sustainable tributary that joined the river as it led water away from the desert to the sea.

Spiritual Epiphany

Jesus and Princess helped the recruits drink, bathe, and refresh in the clear, life-sustaining essence. Tiffany spent quality time signing with her giant friends.

The new citizens watched in awe as Mrs. Chuckles kneeled, tenderly lifted Tiffany to rub her against her bearded cheek, caressed her golden hair, and set her smoothly back to the ground. The matronly Giant then repeated the petting motion on the other humans but left them standing on the ground. It was easy to see she understood and respected their fear. She had Chuckles tell Tiffany of the successful birth of their child and she beamed as she watched Tiffany's reaction as she began to understand the message. The hugging started all over again.

Chuckles grimaced his trademark smile and pointed to the skies and a few far-off Screamers who had been watching with interest but holding their distance. It was bright daylight, and the humans were vulnerable without their hairy guardians. Through signs, the gentle monster told Tiffany that a shallow set of caves was upstream on the little tributary.

They were very near, and there was food nearby. Humpbacks and berries were plentiful. He suggested the Giants escort them to the shelter before they left.

Tiffany and the Pass Giants' love for each other was clear. Jesus and Princess had heard stories of the bond they had built but had never experienced the relationship firsthand. The new immigrants were in awe. For the first time, they saw this race of bipeds as something more than monsters. They saw a new side of their new world. They saw the opportunity for the world I loved so dearly.

***

Roger Haller

51 Pegasi - Sister Tiffany

Tiffany explained to the others and nodded in agreement before anyone could object. The Giants stepped across the stream and headed slowly up the tributary. Tiffany followed, and the rest of the humans waded across the small river to follow. The newly refreshed escapees could now move under their own power but could not move fast.

Still, it wasn't long before the humans were introduced to a gentle hillside rising from the riverbanks, with a lush thicket of the berry bushes the Aardians had come to thrive on.

They found familiar little tracks on the trails that wove in through the berry warren. Within the thorny shrubbery, the Giant's pointed out a dark hollow. Under the cover lay the entrance to a vast cavern with colorful layered walls in ribbons of sandy tan, sparkly silica, green-stained rock, and burnt okra. A small rivulet trickled through the layers to gently splash into the little stream flowing past the brambles.

This cave wasn't just shelter. It felt like heaven to the weary adventurers and their new charges. Princess and Jesus joined Tiffany in her sign to thank the helpful Giants. In unison, they touched the fingers of their right hand to their chin with their thumb pointing up, then lowered their hands toward the Giants in a motion of me-to-you.

Tiffany looked around and grinned at the humans joining her in communication. She was sure this gesture would be a big deal in the future. She signed a 'B' and changed to a 'K' while pulling her hand toward her body. Tiffany then flicked the tips of her fingers out toward the Giants, placing her right hand in front of her chest.

Tiffany told her human tribe, "I just thanked Chuckles and his family and told them we would be back."

Chuckles and family smiled their grimaces, waved, and turned to go. As they disappeared, the Screamers appeared.

Spiritual Epiphany

From the safety of the caves under the berries, they ate some fresh berries and prepared a fresh Humpback to re-energize while the Screamers tried to get them to bolt. The rescuers were well-versed in the tactic, and the escapees were too tired to flee.

During introductions, they learned the story of their new friends, and they all decided to spend another day in the caves to strengthen their new trekkers for the journey back. Tiffany introduced her crew first. Pointing at Jesus, she said, "This is Jesus. He's our best scout, tracker, and guardian. He knows before anyone else what is going on around us."

She pointed at their Princess. "Meet Princess. She has proven to be the most resilient and the best hunter on our team. She has overcome more here and on Earth than anyone should ever have to."

She pointed her thumb back at herself, "I've been here the longest on our team, and I've got a burning desire to keep humans from ever having to experience what you have been through. I'm also the first human to have a friendly relationship with the Giants. As you can see, they can be one of our best resources and, possibly, our best allies on this planet."

The smallest woman responded. "Did you say this planet? Is this not Earth?"

"Yes, that is what I said. We can explain in greater detail as we go, but we are no longer on Earth. We are on a planet called 51 Pegasi d. This is a planet much like Earth, but it is a bit smaller. We have a little less gravity here and a little more oxygen. We have two moons, and we live off the land. There are no Kroger's or Safeway stores here."

Tiffany realized she may have been a bit too blunt, so she continued in a softer tone. "Can you introduce yourself and help us get to know you?"

Roger Haller

51 Pegasi - Sister Tiffany

The small woman looked up through her eyebrows and responded. "I'm Kat… Katherine Garcia is on my birth certificate, but my friends call me Kat. I live in Pueblo, Colorado. I was a bartender in a bar and grill there, but I had just been fired before this nightmare. The owner's girlfriend got me fired. She gave me a hundred-dollar bill and asked me to make change for a drink. It was counterfeit, and I didn't check her, so the cameras caught me not checking, but she denied it was her bill. She said she paid with a twenty. The cameras couldn't tell.

The Owner had been flirty, but he was with all the women. I woke up in this birthday suit in a jail cell, swinging from a tree. Yesterday, a Sasquatch took me out of my cage, put me in with Silas and Michelle, hauled us out into the desert, and turned us loose."

Silas spoke up. "I'm Silas Lyon."

He paused to see if anyone objected to his turn to introduce himself. No one interrupted so he continued. "The dunes were too hot to walk for long, so we dug into the sand under a rock, hoping to wait out the heat. I think we lost a lot of water in that hot sand, but it was better than being on top, and the shadow from the rock helped a lot. The big Eagles were all around, but as long as we were still, they didn't seem to be able to see us."

Everyone seemed to be glued to his story, so he continued. "The desert dunes were a big change from my log cabin. I'm a guide and outfitter from Embarrass in Northern Alberta. I know it sounds like embarrassed, but it's a French word for barrier. It's named after the river, which has many fallen trees and branches blocking it. I guess Embarrass is not really a town; I think Fort McMurry is the closest real town.

Sorry, kind of running on…I just won a yearly contract with a company in Pennsylvania to guide a string of international clients to Moose and Grizzly.

Roger Haller

Spiritual Epiphany

This would be a nice grubstake, and I should be there to finalize the deal."

Silas stopped talking, so everyone turned to look at Michelle. The pretty woman blushed at the attention. "I'm Michelle."

At first, Michelle didn't offer more. She went quiet.

The extended tribe was well on their way downriver in the light of the moons when Princess learned her last name was Sinclair. Michelle was going to be a surprise, but there was nothing I could do to warn her companions.

***

Chapter 24

A New Scout and an Enigma

The new citizens traveled well. They learned the ropes as the hikers dodged the Purple Screamers and harvested from the land as they passed. In two weeks, they were back to the coast. They were also back to insects. Many of the bugs they met were large, and most had no interest in them.

However, they found a couple of species the size of small birds that had a taste for human flesh. Their size made them easy to spot and swat, but they left a mark. Pincers seemed to be the weapon of choice on both, but they didn't seem to leave ill effects other than the nips.

Traveling at night helped. They could stay out in the breezes, and the insects went to bed. Traveling together allowed the rescuers to get to know their charges better. The large man built strength quickly, and it was good to see how quickly he adapted to the trail.

Silas became a pleasant contributor to the camping life. He promptly gathered wood, started fires, harvested, cleaned, and cooked food. He picked up the archery skills quickly and was soon more than capable.

Roger Haller

A New Scout and an Enigma

Kat was a great surprise, too. She often studied a skill for hours. She could improve not only the skill but also on the process in which the skill was used. Katherine was the first to build a rotisserie from a waterwheel made of an evergreen branch with a bundle of evergreen fronds for paddles.

Tiffany felt she would have tried to discourage the idea because of all the extra work if she had discussed it first. However, the tiny dynamo was gone from idea to completed project before anyone knew what she was up to. Kat also quickly became a voice on the team. She had no problem sharing her opinions and ideas.

Michelle was another story. She learned quickly and followed directions. She quickly jumped into a task and soon didn't need direction, as she intuitively knew how to stay useful, out of danger, and out of the way. Princess spent most of her free time with her, trying to include and support her need for distance. Princess understood her more than the rest.

Princess learned her last name and that she came from Halifax, Nova Scotia, on Canada's East Coast. However, Michelle rarely answered a question with more than yes or no, so she was still a mystery when they turned North along the coast. The summer was hot, but the sea breezes helped. They were in waving grasslands again, with little cover, so they traveled in the dark and hid amongst the boulders of the rocky shore during the day. The Screamers seemed to stay far to the East, but the trekkers could hear their angry calls, so they took no chances.

Tiffany asked Princess if she could get Michelle's preferences when they arrived at Moon Bridge. They needed some idea of how and where she would prefer to be housed. She felt Princess had the best chance of communicating with the enigma. Princess agreed and talked conversationally to the quiet woman during the next few days as they walked with only nods or shakes of the head in response.

51 Pegasi - Sister Tiffany

Never demanding a response, the pressure was off, and the mentor found that the woman didn't seem to understand English, or didn't want to admit she spoke English to keep from speaking. She responded to French but with a strange accent.

Princess knew a few French words and phrases from high school classes and a few of her bourgeois parents' friends, but it wasn't enough to make much progress or open the woman to conversation. She settled for visual communication, pointing, gestures, facial expressions, and other body language… until the earth started shaking, and a low rumble like thunder overtook the pedestrian band from the South.

With no place to readily hide but the ocean, the frightened trekkers were headed for the beach when Chuckles and some of his band ran up on the scrambling humans.

"It's Chuckles!" You could feel the relief in Tiffany's voice as she called to the team entering the surf.

Chuckles stopped short of the beach, his face curled up in a snarl. The sea air did not please his sensitive olfaction. Although the snarl kept the humans at a distance, they watched carefully as Chuckles, Mrs. Chuckles, and another Giant set three Screamer skin sacks on the ground and backed away.

Tiffany and Jesus stepped warily up to the sacks. They were moving. At arm's length, Tiffany opened the first bag, and a dark-skinned man peeked out. A woman's head followed. The other sacks soon settled around startled faces, and two people emerged from each. The human tribe doubled as everyone looked back at the retreating Giants. Chuckles waved over his head, but they disappeared in moments.

Four Indian fugitives stepped out of two sacks, and a pale woman and a slight man stepped out of the third. The woman reached back and drew out a whimpering toddler.

A New Scout and an Enigma

Tiffany froze. As the woman stood up with the young girl in her arms, she froze, too, her eyes on Tiffany. Her lower lip started quivering, and tears started flowing. Tiffany was openly weeping now as she stepped toward the mother and child.

"Sister Anne!"

"Ben!"

"You have survived."

The conversation died as the old friends ran to open arms. The humans camped early that morning, facing the surf. They tucked in behind a large volcanic boulder as the moons set. Jesus, Princess, and Silas gathered dried driftwood and built a comfortable fire for cooking and heat.

Introductions began after the sobbing eased. Jesus, Princess, and the new folks were introduced to Sister Anne, who had come to this world with Tiffany, only to be ripped away and to have started a new life far from the seminary she had dedicated her life to.

Life was good for her now. She learned to love the younger Ben, and motherhood changed her direction for good. Anne could think of nothing she would rather do than marry Ben and raise their family in the safety of an Aardian village. The child was walking now but was tired quickly and spent a lot of time in one of her parent's arms.

Ben was excited to see Tiffany as well. They hugged and cried like family. None had heard from any of Ben's family, and Tiffany had to tell them about losing Sister Beatrix. Now that they had each other, they had family again. This was another milestone in an unforgettable new life. When night fell, and the moon rose, thirteen humans headed North along the coast. Twelve adults and a child made good time along sandy shores.

Roger Haller

51 Pegasi - Sister Tiffany

Stories were told, and people began to know each other. Sister Beatrix had taught Sister Anne some French, but it was not enough to get much more information from Michelle.

She did learn Michelle had last lived in the Puducherry region of India for many years, so her French was flavored with Tamil, the native language of the area.

Two of the new Indian refugees in the tribe came from North Central India and spoke Hindi, with English taught as a backup in their schools. They were from New Delhi. The other two were from the Tamil area in South Eastern India.

The new friends traveled well, and there was little friction as they strove to work as a team. Even Michelle tried to be helpful. She could understand simple questions and directions from Sister Anne and Princess, but she still answered in simple yes or no, oui or non. The silent one worried me. She wasn't open with her new tribe.

I wonder how she will react to Jean.

***

A New Scout and an Enigma

The trekkers were getting close to Moon Bridge now. Tiffany consulted her notes and the new map. She told the hikers she thought they should be at Moon Bridge by the end of tomorrow night's trek.

As she finished, Jesus pointed out a glow far out over the ocean horizon. The distant skyline grew red, and streaks of light rose toward the sky.

"Eso es un volcan… Volcan mak nueva isla?

New island?"

Everyone looked far out to the west as Tiffany agreed. "We saw that begin on the way down. I think you are right, Jesus."

As they contemplated, the beach shook.

"Inland. We need to hurry."

Tiffany started to run inland through the grasslands, looking for high ground or boulders to climb. The trekkers didn't think twice. They knew what she meant and joined her scramble. The shaking stopped as quickly as it started, though, and nothing came of the shake.

By morning, they could see the foothills and were now in enough shrub brush to hide. If they stayed still in the day's heat, they would be as safe as Aard gets. Here, they got to know their Indian tribe. Although their accents were thick, the man and woman could speak English, and they could translate using Hindi for the other two women.

The new citizens got to know Rajesh and Shilpa, the two with English skills, and Hema and Lakshmi. Rajesh worked as a page in the Parliament House in New Delhi, and Shilpa was a lawyer who worked her way up the ladder in the Supreme Court. Both positions were viciously competitive.

Roger Haller

51 Pegasi - Sister Tiffany

In contrast, Hema and Lakshmi were friends working in an irrigation company in Tamil Nadu, near Madurai. Hema had risen to architect stature, and Lakshmi was an Irrigation engineer. Both knew monsoons well and were adept at managing, storing, and transporting water.

Hema could also speak French and grew interested in the quiet Michelle. Once introductions were made, she spent much of the trek to Moon Bridge the next night opening up to Michelle. She didn't mind that Michelle didn't answer back much, but Tiffany and Princess noticed Michelle began to get more comfortable with the ever-patient Indian woman.

Silas was happy to see trees again. Although the grasslands were fascinating, he felt safer under a canopy of evergreens. He took equal shifts as lookout, point, and rear guard. Tiffany, Princess, and Jesus welcomed his trail sense and experience. In turn, the prominent Canadian was impressed with the rescuers.

He struck up a quick friendship with Jesus and noticed that Jesus and Princess seemed to be a pair, but he saved his most regard for the regal blonde who appeared to lead the tribe. His years of life alone in the woods didn't dim his intuition, so he took his time getting to know her. He sensed a troubled past and some internal conflict, so he tried to be handy, friendly, and helpful. While taking his time, he did pay attention.

Tiffany was thoughtful, a natural leader, and a listener to her team. He noticed the respect Jesus and Princess gave her without reservation. It was rare to see a leader who was also a friend. Silas wanted to know more about her, but he started by asking questions of Jesus and Princess first. They were friendly and open, and Tiffany listened and responded naturally to the conversation when appropriate. The more he learned, the more Silas wanted to know. Tiffany was tall, beautiful, intimidating, and compelling. He would take his time.

A New Scout and an Enigma

The village of Moon Bridge was excited. When they heard Tiffany's call, they came running. Hugs and squeals of joy ran rampant as old friends connected and new ones were hustled into the little village on the hill.

"Did you see Mac? He just left a couple of days ago to explore the South." Shiv had hoped Mac had met the new folks.

"Nope, It's a big world down there." Tiffany smiled and hugged the happy ex-con and his beaming Stacey.

Dawn was breaking, and the morning meal was hot on the fire. Tea flowed like wine. By now, the village had two large huts with multiple rooms that served as hostels. The new citizens could sleep in beds, sit in chairs, and eat at tables. The immigrants were given clothing. Most wanted robes, but chamois, kilts, and loincloths were popular after a day or two in the ever-present heat. The novelty of full clothing wore off with the weather. Tiffany noticed that Silas quickly settled for a loincloth like Jesus's. That fact pleased her. Then she noticed that she noticed…

She decided to get to know him. Tonight, they would find out what the new citizens wanted. They would survey them to see which village or tribe would suit them best or if some wanted to return to Earth and their old lives. Perhaps now, Michell would need to make a decision that would reveal who she was and what she wanted in life.

The villages had just doubled over the last season, and Tiffany and the team had been a big part of that growth. Mac had brought some folks in. Popeye and Jewels had as well. I was delighted to see that the humans on Aard were thriving. Humans were star travelers now, and I hoped with all my soul that fact was good. I loved this planet, these villages, and these people. I needed 51 Pegasi-d to be the holy grail.

***

Chapter 25

Human Balance

Shiv called Popeye, Jewels, Rita, Julio, Lisa, and Jean to Moon Bridge. He suggested they bring anyone considering options for a place to live their Aardian lives. Mac was well on his way south to explore the territory from where Tiffany and her team had just returned. Along with Tiffany and himself, this team organically became the council of Aard.

This task had been on several of the leader's minds for some time, so he had no trouble getting the visitors to Moon Bridge. Tiffany asked if Shiv would call upon Sirih as well, as she may be of some help with the new Indian crew and perhaps even with Michelle. She was happy to join.

Moon Bridge now had a central hall gathering pavilion, and all of these leaders followed the policy Mac had started, which was where everyone who wanted to be involved was. The evening fire on that first day attracted a broad audience.

Julio introduced Lisa, a friend of Mac's to those who hadn't met her yet. She moved back and forth to Earth and was working with Mac's father and brother to help the new Aardians flourish.

Human Balance

Julio and Lisa interviewed the new arrivals from the last few months. Before discussing where new citizens would homestead, the flourishing Aardians needed to know what the new arrivals wanted. Some may wish to return to their old lives on Earth and pick up where they left off.

The interview panel started with the Indian refugees. While they were talking, Princess, Hema, and Sirih spent some quality time with Michelle. With several people asking her questions, Michelle shut down. Soon, she wasn't even nodding or shaking her head to questions. Sirih noticed first that they were driving her farther into her shell. She suggested she stay and let the others back away to give her and the retreating woman some room.

They agreed, and Hema joined the rest of the Indian folks in interviews with Julio and Lisa. Michelle sighed in relief as the well-meaning ladies strode away. Sirih offered half of the small breadfruit-type fruit she was eating. Michelle happily accepted, and they ate in silence.

Throughout the day, several folks were transported to Moon Bridge. A tight little circle spoke French at a small table on the south side of the village pavilion. While Buzz looked on, Jean was talking earnestly to Charlotte in French. Hilda had come with him, but she had set up a chat with Anikka at a table nearby.

Jean discovered Charlotte was a Psychologist who specialized in traumatic responses.

She was amazed at the percentage of Aardian citizens who had adapted so well to living close to the land after the trauma they had experienced. Princess had been walking by when she heard the words "psycholque" and "traumatize." She asked Jean, "Could I interrupt for a moment?

He nodded, a bit surprised to hear from Princess.

Roger Haller

"Stud, We have a lady who speaks French, but she is from India. I think it's a French colony, Tamil, or something. She has been traumatized by something and does not speak very much. We need to know how to serve her best."

Jean and Charlotte were interested now. They watched as she pointed down the hill to Sirih, sitting with the dark-haired woman who was afraid to look out over the growing group of people, jubilantly introducing and making friends.

"Pouvons-nous l'emmener dans un endroit calme ou je pourrai etre seul avec elle?" Charlotte pointed down the hill to the quiet conversation outside the excitement.

Jean translated. " Can you take her to de quiet hut? Charlotte es de doctor of psycholque. Ma-be she help…"

Princess nodded, smiled, and said, "Sure." She waved Stacey over.

Jean continued. "We jus fin da best place for Charlotte et Buzz and she come."

Charlotte nodded. "Oui, soon… I come."

Stacey and Princess reported to Sirih, who welcomed the professional help and a place to get Michelle a sanctuary. Within minutes, Buzz, Charlotte, and Anikka had chosen to set out shingles in Freedom near Jean the Stud and Hilda. However, Charlotte suggested she stay at Moon Bridge long enough to work out a program for Michelle. Buzz was happy to stay with her and help where he could, but Charlotte waved him off. "No, you go find your best home. I will study more and find where I am needed most." When their chat concluded, Jean let Charlotte and Buzz know they could carry on as they liked, and he would report to the Aardian counsel on their decisions and desires as they formed.

Human Balance

Charlotte stood to head down the hill to see Michelle. Buzz began to join her, but she placed a hand on his arm and said, "Buzz, you stay, s'il te plait. Elle a besoin… she need peu de gens… few people."

"Ahh, yes, I get it. Call if you need me." Buzz followed Jean, Hilda, and Anikka to the council meeting. Hilda and Anikka walked arm in arm. Anikka was feeling much better about her circumstances.

The council was in full attendance, and the family reunion atmosphere was thick with new friends, rekindled relationships, and good times. Julio, Jean, and Shiv, once meeting the new refugees, explained the process and the reason. Once done, they explained in each language that they may be able to send people back to their old lives if that was what they wanted. However, they did warn them that the reason they were here was that someone on Earth wanted them gone. They were advised to think about that before deciding to go back. With a bit of reflection, it surprised no one that there were no takers. The full impact of understanding seemed to wash over the new folks. None of them seemed to have anything to return to.

Outside the council interviews, several conversations were about negotiating, setting up partnerships, and trading, and unlike most family reunions, there was plenty of flirting.

Matt and Jen announced in the pavilion that they would like to spend a week at Moon Bridge and then at Freedom and Willow's Cathedral before returning home to Shangri-La.

The high wooded valley had already felt like home, and they felt that their hut and furniture-building careers were blossoming there. They were keen to help Les and Bill, the other major hut builders, now that they had Tiffany's updated designs to work from.

51 Pegasi - Sister Tiffany

Buzz told the council he was interested in Freedom and Willow's Cathedral. He hadn't felt healthy for the last few years, and the locals in Freedom had told him about the mushrooms. He hadn't cared for mushrooms on Earth, but he didn't mind the blue ones on Aard. He wasn't sure but felt he was already getting better.

Buzz said he couldn't speak for Charlotte. "We don't know each other well, and our communication wasn't the best due to the language barrier. We have been bonding as friends but our circumstances did not get a good start while being directed to mate in the cage. I think I was 'friend-zoned' tonight, and that's okay."

Julio took note of that information to use in his approach when talking with Charlotte.

Sister Anne noted that there were pregnant women and two crawling babies in Moon Bridge. She had a toddler who needed a community with children. She talked it over with Ben, and they agreed this was the place they would like to raise their child. Sister Anne would be referred to as Annie, and Julio offered to marry the couple if they wanted. By now, he had performed a few marriages as the first non-denominational minister of Aard. This fact made the couple very happy.

Rajesh and Shilpa felt they could serve Julio and the leaders on Aard, as they were experienced in politics and the legal system. They thought they could help design a constitution for the new colonies. They would spend time with Julio and Lisa to start, to find out what the leaders had already decided, and then help where they could. They would probably spend most of their time in Freedom.

Hema and Lakshmi gravitated to Stacey, Sylvia, and Adelphi, who were interested in the vast opportunities for agriculture in the grasslands and mountainside.

Human Balance

The villages of Aard were growing up. Agriculture, a constitution, builders, a bartender, and a psychologist. Society was setting in, and support for the PTSD that accompanied most of the citizens to Aard may be critical. I hope the psychologist will find more clients than the bartender. Although, I had a soft spot for Buzz. I hope he finds new legs along with the blue mushrooms on 51 Pegasi-d.

***

Roger Haller

51 Pegasi - Sister Tiffany

The next day would see migration back to their respective villages, new relationships, new skills, new excitement, and new hope for the humans on Aard.

Silas could not help but notice that Tiffany and Adelphi walked arm in arm to a hut after the council meeting. By watching them through the evening, he knew they were close, and he was curious to know how close. Before deciding on his next move, he asked to talk to her, Jesus, and Princess the next day.

Charlotte had already made significant headway with Michelle. Her priorities were to make her feel safe and educate her on what she wanted to do, why, and how. She wanted to make sure Michelle felt cared for and validated. To do this, Charlotte shared the story that led her to Moon Bridge. It was all give and no take so Michelle would feel rapport and trust and that her boundaries were respected.

In French, Charlotte told Michelle about her life before this new world and why she would not want to return to her old life. She told the quiet woman how she had been abused by an uncle when she was a young teen and had to leave her home, family, and church to have an abortion. She told Michelle how her doctor connected her with a safe house that took her in, helped her through high school, and sent her to college.

Charlotte explained that her painful experience had led her to become a psychologist, partly to help her understand and heal herself.

Her degree was her savior.

Then it all fell apart. Her uncle found her and moved to her town. He was trying to restart the sick relationship he had forced on her as a girl. She fought him off in a busy restaurant and found herself naked, in a cage swinging from a rainforest tree.

Human Balance

She explained how she was then forced into a relationship with a man she didn't know and moved to a breeding camp to have children. She then explained that, like Michelle, she had been rescued by Tiffany, Jesus, and Princess. Michelle was glued to every word, her eyes wide, but she did not say a word.

"Je veux que tut e joignes a moi et que to crees une nouvelle vie dans ce nouveau monde."

Charlotte asked Michelle to join her in this new life in this new world. The enigma nodded intently but still didn't speak.

The psychologist asked Michele a few questions in French to see if she could create a baseline.

"Are the clothes you've been given comfortable?"

Michelle looked at her robe. Even though she was shiny from the heat, she pulled the hems of the lapel closer and nodded.

"Do you feel safe in the hut?"

Michelle looked around and nodded.

"Are you tired?"

Michelle shrugged her shoulders, then closed her eyes a moment and nodded.

"If I leave you for tonight, will you be able to rest? Get some sleep?"

Michelle closed her eyes again and stifled a silent sob. "Oui."

"Do you mind if I stay with you in this hut until I find my new home? If that is okay, I will return to sleep here tonight."

Roger Haller

51 Pegasi - Sister Tiffany

For the first time, Michelle smiled and pointed at the second bed in the room. Charlotte stood, kissed her on the forehead, and opened the door to leave.

Michelle spoke more words than she had since coming to 51 Pegasi-d. "Merci, je me sens mieux. Viendras-tu demain pour parler?"

Charlotte smiled softly. "Oui. I will return, and we can talk more in the morning."

Both ladies shed tears, but the tears ran around up curved lips and quivering smiles this time. The talk had helped both.

Charlotte returned to the village pavilion and updated Jean and Julio on her plans. Julio told her that Buzz had gone to the hostel hut to get some sleep and was planning on transporting to Freedom in the morning. Charlotte nodded, smiled, and said, "I'll stay with Michelle until she feels ready to join the village. I feel like I have found my purpose here."

The village cleared for respective beds and quiet reigned over Moon Bridge while the twin beams shone across the mirrored lake. The air was hot and close.

The next Monsoon was nearing. The morning was busy at the transporter post on the hill above the lake. The Freedom and Willow's Cathedral residents took turns for a trip home. Rajesh, Shilpa, Anikka and Buzz followed. Adelphi and Charlotte continued their projects, and Silas got Tiffany to walk with him by the lake. Princess and Jesus looked at each other with raised eyebrows and grins. Across the village, Adelphi noticed and smiled sadly, too.

"Tiffany, what are the chances I could join you, Jesus, and Princess on the trail? I think that is where I belong."

Human Balance

Tiffany smiled up at his rugged face. "As you can see, it's not glamorous on the trail."

He smiled back. "I'd trade all the village amenities in a heartbeat for the human quality in your scouting team. I can cook, too."

Tiffany felt a shiver up her spine… a good shiver. She couldn't remember ever feeling that strange tingle before. She noticed her heart was beating uncomfortably fast, and her palms were moist. Silas was nervous, too. He was suddenly stuck for words. He had only asked for a place on her team… but it felt like a proposal.

"Have you asked Jesus and Princess what they think of an extra scout?"

"No…"

"Well, you had better. They will also be responsible for your training."

He grinned wide, nodded, and trotted off to find Jesus and Princess.

Tiffany watched him go. "Damn!"

I almost chuckled as she looked toward the sky, folded her hands together, and quietly said, "Sorry… Thank you, God. I will do my best not to mess this up."

Later that day, the scouting team and Rita returned to Shan-gri-La. Matt and Ann would follow after their 'vacation tour.' My world was falling together.

***

Chapter 26

Organization vs Individual

The new huts under the evergreen canopy on the mountainside at Shangri-La were a blessing during the Monsoon. Learning from the functionality of Willow's Cathedral, the cavern was also used more. Storage was now moved to a pair of opposing caves deeper into the tunnel, and the large outer cavern was vented for a community fire. The fire vent was utilized for smoking and drying food. One cavern was dedicated to dry firewood. The villagers spent a lot of community time in the open cavern.

As expected, Silas' training went well. He was a natural with the bow and developed the best Atlatl throw. He was smart enough to let his relationship grow organically with Tiffany. Building a friendship was an easy step because she was ready. Leading with mutual respect with everyone helped Princess and Jesus to accept and grow with him.

Jesus was happy to have a male companion, and adding a male that Tiffany could relate to took relationship stress from he and Princess. Suddenly, Tiffany was cheerful more often. The team felt balanced.

Roger Haller

Organization vs Individual

As the monsoon ended, Shangri-la received visitors from the North. Tamir and Emran came into camp. They looked a bit thin and ragged, and their clothes, tools, and weapons were tattered and worn.

The two hadn't had the advantage of boot camp. They were well adapted to a long bow but had no idea where the high-quality arrow shafts and distinctive arrowheads were to be found.

Omar translated their story, and it seems they did well overall. They were able to hunt for Humpbacks, and they had berries, although smaller than they had seen in the South. They were disappointed that Basma had moved on to Willow's Cathedral, to the South.

The two were less contrite now but wanted a meeting with Jesus. They wanted to negotiate a loose partnership with the village but felt more comfortable talking with a man. Jesus was presented but insisted Rita and Tiffany were the village leaders. He would happily join, but they must be in the meeting.

Tamir and Emran were insistent initially, but when Jesus started to walk away, they called him back and agreed. Rita and Tiffany joined, and Rita took the lead.

The men wanted boot camp. They insisted that they would set up an Islam-only village to the North and wanted Tiffany to deliver all Arab-speaking refugees to them.

Rita raised an eyebrow and responded through Omar. She said, "There will be no forced segregation on Aard. Central to the desire of the humans already living on the planet is the understanding that everyone, of any gender, religion, or ethnicity, would have free will. No one could make decisions for another."

Roger Haller

Omar was precise and intent on the meaning as he translated, but he smiled through it all.

Tamir and Emran were silent, but it was easy to see they were angry.

Tiffany reached out and laid her hand on Rita's arm. "Before we give a final answer on this, can we take some time to think it through?"

Omar waited.

Rita said, "What's to discuss?"

"Let's talk to the other leaders a moment before we deliver our answer. I have a couple of ideas to go over with you."

Rita thought for a moment, then looked at Omar. "Please tell them to meet back here tomorrow afternoon. We will have an answer. They all stood. Tiffany hugged Rita and thanked her for the delay.

When they were alone again, Tiffany asked Rita to join her at Willow's Cathedral to talk with Shiv, Sean, Julio, Popeye, Jewels, and Lisa. They were all sitting around a large table in the central caverns within an hour. Tiffany explained their dilemma. "I wish Mac was here for this, but we need to decide as a society. We need to respond to the request from a religious order to create a segregated community on Aard. He wants us to send all believers of Islam to him so they can build their own society."

Julio leaned forward and quietly replied. He was very careful to find the right English words to express his view. "We all here because of that issue. Someone decided we did not fit their type. For my input, I would say the most big issue on Earth come from segregation by religion, nationality, or sexual need.

Organization vs Individual

The search for power uses segregation to get and abuse power."

Lisa's follow-up gained nods from all around the table. "The freedom to be individuals has become the biggest feature that has allowed us a second chance to find happiness, which is why most of us have no desire to live our lives on Earth."

Julio followed up on his thoughts. "Mac say dis subject when we having village meeting. He want us tink 'bout how we regulate new society. We agreed less e mas. We write rules only needed. It now required. I tink dis requess start our negotiation a constitution of human on Aard."

Shiv had been silent as long as he could. "We can't let that bullshit from Earth move to Aard. We have the chance to scrape that shit off."

Tiffany nodded and added, "I think Julio has the key.

The ability to abuse power comes from groups. Mac even wanted us to separate into villages but stay in constant contact so we don't become 'us against them.' Religion, sexual preference, and politics are a personal thing. That's where we went astray on Earth. We demanded that people think like us, look like us, love like us, or be demeaned as bad or even evil. Here, we are thriving as individuals who are not bound to that society's rule. It may become harder to govern as needed, but we can build precedence."

Jewels applauded. "Our first constitutional rule must say that we have total autonomy until it takes away someone else's. We live and die by our actions and decisions. No one can direct us. Instead, someone can speak for us. Remember Abe Lincoln's saying, "Government of the people, by the people, for the people?"

Popeye grinned. "My wife said that. This question should be the first decision the whole colony decides. Everyone here represents several people who look up to them. How long would it take for all of you to get a "vote" from your people to tell you how to vote in this meeting?"

Julio smiled. "I tink we can have answer tomorrow, dis time. Let's go back to our communities to have dat vote."

Tiffany stood, smiling at the ring of leaders around her. "Anyone object?" No one objected.

"See you here tomorrow at the same time.

At last, the community was forced to sit down and discuss a constitution. It seemed the time was right.

I wished Mac had been there to begin the most important documentation of this group of villages. However, I knew he was en route back to the villages and would be home soon. I was sure his voice would be added to the constitution of the humans on Aard.

***

Organization vs Individual

Back in Shangri-La, Rita hugged Tiffany. "That was beautiful. I think I know the answer, but what a concept. Turn leadership upside down. Leaders speak the will of those who look to them to voice their views."

Tiffany and Rita gathered Jesus and Princess on their way to Omar's hut. They told Tamir and Emran about their one-day extension to get their answer. Tiffany explained that the full colony would provide the answer to make it as fair as possible.

This did not please Tamir. His voice was raised and demanding as he spoke to Omar. "What weak leaders depend on the people for direction?"

Omar smiled as he replied, "Alqadat al'adhkia"

Omar turned to the village leaders. "I told Tamir that you are smart leaders. He will wait until tomorrow for an answer."

Tiffany and Rita were in the meeting early the next day.

The answer was unanimous. There would be no effort to segregate communities. The new constitution would be drafted soon, and the first statement would be that society would be based on the rights of all individuals as the primary group before smaller groups of any kind.

Villages would continue to be built from the bottom up. Individuals would collaborate to define what a village should be. Villages would define what the colony would be. The colony would define the human involvement on 51 Pegasi-d. Aard.

Later that day, Tiffany gave Tamir and Emran an answer and three options. "Omar, please be as precise as you can in translating so there is no doubt about what I offer."

She looked directly at Tamir and Emran as she spoke.

51 Pegasi - Sister Tiffany

"Please tell them there will be no segregation in this colony. Everyone will have full autonomy to decide where they live or anything else that concerns their personal lives."

She let that sink in for a moment, but before they could argue, she continued, "You have three options. You can go out on your own to build the life you want, but it will not be part of our society. You see, you, too, have the right to self-direction. Your second option is to interact and collaborate with us for trade, support, and community. However, if you take that option, you will be subject to our constitution."

Tiffany leaned in. "Your third option is to return to Earth, where you came from. We have the ability to send you back to your old lives."

Omar turned to the scowling men and translated.

Their eyebrows went up, and they conferred with each other. They were excited now. "If we go back, can we return here with our families and friends?

Omar translated back to the English speakers.

"No!" Rita's answer was quick.

It was that moment when I realized a few distinct qualities of Rita. She had fully bought into the political philosophy decided by this new society. The fiery red head would be a fierce guardian of the new constitution and she would be a strong leader who was direct and forceful in that guardianship.

After a few moments of silence, Tamir, in particular, became more interested in the third option. He whispered in Emran's ear. At that point, both he and Emran grew excited. They both responded eagerly to Omar until he had to raise his hands to signal enough.

Organization vs Individual

He turned to Tiffany. "They want to know how, when, and where they would go if they went back."

"Where did they come from?"

"Beirut."

"Please tell them we can get them back to that area. However, ask them to think about who sent them here. They had an enemy or competitor who wanted them out of the way."

Omar translated. The looks on their faces told Tiffany and team what they expected. Recognition came to their faces. Tamir and Emran negotiated with each other for a few moments, then asked Omar if they could be delivered to the outskirts of Beirut. They would like to avoid those who sent them here. They asked if they could be transferred to Damour, south of Beirut.

Tiffany said she thought they could, but she would need to confirm. They agreed to meet at Omar's hut tomorrow at the same time. The men left excitedly, talking about their next moves.

Tiffany and the team were transported to Willows Cavern for a meeting with Popeye and Jewels. Popeye agreed and set up a spare transporter for a small strip mall called Damour Village for a very early morning transfer. It didn't matter what time they were to leave Shangri-La. They set up the portable transporter at Omar's hut in the morning. For security reasons, they didn't want to use the cavern.

In the early afternoon, Tamir pushed the little white button and was gone. Although terrified, Emran pushed it a moment later. Both men were standing behind the Qamara Restaurant and Café. It was too early for the businesses to be open, and they looked out of place in the Aardian robes.

51 Pegasi - Sister Tiffany

They crossed the busy highway to the Lebanon post and waited for dawn. The post office had been closed for some time, but several apartment buildings were being built nearby, so they wound through the silent streets to a small apartment building with 'Daccache' displayed in a colorful sign along with a phone number.

They climbed the concrete stairs to the third story, where Emran knocked on a door. After a few minutes of muffled movement inside, a middle-aged woman in a faded jogging suit answered and hugged her strangely dressed brother. She nodded to his friend and led them to a table while she started to warm an old kettle for tea.

They could see the top of the Civil Defense office across the street from the window, toward water.

I was worried. This was so much like the release of Lawrence from Aard. This was possibly even more worrisome due to the international element of the action. Beirut has been the linchpin of a lot of conflict on Earth.

Tiffany and the team did the best thing for the time and probably for their constitution. Still, the ramifications could be widespread if the Global Main Street Revitalization network had not been fully extinguished.

***

Chapter 27

Aard in Anguish

The Constitution was on everyone's mind now. The council hut in Freedom had a lot of attention while the villages met to discuss the topic.

It was quickly agreed that a forum for all was the best way to kick off the topic. It had been two weeks of philosophical discussions already. Still, to their credit, Julio and Lisa captured the input, polished much of the emotion from the conversation, and presented very concise documentation on what the leaders heard from the citizens.

The direction was clear. The human citizens of Aard wanted what humans on Earth thought they wanted but could rarely accomplish. The primary agreed-upon elements of the Constitution were familiar to Americans and other democracies. Yet, they were worried that the translation of those elements by those who wanted power would be their downfall if they could not protect the citizens from grifters and scammers.

They all knew they could not legislate by general vote on everything. There was no sane way the entire population could vote on every change or new rule.

Roger Haller

They would need civic leaders, and that element had already been established organically.

Everyone agreed they wanted a voice and unconditional equality in everything: gender, race, religion, opportunity, and responsibility. Leaders had to be held to the same standards all citizens were held to. This constitutional element led to the discussion about religions, political parties, and any person or group that wanted to control the autonomy of any other individual. Unsurprisingly, that element was the most emotional because most of the humans on this planet were placed here by an organization that did not value their rights as individuals.

The villagers all agreed they had a good thing established with villages that collaborated instead of competing. Jewels, Stacey, Adelphi, and Sylvia had established a process to 'farm in the wild.' Jewels succeeded in the first level of domestication with the humpbacks, capybaras, and aardvarks, where enhancing their habitats enhanced the food supply. Animals began to see humans as assets but not as predators. Adelphi, Sylvia, and Stacey were successful in the same manner with the flora.

Sylvia recruited Hema and Lakshmi to introduce sustainable irrigation projects that started at the Lower Falls. During monsoons, surplus water was sent to holding pools that could be used in the grasslands to the south of Bitter Water during drier seasons. This team didn't need new rules, but they suggested that precedent could be a good way to ensure sustainability in the future.

Julio warned that they best not build too many rules, but they also needed to ensure that the process for new regulations and updates had to be vetted and agreed to at a granular level. He introduced and explained 'Kotter's eight stages' to the citizens. Things would change. People would change. Environments would change. His voice was heard. The new constitution would be short, flexible, and visible to all.

Aard in Anguish

Someone applauded his statement from the outskirts of the council hut. Two people clapped. Rajesh and Shilpa stood up. Shilpa said slowly and carefully, "This is a historic time. It is best to move very slowly and use little ink."

Rajesh added. "Creating a law is much easier than deleting or modifying it. You have time." Julio took more notes as Lisa leaned in to discuss the new voices.

The meeting ended with a promise to reconvene in a few weeks to review a suggested document. Tiffany, Jesus, Silas, Princess, and Rita sat to one side of the council fire, planning a return to Shangri-La. They were in no hurry as the transporter would be busy much of the evening.

Jesus was keen to take a trip north along the shore above Shangri-La. Tamir and Emran had not been open to what they had found in their exploration. Silas was anxious to make a trip now that he was almost through boot camp in Shangri-La. Princess felt he was ready. She was prepared for the next trek, too. Life on the trail made her happy. This was probably due to her camp partner, Jesus.

Tiffany smiled. Trekking with Silas may be an interesting change, too. As the scouts planned, Rita was quiet, but Tiffany noticed and asked her what was on her mind. The redhead was a striking image in the firelight as she contemplated. She slowly looked up from the flickering embers. "Just a little concerned about Marcel and Patrick. The two you brought into camp as Mac was leaving. I'm getting reports that they display some characteristics that may lead to friction."

"What's going on?" Tiffany was concerned now.

"The word in the village is they are building a still in the woods. Don't get me wrong; I miss a little nightcap occasionally, but other characteristics add to the mix.

Roger Haller

It seems they're full of grandiose adventures in the Middle East as mercenaries. They seem to have a history of selling guns and alcohol. I think they may see opportunity here. They are also womanizers. I don't see anything wrong with flirting, but the ladies feel a bit creeped out over their advances. Romance doesn't seem to be involved."

Tiffany thought for a moment. "I've been uncomfortable about a few of their remarks too."

Rita shrugged her shoulders, "They haven't caused trouble and seem to be trying to make friends. ... just not sure of their motives yet."

"Good insight. Thank you. I think we can all keep a closer watch." Tiffany laid a hand on Rita's shoulder. "Thank you for sharing." The rest of the team agreed to watch them closer.

Adelphi walked up to the scouts, and as she did, Tiffany stood up to receive and respond to her hug. "Adelphi, I don't know if you have met Silas or Rita yet."

"Hi Rita, yes, we have met. And Hello, Silas. It is good to meet you. I hear you are joining Tiffany's Scouts."

"It's good to meet you, Adelphi. Tiffany has told me much about you and your skills."

"I'm sure it's not all true, but please look after her on the trail. She has always had Jesus and Princess, but she means so much to me, and I hope you help keep her safe, too."

Adelphi smiled warmly and hugged Silas where he stood. She hugged the rest of the crew and sat down. "I need to visit Shangri-La soon. Some of the old papers from the tower cabin suggest there may be some of the bleeding flowers near the coast above you. Sylvia and I may need to trek up there."

Aard in Anguish

"It's funny you should mention that, my friend." Tiffany added, "We were just talking about a trek north along the coast. If you give us some requirements, we can do a reconnaissance for you."

"I won't be able to go until after the next monsoon because of the experiments I have going on now, but I can give you a list of things to look for and how to preserve some evidence if you could help."

Another monsoon was approaching the expanding humans, so preparations had started. The trek north may need to be short this time.

"I have an early morning." Adelphi rose, kissed Tiffany on the cheek, nodded her head, and smiled at everyone. "By the way, Charlotte seems to be making progress with Michelle through boot camp. Archery seems to be bringing her to life. Oh… and there are now two babies walking in Moon Bridge." She smiled big with her news bulletin. Adelphi made her way to the hut across the compound she shared tonight. She would be back in Moon Bridge in the morning.

I observed no animosity in the conversation. These people all cared about each other. However, I have the same reservations about Marcel and Patrick's characters. I have met a few like them on Earth.

They may be cause for a rule or two in the new constitution, but that needs to work itself out.

The fantastic news may also create some new rules. Humans have now been born in two star systems.

***

Roger Haller

51 Pegasi - Sister Tiffany

The village finalized preparations. The wet season would drive the humans into shelter for a few weeks. We got the news that Mac was back in Freedom.

Tiffany spent much of the evenings getting to know Silas. His parents had passed away when he was young, and he had no siblings. She found Silas had an ex-wife in Calgary and a grown son and daughter. He had nothing wrong to say about his ex, but she had moved on before he was ready, so it was a broken heart that took him to a solitary life in Northern Alberta. He had no issues with his son and daughter, but they had busy lives in the city and didn't try to stay involved. Silas admitted he was part of the problem as well. They all lived in the city, and he couldn't handle a life on concrete. He had reached out by letter a couple of times, but he had no use for a cell phone or social media, so his lack of social life was part of the problem.

Tiffany opening up. She told her story, and the tall Canadian was shocked. He couldn't picture her in a habit, but he could easily see her as a missionary. Tiffany's eyes welled up and spilled over while she told her story. The gentle giant took her in his arms and kissed her tears away.

Tiffany melted and sobbed in his embrace for minutes, letting her emotions flow. Until now, her life had been about loss. Silas was not surprised. He knew from talking with her that she carried a heavy burden. He encouraged her tear flush, and when she looked up at his face through blurred vision, she could tell he was also contributing to the tear stream.

She reached up to wipe the corners of his eyes, but the motion turned into a kiss as she held the sides of his head. Tiffany experienced complete intimacy through romance for the first time. Silas proved to be a slow and skilled lover. They held each other and whispered softly through the night.

Aard in Anguish

The next morning, as they went about their day in the village, they noticed everyone smiling at them. It appeared evident that their relationship had changed. The day was well spent. The Pegasi sun shone, and steam rose from the dew in the camp. A festive atmosphere encompassed the crowd around the cooking fire that was placed just outside the cave. It would be a quick change when the rain hit. Jesus and Princess teased them gently about their new bond, and Tiffany was happy to tease them back.

The ground started shaking, and everyone dashed away from the rock face and around the cave. Rocks and dirt were falling off the mountain. Dusk was upon them, so knowing where they would be safe was hard. Finally, the village gathered near the river in the valley. Screamers were screaming, but far away, the darkness was falling quickly.

The shaking stopped soon, but small tremors kept them from returning to the village. The stars came out, and so did the moons in due time. Everything seemed back to normal except for the far-off screaming of the Screamers.

The night was long but uneventful. The village returned to the huts and cavern on daybreak. One hut was damaged by falling rock, but nothing else was affected. Checking the caverns found all good.

Tiffany and the rest of the scouts stepped through the tunnel to the South side of the portal. There was a far different scene in the South. The sound of panicked Screamers migrating overhead kept the scouts in the mouth of the tunnel. To the south, massive gray and black clouds billowed Eastward. Their hearts sank as their friends to the South seemed engulfed in the darkness.

Tiffany hurried back to the Transporter with her team on her heels. She scribbled a quick note and sent it to Willow's Cathedral. " We are safe. Please respond. – Tiffany."

51 Pegasi - Sister Tiffany

She sent the same message to Moon Bridge.

They received a response from Mac almost immediately. "Willow's Cathedral seems safe, but we are not all accounted for. I will update when it is safe to join us. – Mac"

There was finally a reply from Moon Bridge... or at least from the villagers of Moon Bridge the next day. "I hope this note finds you safe. We have escaped to the South, out from under the ash. We will be alright, but need to build in the rain, - Kels."

The Western skies turned black. The new monsoon was upon the humans of Aard. A week of torrential downpour muted activity, so messages back and forth between the other villages were sporadic and short.

There would be much to rebuild, but with every rebuild, there was improvement.

Shangri-La was unchanged but Freedom and Moon Bridge would need their help. I did not yet know how many more memorials would need to join me at the Landing Pond, but I knew the communities would survive this tragic turn and flourish.

Mac, Jean, Shiv, Popeye, Jewels, Tiffany, Adelphi... everyone was evolving. Life continued as it changed. They all struggled with their internal conflicts as they dealt with the external ones. Still, they woke every day and challenged their obstacles. Human life on Aard was normal.

The communication showed no regret but for the lost villagers. The transporter notes were positive and promising. Rebuilding was already busy in the rain. My people are strong.

***

Chapter 28

Reckoning

Jesus suggested the scouts hold off on their Northern trek until they could be sure Freedom and Moon Bridge were self-sufficient. The rest of the scouts agreed that the Aardian family was the priority. Shangri-La finally got the conditional all-clear from Willow's Cathedral, so the scouts were transported from cavern to cavern.

No one had heard from Ann, Sirih, or Marus yet, but most were out searching when the scouts arrived. Dr. Tim remembered that Marus had been net fishing with a canoe he had built. The rain was still a powerful obstacle, but it was beginning to slow. It was helpful in another way.

The smoke and ash from the eruptions were cleared. The only volcanoes that seemed to affect them were the new island seen offshore and slightly to the South and a plume from over the western horizon that they rarely saw in the overcast.

A new search party was being formed to work up the top end of the delta, where they had to stop searching when the weather hit. The search party would work up to the lower falls in the driving rain.

51 Pegasi - Sister Tiffany

Two new people were added to the search. Phil and Theresa, who Mac had brought back to Moon Bridge from the South, had migrated to Freedom when Mac returned.

Theresa was a veterinarian from Henderson, Nevada, and gravitated to Jewels. Phil was a gregarious mystery. When asked where he was from, his standard answer was, "Everywhere." He had a French accent, but Jean couldn't place his dialect. He was happy to be involved and quick to join the search.

Silas found Ann. She was mostly buried in mud, but a flash of purple Screamer feather alerted him, and he dug out a foot first. By the time the rest of the searchers reached him after his call, Silas had her unburied, but it was far too late. He and Jean wrapped her in a Screamer hide for her trip home.

Closer to the falls, they found the overturned remains of Marus' Canoe beside a large non-native boulder. The stern of the small boat was crushed, but most of the canoe was free. It was upside down, and when pulled out, they found Marus wrapped around Sirih. Both his legs were broken. There were marks and evidence that showed how he had pulled leaves and debris around them to keep some of their heat.

As the rescuers pulled them out into the rain, they found Marus' life had ended, but Sirih was still alive. She had a broken right arm and scrapes and cuts down her back and right side, but she was still breathing. Sirih took precedence, and she was wrapped and carried in a sling between Princess and Jean back to the cathedral, where Dr. Tim had been alerted.

Silas and Popeye did the same with Marus but needed help from Jewels and Theresa. Mac, Tiffany, Phil, and Jesus managed the retrieval of Ann.

The cathedral was somber that night, and the torchlight near the vents reflected off many tear-washed faces. Dr. Tim, Maritza, and Adelphi worked without rest.

Reckoning

Phil made his presence known by helping Oliver ensure everyone found a new cup of tea, a snack, or a place to rest. It wasn't lost to many that he was naturally doing many of the tasks Ann had accomplished so well. When nothing more could be done that night, Mac sat with him and tried to open a conversation.

"Thanks for all your help with our loved ones, Phil. You blended into the village so well. We don't know much about you, but please, tell us how we can make this village a special place for you."

Phil smiled his trademark smile and waved his hand over the scene. "I already feel like family, Mac. Let me know what you need, and I will work toward filling any gap. I am a generalist, so I have a lot of world experience in many areas. I'm happy to be what you need me to be."

"Fair enough, just help where you can, and when a role strikes you, let us know so we can help you achieve your goals."

"I understand, Mac. I've led many paths, so I know why you need to see my natural direction. I'm sure I'll fall into place where needed most."

Mac let it rest there. He wasn't going to get any farther tonight. Dr. Tim came into the hall and let everyone know Sirih would heal. Along with her broken arm, she had a fractured rib and a punctured lung. She was stable, sleeping soundly, and would be open to visitors later tomorrow.

Adelphi joined and informed the hall that Marus and Ann were ready to join Willow at the memorial as soon as could be prepared. There was no shortage of volunteers to manage the memorial in the morning. This planning brought Mac back to his last view of the landing pond. "We have work to do, folks. As well as the graves, we need to rebuild the bench and chair. I'd love to create some headstones somehow."

51 Pegasi - Sister Tiffany

"I can work stone, Mac. I know we have hammers, but do we have any chisels?" Everyone turned to look at Phil.

Jean, said, "Oui, nous avons des ciseaux."

Phil responded, "Super. Dans combine de temps pouvons-nous les recevoir? Avez-vous une meule a aigiser?

Embarrassed that he had naturally started the conversation in French, Jean translated. "I just tell Phil we have de chisels, and he ask for a sharp-en-ing wheel. We have dat, too."

He looked back at Phil. "We use them in da cathedral. We get them early to go, oui?"

Phil nodded, and the plan was set. Everyone went to find a bed. It had been a long day. By morning, the rain had subsided to light showers, and steam lifted from the landscape as the sun warmed the Landing. The jagged crack in the earth had filled with water, and the pond was back where the small creek widened as it found its level before tumbling back into its old steam bed.

Across the pond to the south stood the old fire rock where the landing hut had stood. On the North side lay the ashes of the bench and chair, and beside the ashes towered a new granite rock, blackened from its launch from the new island. The rain had already washed streaks down the sides, making it look like the rock was crying.

Phil asked Mac if he minded if he carved names in the massive stone.

"Good idea… it seems Aard delivered it for that purpose."

Mac gave him a list of names, beginning with Ann: just names and end dates. Most of the birth dates were unknown.

Reckoning

On this day, Ann Bennett, Kia Agoyama, Marus Nikolaidis, Randy Weinstein, and Sharon Rowlands were the names added to the boulder. Shale flagstones were placed in a path around the large rock, and a little flagstone plaza was built at the pond's edge.

Jean, the Stud, had already started building the willow-backed bench and chair, and the crew got busy building a new two-bedroom hut by the fire rock. The Memorial Landing would live again.

Now that the clouds were parting, the villagers could see smoke from the new island, floating East south of the delta. Three more, bigger plumes rose in the Screamer mountains and streamed East over the land of the Tower Giants. They would be uncomfortable in the sulfur smoke.

Far out to sea, they could see another plume rise from below the horizon. The humans of Aard were sure that was a sign that the Island of the Bleeding Flower was active. Freedom was packed with people for the funeral, and the next day, with all prepared, Julio would lead a ceremony as Ann and Marus were laid to rest with Willow.

My memory was getting company.

At the back of the crowd, I watched Dr. Tim with his head lowered and tears streaming down his face. His horn-rimmed glasses were misty. The gentle doctor had been much closer to Ann than most knew.

***

Roger Haller

51 Pegasi - Sister Tiffany

Phil had worked late into the night. While everyone was preparing, he slept in Willow's Cathedral. When Julio was about to start the ceremony, Jewels was asked to fetch him to dedicate the memorial. The crowd stood in a semicircle around the boulder, and two graves were ready across the flagstone path.

Julio called Phil to the front of the rock, where the names and dates had been masterfully carved. Julio introduced him but stopped to ask his last name for the ceremony.

" Sinclair… I am Phillipe Sinclair."

Tiffany tried to remember where she had heard that name before. Someone else had that last name. Her thoughts were interrupted by a deadly whistle, a thud, a grunt, and a gasp from the crowd. Phil tumbled back against the stone, then tilted forward and fell on the arrow that just stole his life. The deadly accuracy of the arrow meant its target had no chance for last words.

All eyes turned to the hillock behind them, where the Landing Pole had been, and Michelle stood by herself with her bow dropped to the ground. In the eerie silence that fell over the audience while they tried to make sense of what just happened, Michelle said, "It's finally over."

Princess ran to grab the bow. There were no other arrows or weapons. Shiv grabbed her arms to ensure she didn't do anything else or run. Charlotte ran to her to hold her from crumpling to the ground, and Theresa stepped forward, standing over the dead man. Maritza and Dr. Tim were trying to attend to him.

Theresa said, "She did what she had to do. No one else is in danger."

With the situation beginning to feel under control, the crowd now looked to her.

Reckoning

She pointed at the man, still bleeding out on the flagstone. "I have been his prisoner since the cages." She pointed at Michelle. "She was his wife. Michelle had to watch him slaughter her family in Tamil… Southern India. His brother is still trying to get the fortune Michelle's family had built. Phillipe sent Michelle to the cages, and his brother double-crossed him to get us here. I was his brother's wife. I was sent to the cages after him because I knew what he had done."

She looked sadly at Michelle. "Those brothers were the masters of charm and deception. I am so sorry, Mon Ami… May I hold you.?"

Michelle was crying silently, but she nodded and held out her forearms as much as Shiv would let her. Shiv looked around. Mac nodded, and he let her go. The sisters-in-law hugged. Adelphi stepped up to the fallen man. "Silas, Jean, could you please help me remove Monsieur Sinclair? I think he will need a different grave site."

As they removed him, Adelphi said, "Julio, will you please continue the service?"

He did.

The eulogies were read in broken English, and Ann and Marus found their rest beside Aardian pioneers who had gone before. Before returning to their respective villages, the Aardian Council met in Freedom. They suggested that those interested stay to hear or participate if they wished. Adelphi, Silas, Rajesh, and Lakshmi stayed to observe. They started with a long conversation with Michelle and Theresa. Charlotte stayed with them to begin a course of therapy, as both women had far more oversized loads than anyone should need to carry alone.

They learned the full story and found corroboration from a pair of their Indian immigrants.

Roger Haller

Hema worked with Philippe extensively as he represented the French firm that provided many of the projects she worked on. She did not know him socially, but in business, he was known as a charismatic but driven leader in the irrigation company.

Hema never met his wife, Michelle, until they were freed from cages together. She hadn't known he was in Freedom since she and Lakshmi had been busy with Stacey and Sylvia on the flume project. Lakshmi knew him as a self-important business manager who had no interest in the people doing the work. She didn't like him and hadn't seen him since Earth until they attended the service for Ann and Marus.

Theresa asked to go back to Moon Bridge with Michelle and Charlotte. The ladies asked if Charlotte could help them become good citizens, and neither wanted to be near the resting place of their tormentor.

Once the ladies left, the council dealt with another reality for their constitution. I watched an important milestone of Aardian history. Where do you draw the line when killing another human being? So far, Larry was the first, and Howard was next, although his end came from a native creature. Both were self-defense for Freedomites.

Today, we all witnessed and participated in a killing, a defense, a judgment, and a verdict in the same event.

Julio reminded the citizens. "When we firs organize, we say, no law 'til it needed. Today, I not see need for new law. Did anyone else?"

Mac, Tiffany, Jean, and Shiv agreed. Lisa said, "I agree, but shouldn't we document that agreement as a precedent to follow should something like this come up in the future?"

Reckoning

The council was silent for a few moments while everyone weighed her words. Julio answered, "Ma-be, but dis es la primera.. the first.

If it happen more, I tink it would be diferente. I tink ma-be malicia. It be diferente. Ma-be self-defense, no?"

Lakshmi voiced her opinion. "I like that you write few laws. Crime is sometimes subjective.

The legal system interprets the laws because each time is different. No two actions are the same, so the same result may have a different verdict. As much as you can, you should see every case as unique. Judge on the merits of the actions at hand."

Lisa smiled. "Thanks, Lakshmi. I see your point."

Tiffany caught Mac before the conversation moved on and whispered. "Could I chat with you later, Mac, please?"

He smiled and said, "Certainly, Warrior."

The council agreed the case was closed, and the council ordered tea. The Aardian Council had a lot of growth to do, and I felt Lakshmi and Julio had similar approaches. I could tell they would have many decisions to make in the future. Some will not be popular, but starting as transparent as they have been will help.

It also helps that they have agreed to follow the voice of the villages instead of dictating to them. They may be able to achieve better than 50-50 favorability for a while yet.

***

Chapter 29

Off World Collaboration

Mac joined Tiffany for a huddle away from the council fire.

"Thanks for joining me, Mac. I just wanted to know if we could follow up with your family in Seattle to see the status of the Global Main Street Revitalization Organization. You and I brought some new folks to our villages in the last while, and the event today makes me realize we may have imported some trouble."

Mac nodded. "Phil was a prime example of the danger. He seemed like such a good fit. He died here without a very deep investigation because of the word from a few people close to him."

"Yes, Mac, and we have a few more we need to know more about. I am the biggest proponent of saving everyone transported to this world, but we have no way of vetting them.

I'm worried about Marcel and Patrick, who you found when you headed out on your tour."

Off World Collaboration

Mac nodded. "Agreed. They still make the hair stand up on the back of my neck. We have a couple of promising immigrants in Freedom, in Lakshmi and Rajesh. They may be beneficial in building the template for our society. However, we know very little about them."

"Mac, can a few of us visit your father and brother? We may find a way to do a background check on some of these people and perhaps fend off some nasty surprises like today."

Mac smiled sadly, "You make great points, Tiffany. I've been considering a visit to Earth, and your train of thought fits mine. Who would you like to go to get this background check?"

"Well, Mac, Normally, I'd be happy to leave it up to you, but to fit in with the transparency we have been asking for and the need to share your load, we should open the trip up to the leaders… The Aardian Council… Popeye… anyone else concerned with immigration and our judicial system… What do you think?"

"Great approach. Since it is perhaps, sensitive to some around the fire tonight, I'll reach out for a special meeting with the leaders. Will you stick around if I can get us together in the morning before the leaders return to their beds?"

"Absolutely. Thank you."

The council had a quick breakfast meeting in the morning, and a trip to Seattle was arranged for five of them. Popeye, Lisa, Mac, Tiffany, and Rita chose to transport. There was no reason for any delay, so Mac went first to ensure the MacAdams were ready for company. He sent back a paper note that suggested a couple minutes between transportations, and within an hour, the travelers were sitting around a large desk on the second floor of an old canning plant in South Downtown Seattle.

Roger Haller

51 Pegasi - Sister Tiffany

Introductions were made, and Evan and Tony MacAdams were introduced to Tiffany Henderson, Paul Sutler, and Rita Gleason. Mac then updated his father and brother on the earthquake and volcano disasters they lived through. He told them of the loss of Ann and Marus.

Mac had prepped his father and brother on the recent development with Phillip and Michelle so they would be ready with suggestions and ideas for the Aardian team.

Evan took charge. "Welcome back, Tommy. Welcome Tiffany, Rita, Paul, and welcome home, Lisa. We hear you and think we have some answers."

He nodded to Tony. "Tony may have some suggestions too. He has a little technology to run you through, that may help you understand the opportunities. Just before we start, does anyone have any questions?"

Everyone was happy to hear what the MacAdams family had to offer, so he was met with shaking heads. He looked at Tony, "Ready?"

Tony smiled wide, "Yes, folks, I have some things to show you. Please watch the screen on the wall."

He pressed a button on a remote, and the screen lit up. Shortly after, a spreadsheet filled the screen. "Here is the file we started when we learned about the Global Main Street Revitalization organization. As you can see in the blue font, many of the names in column B have been eliminated. You may recognize Howard Thom near the top, along with his rank and final status. Lawrence Hempler was added late because he joined late, but you see his status, too. You don't have anything to consider with the blue font rows. That signifies they will never be a threat again.

Off World Collaboration

The rows in black are incarcerated in various prisons around the world because they were indicated in the disappearance or deaths of people who have been sent to 51 Pegasi-d. Some of them have died trying to avoid prison and were moved to blue font with details in a column off-screen.

I'd like to bring your attention to the rows in red font. Those people are missing and actively being hunted. We suspect most are still on Earth and will be found, but we know some are on 51 Pegasi-d. We have also learned that some of the leaders of the GMSR have a transporter working that does not involve the natives of your planet. You will probably encounter them at times, and their goals are nefarious. They want precious metals and gems from your planet.

They have learned where some are and have been transporting to places with mines. One place they used to transport to was the island off the coast near Freedom. They want to get back to it. We found documentation with maps at one of their headquarters. Any questions so far?"

"Whew!" Tiffany exhaled. "That is a lot of information. They may not know it yet, but the Island of the Bleeding Flower may be fully engulfed in a volcano. I think three other mainland volcanoes may be compromising the Tower Giants and the human building at the base of the old tower."

"Thanks for that information." Tony continued. as he took notes, "We will investigate traffic to and from those locations. I have built a sensor that tracks transports and have planted it at the known sites. I'll show you my dashboard when we are done with the spreadsheet. I want to get us back to the red font momentarily."

"Before you do, Tony, any chance we can get records of that activity? I'd like to know where best to watch for people who may be harmful to us on Aard?"

"Happily, Tiffany, I've already got that information. For instance, several transmissions have been to the island we spoke of. There may be some humans there now. There have also been a few transmissions North of your Shangri-La, against the coast, and a few to the mountains West of the Southern Giant's teleporter, which you say has been abandoned. I'll get copies of those reports, including coordinates, names, and pictures of who we think may be transporting due to where they transport from. This is all being tracked in our database and reported on my dashboard."

He applied a filter to the sheet and pointed at the name column on the screen. "There are no guarantees, but do you see names you recognize? They may not use their real name, but they probably don't see any disadvantage with using it at this point. I am working to get photos to go with them so we can identify bad guys without names soon."

Marcel and Patrick did not come up on the list. However, Phillipe Sinclair and his brother Bernard were listed in the red font.

"You can move Phillipe to the blue font. Our village is burying him today. His wife ended him with a well-placed arrow yesterday." Mac's face looked worn as he relayed the information. It wasn't lost on anyone when Rita, who sat next to him, reached out and placed a comforting hand on his shoulder. Tony noticed that they had matching amulets hanging from their necks. He decided this meeting wasn't the time to mention it.

Mac smiled at Rita, then continued. "The brother's wives are consoling each other in Moon Bridge. It would be most handy if we could get a picture of him. Can we search for a few names to move on, though?"

Tony nodded. "Sure."

Off World Collaboration

"Please look for Rajesh Sharma or Shilpa Bajwa from the New Delhi area and Hema Akkineni and Lakshmi Anthony from near Madurai in Tamil Nadu, India. They all appear to be powerful additions to our tribes." Mac hoped they would not show in the spreadsheet. The search came up blank.

"Do you have a Gerald? From Oregon… Canyonville, maybe? I don't have a last name."

Gerald Wilson came up. Current location unknown.

"He's on the FBI's most wanted list. His last known location was Roseburg, Oregon. I'll look at my sensor data to see if transporter action launched near there and where it landed." Tony pointed to a map a link had produced. Tony was also able to provide a picture of Gerald.

Mac's eyes lit up. "Can we get a few copies of that mugshot?"

His brother nodded.

Evan commented. "These results aren't final, but they are a good baseline. We will continue to research these folks. See if you can get me last names of Marcel and Patrick, please. Until we hear more, we will focus on Bernard Sinclair and Gerald Wilson. They seem to be the present threat, but I'll relay the message to those who know that The Island of the Bleeding Flower is now an active volcano. I'll 'leak' the information to the scrambling remnants of the GMSR to see if it changes any activity."

Tiffany asked, "Do you have a record for Joseph Kony or Father Lukwiya ?"

Surprisingly, Lukwiya turned up, inprisoned in Washington, D.C. The Catholic Church had turned him in as he was trying to re-estabilsh in in the US.

Roger Haller

51 Pegasi - Sister Tiffany

He was wanted in multiple countries for genocide, among other charges. Joseph Kony was listed too. His location was unknown.

Tiffany was excited now. "Is there any chance we can get a list, diagram, or map of the active teleporters the Giant's suppliers aren't using? It seems that era is over now, but we have a new challenge from humans on Earth."

I had mixed emotions listening to this conversation.

The Giants and other natives were becoming less of a threat to humans on the beautiful planet that became my home forever, but humans from Earth were becoming the 'enemy'. I guess they always were, but the ideal of the perfect second chance for humanity was becoming a mute point. Humans were and will always be human.

I decided to focus on the beautiful side of humans, and noticed the look in Mac's eyes as he smiled at Rita.

***

Off World Collaboration

"You'll have a copy waiting in your Willow's Cathedral teleporter room when you return." Tony beamed at the smiles around the table. Tea was served, and a less formal visit took over.

Tiffany finished her tea and stood. "Please excuse me, folks. Finally meeting the famous MacAdams has been great, but I need to be home. This is the first time I stepped back off Aard, and I'm homesick." She hugged the MacAdams and stepped into the little transport closet. Popeye followed soon after.

Lisa stepped into Evan's office to get some updates on what he, Tony, and Pam had produced for the freight exchange. It seemed they may now have a small market to begin introducing Aardian gems to under-served countries that could use a hand up. In return, Aard could benefit from hand-built tools, housewares, and materials that are simple and close to the Earth.

That left Tony, Mac, and Rita drinking tea around the old steel boardroom table. Tony took his chance. "Mac, you and Rita have an amazing pendant. You two an item now?"

Embarrassed, the two looked at each other, their pendants, then at Tony. "…No… w we seem to have the same taste in pendants." Mac stammered.

Rita shook her head and smiled. "It seems a bigger power made us pick these out of the water in different places. I can't imagine being without mine."

Mac laughed now, "Same…"

Tony laughed, too. "Sorry, didn't mean to put you on the spot, but I think I know the higher power." No one answered, but everyone knew who he meant.

Roger Haller

"With that, tactless brother, I think it's time I got back to Aard."

Rita rose, took her last sip, and said, "Me too."

"Sorry, guys… I spoke out of turn. You know me. Something just made me blurt out what was on my mind."

"Don't worry, Bro. I know. I'd stay and give you a hard time, but I have a Transport landing to put back together. By the way, do you have any extra transporters? I think we are down to a couple spares."

"I've been able to reverse-engineer the transporters, Tommy. I have a couple almost ready, but I need to test them further first. I should have some for you in a couple weeks."

"Nice, I want to build the old Landing Pole again. The Landing Pond is my home; I think it wil be secure for some time now."

They got hugs and transported back to Willow's Cathedral. Lisa was going to transport later, after her visit with Evan. Before returning, she wanted to connect with Tony and Pam, so she would probably spend the night on Earth.

Back at the Cathedral, Rita pointed at Mac's pendant. "Mac, is it my imagination, or is that gem glowing?"

He looked, then at hers, then back at his. "Yes… yours too. I wonder if it has something to do with the transport."

"Mac, would it be an imposition if I drop by the memorial and Landing to see what your plans are for the place?"

He looked back at his pendant, then at hers. "It would be my pleasure. Let's update the Council and hike up to the memorial."

Off World Collaboration

They soon had an audience with the Aardian leaders to tell them what they had learned. They showed a detailed map of human-controlled transporters that matched the Giant's camps but also set humans down in a few places where the Giant's were excluded.

One of them was on the Island of the Bleeding Flower. Another interesting location was north of Shangri-La, near the coast.

They climbed the handy vent tube to the Landing Pond an hour later. The pond was different now, yet somehow even more relaxing and inviting.

"Can I make you dinner?" Mac smiled as he pulled a bow and quiver from a stash.

Rita grinned wide. "As long as I can build the fire and help cook."

Another hour later, they were roasting Humpback, Aardian legumes, and eggs in a stomach pot over a cozy fire by the fire-rock. The first fire since the war of the Giants.

Perhaps Tony had seen it before they did. The time had come. They spent the night in the unfinished, new Landing cabin. Both felt a passion that night, that they hadn't imagined they would find again in their lifetime. Neither felt shame or remorse. Instead, they felt the promise of a future.

My plan was well-engaged. My soul was happy. Mac deserved this chance, and so did Rita. Both had focused on other people's success for so long that they forgot to reach for their own. She was going to be a challenge, though. I had been used to dancing backward in high heels, but I never challenged my comfort zone. I never struck at the glass ceiling with enough force to be noticed.

Roger Haller

51 Pegasi - Sister Tiffany

Rita has and will continue to hammer. Now, perhaps, she won't have to, so much. Now, she may have found someone and somewhere to enjoy life.

I smiled. This is how it is supposed to be. As they began noticing each other in a new light, I glowed and brightened my surroundings. The amulets around their necks glowed to match. I was going to enjoy watching this relationship blossom, but tonight, I had other places to be.

***

Chapter 30

Attitude Adjustment and Gerald

Mac and Rita grew close over the next few weeks and were often seen together at the new Landing and Shangri-La. No one could be certain how close, but it was easy to see they were happy. Mac was also planning to join Tiffany and crew for a trek North to the coordinates for the Northern transporter Tony had identified.

As they planned, Adelphi joined the team. She was determined to investigate the report that a crop of the coveted Bleeding Flowers may be found there. Rita remembered to warn Mac and Tiffany that Tamir and Emran had camped to the North of Shangri-La and had been closed-mouthed about their time there.

Mac supplied the two Shia names to Tony for consideration in his notes and let him know they had been transported to Damour, south of Beirut. During the planning, Rita came to pull Silas aside. They talked quietly at the side for a moment.

51 Pegasi - Sister Tiffany

Rita left, and Silas excused himself from the planning as he had an 'appointment with a couple of moonshiners.' Although the team chuckled at his explanation, they wondered what he had up the sleeve of his robe.

Silas had asked to be alerted when Marcel and Patrick came into the village. His opportunity came as the pair came looking for a fruit press. He met the moonshiners at the storage cavern.

"Guys, I'm curious about your operation. I'd like to visit to see where I could help."

Marcel, in particular, was suspicious of the offer and looked up at the towering Canadian, who grinned back at him.

"We don't need any partners."

"Don't worry, boys. I don't want any action. I want to help. Consider me a mentor or consultant if you like. I want your enterprise to succeed and I'm here as a free advisor."

Marcel repeated with an edit. "We don't need any help."

"Yes. Yes, you do. You see, you are off on the wrong foot, and I'm here to smooth your path so everyone wins."

Patrick took his turn. "Marcel said no. Get lost."

Silas smiled, put his fingers to his mouth, and whistled. Jean the Stud, and Shiv stepped out of the transporter cave to join Silas.

Marcel and Patrick got quiet as they took in the tattooed, snarling, bald ex-con standing between twin towers.

"Let me explain, guys." Silas said, "Have a seat."

Attitude Adjustment and Gerald

He didn't wait, but they sat on rocks while he carried on. "You see, we have a nice thing going here on Aard. We have built a clan based on respect. We respect each other as individuals, friends, family, partners, and warriors who count on each other for our lives."

He let that sink in for a moment, then continued. "We have several reports that you two have forgotten your manners a few times. In particular with our women folk. You could be having this talk with a few of them right now, with the same results, but we're not sure you are ready for the swiftness or severity of their advanced self-defense training."

Marcel started to object, but Jean raised his hands.

Silas continued. "We agree that you might have brought something we can all use, in moderation, with your fermentation process and still. However, we also agree that we must approach alcohol from a far different point of view than we did on Earth. It truly is handy for medicinal purposes and stress relief in small qualities, but it kills when overused. We're here to show you how you can be successful members of our society before you are simply a story we tell around the campfire in the future."

He stepped forward. "Do we understand each other?"

Patrick stood quickly but sat promptly as Marcel pulled him back to his seat. Marcel was a bit more polite. "What do you propose?"

"Show us your operation."

"We've worked hard on this…"

Jean stepped toward him. Very slowly, in his best English, he explained."We all work hard on dis world.

51 Pegasi - Sister Tiffany

We have no time to do what you are doing, so we don' have any need to take your work. We do need you to be good citizen…, oui?"

Marcel tugged Patrick's robe sleeve, and the concerned men led the imposing leaders to their work camp. The operation was small, but they had scavenged enough copper from storage to make it work. Patrick was the mechanic, and Marcel the chef.

Patrick showed three five-gallon copper pots, joined with copper plumbing pipe from top to top to top. Patrick explained the first pot, which had a coffee can fitted tightly on the top. "This is our still. The mash is in the bottom, and the steam is captured in this dimpled can. The pipe runs from the can to the next pot, the thump keg. The next pipe runs from there to the worm pot. We keep cold water inside that pot, covering a coiled copper pipe that joins the spigot. That's where the vapor becomes liquid, and shine comes out."

Marcel followed with some insight into his recipe. "We're getting grain from the fields below, but we have to harvest it at night because of the Screamers. It's pretty good. It's not quite wheat… more like barley. That is good for us because we malt some of it to get a nice taste from the end result. We have some glass measuring cups, so our recipes are getting locked down." He pointed at three small huts they had built. "One is our home, one is our kiln for malting, and one is our aeration room."

"Nice work, guys." Silas thought it was time to show a friendly side. "What about the fermentation process you've been using for the wine I've heard about?"

Marcel continued. This was his favorite area of expertise. "The basketball berries are the best. Their natural yeast is stable and easy to use. The sugar content in the berries is through the roof. It's a natural for wine.

Attitude Adjustment and Gerald

We are experimenting with other fruit, too, but it will take some time."

"Okay, guys, here's how it's going to go. You two are now the conscience of alcohol on Aard. You will be the liquor control board, ensuring your products are used moderately and not abused. We will help you get what you need to provide for the communities growing around you, but you will be pillars of the village. You will control the alcohol content to under 5 percent on the wine and under 40 percent on the spirits. We can ask Popeye and Lisa for better measuring instruments to control it more tightly. In return, the people of Aard will take care of you. Are you good with that arrangement?"

Marcel and Patrick were nodding happily. They agreed to be model citizens.

The three enforcers left the excited moonshiners to their chores and headed back to the trek planning meeting.

"You think they can keep it straight?" Shiv looked dubious.

Silas grinned. "They have the incentive now, but if they don't. Aard will simply be dry a little longer."

The enforcers chuckled. "I hope it work. I like some wine wit humpback, Oui?" Jean was beginning to enjoy the company of the big Canadian. Shiv was growing an appreciation for him, too.

Hmm. I wasn't expecting this. Aard is growing up. Of all the things I expected to be introduced as the new citizens grew on their second planet, alcohol wasn't on my list. I used to enjoy a glass of wine, an occasional beer, and even a sip of spirits on special occasions, but I had never missed it on Aard.

***

Roger Haller

51 Pegasi - Sister Tiffany

Tiffany, Princess, Silas, Jesus, Mac, and Adelphi scrambled up a rocky trail to a headland overlooking the sea west of Shangri-La. There had been no screams from the massive purple raptors in the East since the volcanoes erupted. For now, they were free to travel in the daylight, and the vista from this headland made it more than worthwhile.

The trail was well-worn from wildlife, but the recent rains had wiped it clean. The path was bordered by scraggly, tough shrubbery and bent, gnarly evergreens tortured by the sea winds. They could see a wall of taller timber to the north and felt they could be there in time to camp for the night. Much of their trail topped tall cliffs to the sea below, like the headlands at Willow's Cathedral.

Tiffany shared her thoughts. "There are several trails to the beaches below. I've been out here this far, but there is a lot of exploring to be done down below when we get the time."

"Agreed. I wouldn't be surprised to find more caverns like we found at Willow's Cathedral." Mac was intrigued.

Jesus noticed a path heading across the headland to the East. There were animal tracks he had not seen before. He called everyone over. "Is dis gato o un perro?..cat… dog?"

Silas responded, "It could be either… not fresh enough to know for sure, but there are claw marks… A cat on Earth might have them tucked in, but this is not Earth."

"Looks like maybe the size of a coyote or tame dog back home, but not too deep in the soft dirt," Princess observed.

"Look ahead." Tiffany pointed at one of the tough shrubs against the trail. A sharp edge had cut it back. "Someone with a steel blade did that."

Attitude Adjustment and Gerald

The scouts moved more cautiously now and stopped talking. They made their way down the trail to a thicket of evergreens. Under the canopy of the trees, they found a primitive shelter with a torn Screamer hide that used to be a hammock. No one had been there for some time, and the only tracks were their paw discovery and a few humpback tracks.

"I think we found Tamir and Emran's home, but it doesn't look like they planned on making it permanent." Tiffany sounded relieved.

"I guess we can continue North, then." Princess was eyeing up the wall of taller trees to the North. "Not sure this would be safe enough if the Screamers come back, and I'd like to get to know Fido before we get too comfortable in his home."

"Good idea, Princess." Mac was happy to keep moving, too.

They did make camp in good time and had a comfortable dinner around a cooking fire under the trees. The trail North was a bit more distinct here because of undergrowth, and something bigger than humpbacks kept it clear. Probably something bigger than the canine track they discovered.

The trek continued North along the coast for another two days with nothing unusual but for the night sounds. The scouts noted a regular low squeak from something around them at night. Occasionally, they heard some distant grunts, but they stayed distant.

It seemed they didn't want anything to do with the humans. Another noise of note was a high-pitched buzz, almost a hiss. It moved quickly through the night without concern for the trees or obstacles but never got close enough to identify.

The trail had been climbing slowly, and the hikers could now see mountain peaks in the north. On the fourth day, the trees got smaller, and the climb steeper.

Roger Haller

There was less undergrowth, but still no Screamers. They found another trail to the East, dropping into a cozy little valley with a lake between mountain ridges.

"This valley is calling to me." Princess laughed.

"Me too." Adelphi saw a lot of potential.

Standing on a high ridge, the glistening lake below looked like a postcard from Banff in Canada.

"Looks like Lake Louise." Silas was impressed.

As they descended to the lake, a massive, fresh landslide came into view to their North. At the same time, a lush, green hillside with blood-red flowers opened up to their South.

"The flowers! Bleeding Flowers!" Adelphi, smiling widely, pointed to a blanket of emerald leaves and ruby blossoms. The trekkers now understood the high-pitched buzz. Yellow Pollinators, the size of hummingbirds, were sweeping from flower to flower.

The noise was constant. Their wings were blurred as they ignored Adelphi, who joined them in milking the precious fluid from the flowers. She had a small bottle from her tote sack full in moments, and another started.

Tiffany and Mac made camp in the trees while Princess swung her bow to her back, hooked it on her quiver, and then joined Adelphi. Jesus and Silas split off to explore the slide.

Everyone turned to look when Jesus yelled, "Transporter!"

Mac and Tiffany started running toward the excited scout, pointing to the bottom of a long, golden mineral vein gleaming yellow in the bright light.

Attitude Adjustment and Gerald

Silas yelled, "Humans!" and a shot rang out. Silas spun and dropped among the boulders of the slide.

Jesus yelled, "Silas!" and leaped toward him. Another shot rang out, and Jesus dropped to the ground. A third shot tore through the shock at the edge of the slide, and a puff of granite dust followed a slug upward with a high-pitched whistle beside Tiffany.

A dark shape disappeared at the bottom of the golden antenna, and another man prepared to push the button. Yet another man raised his arm to shoot again, but the slick whistle of an arrow ended in his chest, and the gun fell to the ground. Princess rarely missed.

Before anyone could load again, the other man had pressed the button and was gone.

Tiffany reached Jesus first and called Adelphi to see if she could help. She was not hopeful.

Jesus had a hole in the right side of his chest that was bleeding out quickly. She reached behind and covered an exit wound with her hand. It was bleeding worse. Jesus was silent, but she read the terror in his eyes. He knew how bad this was.

Adelphi dropped to her knees, pulled blood-red liquid from her bottle with a glass and metal syringe, and drove it deep into his wound. She expressed the liquid into his chest as she drew the needle out. The liquid mixing with his blood gelled instantly, and she repeated the procedure on his back.

Jesus was still awake, but his eyes were heavy.

"Morire hoy?"

Adelphi looked deep into his eyes and said, "It's up to you. Fight."

Roger Haller

51 Pegasi - Sister Tiffany

Princess was now cradling his head. "No, no moriras." Her Spanish was getting good.

Adelphi looked Princess in the eyes.

She dug out her water flask and said, "Make him drink. Make him cough and make him stay awake for now. She stood and headed for Silas.

Tiffany had gone to find Silas. Her heart was beating hard in her ears. This can't happen now. She found him sitting on a rock, pulling his robe cord tight on his right upper bicep to stem the rivulet of blood running down his arm. She finished tightening. "Are you able to walk, Silas?" He was bloody, and he was pale, but he nodded.

Adelphi met them after a couple strides and sat him down again. She administered the bleeding flower serum to his arm wound in the same manner. The wound gelled and clotted immediately, and she removed the tourniquet.

Adelphi said, "Give him lots of water." Tiffany lifted out her skin flask and helped him drink. Color started to return to his face.

"You will be okay, but we must get Jesus to Dr. Tim now."

Mac came back from the man holding Princess' arrow, with the transporter under his arm, and said, "Gerald. He no longer has a pulse."

"You know him?" Tiffany was shocked.

"He was part of the organization that sent us here. He sent Willow to Aard. I hoped to meet him one day."

Mac took stock of the condition of the scouts and started building a hammock to carry Jesus with. Silas stopped him.

Attitude Adjustment and Gerald

"I am alright. I can't do much with my right arm but tie Jesus on my back, and I can carry him. My legs and back are strong."

"But…" Mac began to object, but Adelphi interrupted him.

"Silas is right. Jesus is better off upright. He needs to cough up blood. He will breathe easier. If Silas can manage, we can carry his pack and weapons."

"Okay, let me make a quick change on this transporter before we get moving. I want to ensure anyone trying to join us doesn't get here." Mac opened the box quickly and closed it again almost as quickly.

The wounded scout party walked all afternoon and through the night with short breaks. Jesus dropped in and out of consciousness a few times but seemed to gain strength and, on the fourth day, was awake when they walked into Shan-gri-La.

Adelphi transported while they were preparing him for travel, and Dr. Tim and Maritza were waiting for him when he got to the cathedral. Princess and Tiffany transported directly after Jesus and Silas.

By the time they got there, Jesus was under anesthesia, After a quick inspection of Silas' arm, Dr Tim turned him over to Maritza and Adelphi. "He'll be fine, the slug didn't hit bone or an artery. I will be busy with Jesus, though. Pray for him."

Princess sat on a small bench in Dr. Tim's emergency room. She wasn't about to go anywhere.

Dr. Tim handed her a clean robe, and mask. "If you are to stay, you will need to help me protect Jesus. You may not like what you are about to see. I need to repair some damage and Jesus will be asleep and intubated. Do you understand?"

Roger Haller

Princess nodded and suited up.

Dr. Tim pointed at a small fire with a boiling kettle. "Pour some of that hot water in that small basin, use some of that soap, and wash your hands carefully. You may need to help."

Maritza helped her scrub and set up. Princess became the newest member of the Aardian hospital staff.

Tiffany, Adelphi, and Silas took a seat in the main cavern, to discuss plans for the future. Silas thanked the Greek beauty and hugged her close. "Thank you for the quick attention to my arm. I feel like it is already healing. Thank you, also for understanding my relationship with Tiffany... I know you've had a beautiful history, and I don't want that to end."

Tiffany was stunned momentarily, "Uhh."

Adelphi smiled wide and took advantage of her lover's loss of words. "Silas, that woman means the world to me. Her happiness is my first priority, and you are in a position to ensure that happiness. I will always love her enough to honor that happiness. I know she is protected by your love on the trails of Aard, and by your heart. That is good."

She turned to Tiffany, who was still watching with wide eyes and gaping mouth. "You are luckier than most, my love. You have two hearts dedicated to you."

Adelphi smiled wider now, "...And if you ever feel the need help with this handsome man, I'd be happy to do my share." She winked at Silas. "That goes for you too, Scout. I'd be more than happy to snuggle you both when you get trail weary."

She laughed from deep in her heart, spun on a heel and headed for the transporter. "I'm off to see Stacey and Sylvia. We have work to do on this medicine." She was gone before Tiffany could respond.

Attitude Adjustment and Gerald

I giggled happily to myself as Tiffany and Silas sat stunned. They smiled at each other. Adelphi just opened up a whole new chapter of their relationship. Silas wasn't sure how to react. Adelphi was a stunningly beautiful woman and as his shock subsided, his hormones and Tiffany's reaction left him with very little control of his facilities.

I snorted as Tiffany delighted in the dazed look on her lover's face. "Don't worry, big guy, I won't let her hurt you. But... You had better build up your stamina..."

She rolled back her head and Willow's Cathedral had never heard Tiffany release such a powerful belly laugh before. Everyone in the caverns smiled and chucked as years of anguish, stress, and tears released in a rush of happiness. A life of service had just won a spectacular reward of love.

Tiffany stepped out of Willow's Cathedral with Silas. She had a lot to absorb. The tall Scandinavian ex-nun had many thoughts and feelings in uncharted territory.

She knew how much she loved Adelphi, and she was beginning to understand a whole new type of love with Silas. Tiffany was confused, excited, scared, but recharged. I watched as the tornado of clashing storms that was Sister Tiffany closed her eyes and took a moment to talk with Sister Beatrix and Julian of Norwich. She had reached a new milestone. Her religion was no longer a problem. If her lord and savior could be androgynous, and God created mankind in his or her image, Tiffany's love was what was important, not which gender she loved. Her next challenges would be conquered with Silas... And with Adelphi.

I smiled. Perhaps love is the answer after all.

***

Roger Haller

Chapter 31

A Gun and a Goldmine

Back at Shangri-La, Mac set up a workbench on Rita's table and opened the transporter again to disarm.

"What did you set the receiver to?" Rita leaned over the work with her hands massaging Mac's shoulders.

"I just spun the receiver dial. The bad guy's transporter will think it's sending to the old coordinates but until I recalibrate, I sure wouldn't want to push their button. They could land anywhere in the Milky Way.

Each transporter has two settings. One of them the source and one the destination. The button, when pushed sends a call to the destination box, collects the destination coordinates in a handshake, the destination box confirms and the transport is launched.

Once I set it for our use, I'll take it back to the landslide. Adelphi will need those flowers, but I suspect there is something much more valuable to Earth in that little valley."

A Gun and a Goldmine

Rita stood as Mac closed the Transporter box. "We can head back as soon as you are ready. I want to know everything I can about that valley."

"Yes, there is another reason I need to get back there." Mac produced the hand gun he had confiscated from Gerald's dying hand. The ominous flat black Glock looked out of place on the rustic table of Rita's hut.

Mac looked sad. "There is a machine designed to kill people on Aard. I'm torn over what to do with it. There are still two rounds left in it."

He was silent for a moment. "My first instinct is to throw it into the sea, but my second instinct is to consider those who brought it here. They will be back and they have no problem killing humans with it."

Rita picked it up, ejected the clip, and pulled back the ejector housing a couple times to empty the chamber and ensure the gun was dead. She dropped the gun, clip, and bullet back into Mac's paperboy sack. "You don't have to make that decision alone, Mac. Tiffany and Silas will be here soon. Let's talk it over with them, then take it up with the council. Let's get some consensus".

Mac looked up into her eyes. "You're a smart cookie. You also know how to use a Glock.

"Gerald was lucky this gen-4 has been upgraded. Someone changed the ejector. He likely would have been ducking his own brass and could have jammed up if it the ejector hadn't been traded out properly."

"It sounds like I need to learn much more about my lover."

"Yes, my man, you do, but there is lots of time. I'm loving what I'm learning about you."

Roger Haller

She continued, "I think I've been looking for you far longer than I knew. From what I've learned of you so far, I promise, you won't regret getting to know me better. Hard life has educated me and you are the first man I've gotten to know that I didn't think I needed to defend myself from."

Mac studied the deep blue eyes gazing down at him as he sat over the transporter. "I'm happy you feel that way, Rita. I've had one lady trust me enough to teach me how to live an unconditional partnership. I lost her, but I feel that unconditional love she taught me, was to prepare me for someone like you."

"Ready for your next lesson?" Rita's grin was wide.

They both laughed as Rita kissed his head, then nibbled on his ear. It has been a long time since Mac felt a connection this deep. He stopped thinking as his body took over.

As Mac stood, Rita pulled him into a warm embrace. They had better things to do now. She led him toward the bed in the corner. About half way, they forgot everything they had been talking about. Emotions and hormones took over. Lost in a galaxy of freckles and a universe of flowing red hair, Mac launched into a new world of space and time travel. There was no sense of time. The universe was very local and immediate.

Rita was a proactive lover and she took it up a few notches. She applied a new level of passion that took Mac back to school. He forgot all lovers before. He didn't have time to reflect and he didn't care. All that mattered was the envelope of their passion.

The sun had not set yet when Rita led him from the table, but they woke, tangled and disheveled in the light of a new day. Bleary-eyed and unsteady, they climbed the hillside above Rita's hut to the mist of a feathery little waterfall. The veil of cascading water flowed over the granite rock wall.

A Gun and a Goldmine

It collected in a cozy pool of cool, green water before it tumbled down a little stream to the river below.

Dropping their loincloths at the rocky shore of the pool, they bathed and washed each other to a crisp and energized day. They were joined by Tiffany and a patched up Silas as they walked back to Rita's hut.

"You two look bright eyed and bushy tailed." Tiffany was in a very good mood. This was a nice change from the brooding Viking who had struggled with such a heavy load of emotions.

Rita was quick to respond. "You too look much the same, but for the sling." She pointed at Silas' wounded wing.

Mac's right arm was locked with Rita's but he extended his left to Tiffany, "Join us for breakfast, you two. We're about to head back to the landslide for a couple of chores. Do you feel like a short trek?

"I was just about to ask when that was going to happen. With Jesus and Princess off the trail for a bit, I was hoping you might want to go back and check out that little valley. I think it may have some potential. It may even make a nice, new homestead for our expanding citizens."

They stepped into the Rita's hut as Mac said, "Let's have a little chat before we go up to the cooking fire for a little breakfast."

Mac and Rita filled the scouts in on the transporter plan, and the Glock.

Mac got serious. "That landslide is gong to be dangerous for a while. The GMSR, or what ever they are now have the coordinates and they have value in the place. We have to break that connection and possibly the people who know about it."

Mac, continued. "We'll probably need my father and brother's help. Tony will have some records. I will need to visit the bad guys in their house."

This caught everyone's attention.

"I think we need to strike while the iron is hot. They may be missing a key person or two." Mac explained the adjustment he made to their transporter destination control.

"Today I want to visit Tony, then I think we will be prepared for a visit to the slide. His information may prepare us for a visit to the bad guys."

Everyone was getting concerned now. "Let me come with you." Silas wasn't about to let Mac address the bad guys alone.

"One step at a time. You're welcome to join me in a chat with Tony, but we may be better off with a slim profile when we visit them."

After addressing a few objections from Rita and Tiffany, it was decided they'd all visit Tony to get a better read on the nature of the danger and perhaps the best way to approach a permanent solution to access to the rock slide.

It became obvious to me that Aard had a diverse set of leaders now. Mac had successfully ceded leadership to the council. He knew it and embraced the mixed set of views as a positive. Even though, Julio, Jean, Shiv and some of the new leaders weren't included today, they would be. Right now, the GMSR was pulling the Aardians together to face the new enemy... From Earth.

With an uneasy truce, the team headed for breakfast.

***

A Gun and a Goldmine

The team sent a note to Tony, and were happy to get an almost instant reply.

"I had been trying to figure out which transporter to ping. I've got some news. I'm at the canning plant, come on over."

Within a half hour, the four Aardian leaders were sitting around the Seattle board table with Tony's dashboard on the screen overhead and a pot of coffee and one of tea ready to pour on a sideboard. Everyone's attention was on Tony's sensor chart. Highlighted was the newest destination. The site was now called the 'Slide Landing'.

It turns out it had been busy from three locations on Earth. Eugene, Oregon, Aragalur, Tamil Nadu, India, and Besancon, France, near the border with Switzerland.

Mac sat up straight. "I'm seeing the pattern. Gerald was from central Oregon, and we have some new folks from Tamil Nadu, including Mrs. and the late Mr. Sinclair."

Mac's brow furrowed. "I've been trying to remember where I heard of Besancon... Stud! Jean came from there."

Tiffany started. You mean Jean may have something to do with these travelers?"

Mac stood, walked over to the sideboard and poured a coffee. He looked back at the table of startled Aardians and his brother. "I expected Gerald to show up one day... We now need to consider Phil's brother... and someone from Besancon sent Jean here."

Tony stood to get coffee on that note as well. "Tommy, that site has seen action since you scooped the transporter. Someone knew the coordinates and traveled with their own transporter. We have seen a new fingerprint with the scanner and the landing has been used only once but they are back."

Roger Haller

The coordinates and timestamps of the last visit were on the overhead screen. The last visit was from Besancon, France, and it was two days ago. The visit included one visitor and they only stayed an hour.

Tiffany said, "Jean. We need Jean to advise on the trip to France."

Mac agreed, "Yes, but we need to do this right away."

"Let me go get him. I'll be right back." Tiffany looked to Tony. "Can I transport to Freedom?"

"Yes, Take that transporter by the coffee pot. Tuck it under your arm and press the button. You can leave it at Freedom. I've been working with Popeye to set it up in a sandstone cave in the slate wall with a great copper deposit. I'll ping Popeye to connect it to an antenna he has been setting up there. He and Jewels are there now. Once set up, you and Jean can use it to come back here."

In moments, Tiffany was gone. Transporting off Aard was against her nature, but her reluctance was trumped by her need to protect her new world.

Back at the table, Mac suggested that Oregon may not be as relevant with Gerald out of the picture but they needed to continue to monitor. Tony nodded in agreement. "We continue to monitor every location we become aware of. No telling how many people know of Transporters and off-world treasures. Humans will always be human."

Tony's last statement was not lost on anyone.

A Gun and a Goldmine

In particular, Mac was acutely aware of Aard's biggest challenge. Humans were now Aardian's most dangerous threat. That challenge would most often come from Earth, but immigration was more art than science. At any time, Aard may introduce the wrong roll of the dice. Anyone she saves, anyone Popeye brings in, anyone who escapes the GMSR could be their downfall.

Standing at the base of the slate cliffs at Freedom, Tiffany felt the same revelation as she stepped up to Jean, the Stud and Hilda.

"Jean, we need your help. Someone from Besancon has been to the landslide North of Shangri-La. Mac is set to transport to their transporter location. We need to know what he should expect."

Without hesitation, he said, "Where is he? Lets go."

"He's in Seattle with his brother, Silas, and Rita. Popeye is setting up Freedom's transporter. We can be back there in moments."

"Can I come?" Hilda was now concerned.

"Certainly."

They gathered around Popeye and Jewels.

While Popeye set the antenna connections, she explained the new concerns and plans. "Can you please let Julio, Shiv, and anyone else know what we are up to?

Popeye nodded. "The transporter is ready. Push the button and you will be in Seattle's landing closet."

"Thank you." Tiffany hugged Popeye Paul and Jewels and was gone. In short increments, Jean and Hilda transported too.

Moments later, Jean went over the map with the team, and Tony had pinpointed the longitude and latitude times to an industrial equipment lab near the rail station, just North West of Besancon citadel. Tony pointed out that this finger-print sometimes left coordinates from the Besancon Astro-nomical Observatory. The observatory was only about three kilometers Northwest of the citadel.

Everyone watched as Jean's uncomfortable memories swept across his expression. "My las memory on Earth was da words de ma petite amie... My girl-fren tru my tears. She was leaving for le machinist who has family money."

He looked quickly at Hilda, who rubbed the back of his neck. "Life much better now, but she was not sure... I tink she get help... I know who send me now... Andre Sinclair."

All eyes widened now. Sinclair. Another Sinclair. Tony did another search of his database, an Andre came up, but the record was not complete. They did not have a last name. His location, however, was Besancon, France but the law agencies had not been able to find him. Now with this new information, Tony was going to update his father. He promised an update back to the Aardian's when he had one.

Jean said, "We must go now. We must stop all Sinclair."

A Gun and a Goldmine

Mac laid a hand on his friend's shoulder. "Stud, we must be careful to respond rather than react. Will you spend a little time with me, my brother, and my father planning our response? We must get it right."

Jean nodded so Mac looked at the rest of the Aardians around the table. "We also need to defend the landslide, the Bleeding Flowers, and Aard. If Jean and I go to the source, could some of you take on the visitors?"

Hilda, with a child at home, began to tear up. Jean pulled her into an embrace. Rita, Tiffany, and Silas were also in a state of shock at the speed of this development. Silas broke the silence. "I can handle the landslide, Mac."

Tiffany added, "Not without me."

Rita saw the writing on the wall. "This is what retirement looks like, huh, Mac?" She was only half kidding.

Jean enveloped Hilda in his large frame. "Je reviens tout de suite, mon amour... I be right back.

A few more tears and she was off to worry with her child. She stayed silent but her tears spoke loudly. Tiffany and Rita hugged her tight when Jean released her. Soon, all were back on our home planet, but for the MacAdams and Jean. I didn't like this at all. Humans, gold, diamonds, and a gun. What could go wrong?

***

Roger Haller

About The Author

Roger Haller

Roger Haller has always been fascinated with the interaction of characters in challenging environments. From the Native North American stories published in his first Novel, 'Guardian of the One' in 2008, through the stories that were published in the global anthology, 'Satirica', also in 2008, and 'Garage Angel', published in the Spec-Fic Anthology, 'Thank you, Death Robot', in 2009, the vivid characters driving his stories have been his trade-mark.

Roger was born in Tillamook Oregon, then raised in a Native family in Southern British Columbia, timber and cattle country. Since 2000, his home has been Western Washington and he currently resides with his wife Joni, on a small hobby-farm in Monroe, Washington.

Cowboy Logic Press Books
By This Author

'Guardian of the One' Imagine the universe as a single entity to which all things are attached. Follow a Native American legend as the new Guardian of the One begins the task of bringing the world back to this understanding. Many powerful entities can not let this happen. Watch Gadge and Sammy, his Dreamer, as they unravel the mysterious links of the soul. Are they in time to save the wobbly cycle of life?

- 51 Pegasi - Black Mac
- 51 Pegasi - Sister Tiffany
- 51 Pegasi - Shiv
- More to come

Other Books by Cowboy Logic Press

2008

'Satirica' A post apocalyptic speculative fiction anthology by Cowboy Logic Press. Edited by Dudgeon and written by

these fine global writers:

Joshua Allen	Bill Housley
RJ Astruc	Dan Kopcow
Jaspn K Chapman	Dan Marcus
Gary Cuba	Paul Mannering
Lawrence R Dagstine	Thomas L Martin
John Parke Davis	Edward Morris
Steven J Dines	Mike Philbin
Dudgeon	Anden Sharp
Victor Giannini	Kevin Spiess
Roger Haller	David Thorp

2009

'Into the Dark - Escape of the Nomad by Bill Housley

A captivating Sci-Fi for the whole family. Bill wanted to see Science Fiction that everyone from the teen to Grandma could enjoy. He succeeded spectacularly.

Cowboy Logic Press Books

Hot off the Press and About to Launch:

The Life and Times of Ken Sharp - A memoir of a hands-on life. Born on the wrong side of the tracks and living life as it comes. Out Now in paper and Kindle!!!

51 Pegasi - Sister Tiffany - in your hands now. Get to know Sister Tiffany and some high-power new characters as the adventures on Aard continue.

Terrebonne - The Drog - An amazing chapter book for the newly launched reader. John P. Lewis masters the art of logic from the mind of an eight year old. Wendy Bazuta sets a new high-bar for chapter book characters. You're going to fall in love with this crew.